FATAL REACTION

ALSO BY BELINDA FRISCH

Cure (Strandville Zombie Novel: Book One)
Afterbirth (Strandville Zombie Novel: Book Two)
Better Left Buried
The Missing Year

FATAL REACTION

BELINDA FRISCH

THOMAS & MERCER

Text copyright © 2015 Belinda Frisch
All rights reserved.

Published by Thomas & Mercer, Seattle

www.apub.com

Amazon, the Amazon logo, and Thomas & Mercer are trademarks of Amazon.com, Inc., or its affiliates.

ISBN-13: 9781477830123
ISBN-10: 147783012X

Cover design by Marc Cohen

Library of Congress Control Number 2014958624

Printed in the United States of America

To my loving husband, Brent, the cornerstone of my life, who supports my talent unconditionally and believes in me even when I don't believe in myself. I couldn't do any of this without you.

In memory of my grandfather, Robert J. Seitz

CHAPTER 1

The neon sign of the Aquarian motel flickered against the dark morning sky. Six inches of fresh snow blanketed the rows of dilapidated cars, making the ill-reputed slum look only slightly less depressing.

Sergeant Mike Richardson was the second to arrive on the scene. Harold Cooper, whom most people called "Coop," stood questioning Samuel Roberts, the Aquarian's manager, under the overhang in front of room 11. The severity in his normally cheerful expression foretold of the bleak scene beyond the door.

Coop, dressed in the requisite blue uniform and a heavy jacket zippered up to his chin, shivered and jotted down notes. His breath puffed out in white clouds as he spoke. At six foot two and a lean one hundred seventy-five pounds, his body wasn't built for such extreme cold.

Samuel, known throughout the department for drug-related incidents and petty theft, wore nothing but a food-stained white tank top and a pair of tattered, acid-washed jeans. A good four inches shorter than Harold and at least forty pounds lighter, Sam couldn't afford to lose the calories his crack addiction burned.

He bounced up and down, scratching at his long, thin neck hard enough to leave raised red trails dotted with blood.

Mike zippered his coat and warmed his hands in front of the patrol car's vents, savoring the last bit of heat. The digital clock on the radio said it was 1:15 a.m. Thirty years on the force and as many run-ins with Samuel told him that nothing good happened at this hour, and never at this place. Shutting off the engine, he grabbed a pad and pen from the passenger seat.

"Hey, Coop." Mike tucked his face into his collar, and his breath reflected off it, freezing in crystals on his salt-and-pepper beard.

"Hey," Coop said.

Mike, eager to get out of the cold, went immediately to the strung-out man casting back-and-forth glances across the parking lot. "Samuel, how're you doing?"

"I'm g-g-good." Sam brushed a knotted strand of greasy blond hair back from his heavily stubbled face.

"What happened here?" said Mike.

"I—I—I don't know what—what—what happened. I keep tell—tell—tellin' Officer Cooper, b-b-but he w-w-won't let me leave." Sam's parted lips were turning blue.

Samuel launched into a string of denial Mike had seen coming before he even started his line of questioning. In all the times Mike had been called to the Aquarian, no one had ever seen anything.

Mike noted several newly missing teeth and one on the verge of falling out. The few that remained varied as much in color as fall corn, ranging from yellow to brown. Samuel twitched and picked at his skin. Mike knew if he didn't get him to look at the scene with fresh eyes, he would be unlikely to remember anything later. He set his hand on the doorknob, and Coop grabbed his arm.

"Wait. There's something I need to tell you before you go in there."

Sam's bloodshot eyes went wide. "I—I—I don't want to go b-b-back in there. I—I—I did—did—didn't see anyone. I swear it.

I—I—I just found her. Sh-sh-she was supposed to check out. I'm tellin' you. I don't know anything." He backed away as if getting ready to run. "P-p-please. I—I—I just want to go to the office."

"All right, Sam. Take it easy." Mike took several slow steps toward him and softened his tone. "We won't go back in there. Tell me what you saw. Did you notice anything out of place?"

"I—I—I only went in there to clean."

"At one in the morning?" Mike raised his eyebrows.

Sam's vacant stare fixed on the scab on his arm that he wouldn't stop picking at.

Mike drew a deep breath and looked up. Six new security cameras, half rounds with smoked lenses, had been mounted along the motel's overhang. "Sam, when did you put in surveillance?"

Samuel's roving stare moved faster, casting back-and-forth glances across the escalating scene.

"Sam! When did you get cameras?"

Samuel refused to answer.

Two more patrol cars arrived. The sirens and swirling lights drew the inevitable crowd. Men and women, most of whom called the motel home thanks to the county's Section 8 program, filed out of their rooms. Mike suspected the few doors that remained closed belonged to recent parolees looking to avoid trouble.

A little girl, wearing a pair of pink blanket sleepers with the feet cut out, rubbed her eyes. Her overweight mother exhaled a cloud of cigarette smoke and pulled the girl to her side.

"What's goin' on?" she said. "I got a kid trying to sleep in here."

"I'll be with you in a minute, ma'am." Coop waved the growing crowd back. "I'm going to need to take statements from all of you, but for now it's best you go back inside."

These people knew the protocol, and Mike expected no more information from them than he had gotten from Samuel.

Blood welled up from the now-open wound on Samuel's thin forearm, and he clenched his teeth; Mike guessed he did this involuntarily. Samuel's big toe wiggled through a hole in his gray-white sock, and his skin glistened with sweat.

Ronald Graham stepped out of his patrol car, his coat taut over his bulging belly and his plump face buried inside his collar.

Mike waved him over. "Ron, take Samuel to the office. Get him warm, make him some coffee, and get his statement."

"Will do. Come on, let's get you inside," Ron said to Samuel, and gestured for Mike to look over his shoulder.

A white van with the Channel 9 logo emblazoned on the side parked in the shadows of a burned-out streetlight. Terri Tate was relentless and, no doubt, had sprung out of bed to scoop the story.

Mike suspected someone on the force had been tipping her off for years.

"Coop, deal with that, would you?" Mike turned the doorknob of room 11 before Coop could stop him.

The scene was quiet and heavy with death. Suicides had a different feel to them, a kind of vacant sadness that sucked its witnesses in. Mike had seen several, and each left him feeling momentarily hopeless.

He took a minute to adjust.

An empty pill bottle sat on the bedside table next to a drained bottle of vodka. A jilted, seventies-era orange lamp cast a pale light across the tattered carpet, illuminating the grisly sight of a woman's lifeless body just feet away. Her long hair draped over most of her face, dried vomit visible at the corners of her mouth. Her left arm faced palm-side up, a teal ribbon tattooed on the inside of her wrist. Mike gasped when he realized what Coop had been trying to tell him. The tattoo was a tribute to Sydney's recent victory over cancer. Mike had been one of the few people nursing her back to health after her hysterectomy. He fought back the tears. Having no children of his own, he had done his best to step in as a father to Sydney and her younger sister, Ana, when their own father, Mike's partner on the force for twenty years, and their mother, were killed in a plane crash. Seeing Sydney lying there was as crushing as if she were his daughter.

Mike, mindful of protocol, pulled on a pair of shoe covers and gloves, and checked Sydney for the pulse he knew wasn't there. Her body was stiff with rigor mortis, and her skin was cold enough that Mike felt the chill through the latex gloves.

He briefly considered why Sydney, who lived only a few miles away, would be at a place like the Aquarian. There was no viable explanation. Suicide came quickly off the table, and homicide took its place. Mike formulated mental checklists, sorting scene details and compiling a short list of suspects. Local firefighter Anthony Dowling, whom Sydney was in the process of divorcing, was at the top.

The motel room door opened, and several of the Aquarian's more brazen tenants moved in for a closer look.

"I'm sorry, Mike." Coop's condolences were nearly lost in the chatter.

"Get them back," Mike said. "Get every single one of them away from here, but no one leaves. You understand me? I don't care what their excuse is. Everyone gets questioned."

Coop nodded. "You heard the sergeant. Everyone get back and line up. I need your names." He tied a piece of crime-scene tape to a chair near the door and commenced roping off the area.

Mike radioed back to the station. "This is Sergeant Mike Richardson. I need the coroner at the Aquarian immediately. There's been a murder."

CHAPTER 2

Paramedic Anneliese Ashmore blasted the heat in the First Responder Jeep and waited at the drive-through window for her fifth cup of black coffee. Working twenty-four hours straight had her fighting exhaustion and the boredom that came with a relatively quiet shift.

The unpredictable New York winter had settled in, and the temperature was well below freezing. It was snowing—the kind of heavy flakes that made it hard to see past the immediate glow of the headlights, and that cut visibility even more under high beams.

A gauntly thin clerk, with dyed hair tamed only by her uniform visor, reached through the drive-through window and took two singles from Ana.

"You can keep the change." Ana smiled and tucked her auburn hair behind her ears.

The woman smiled back, handing her a bitter-smelling cup of coffee undoubtedly hours old.

Ana tossed an empty onto the passenger's side floor, replacing it with the full one that she fit into the cup holder. The Jeep lurched forward and crushed the freshly fallen snow beneath its tires. A police cruiser sped past her and pulled into the Aquarian motel parking lot, a block down the road. An ambulance from her station followed.

Ana checked her radio, and, finding it operational, wondered why a call had never come.

Eager to break the monotony, she went to find out.

———

The bitter February cold ripped through Ana's open uniform jacket as her gloved hand struggled against its stuck zipper. She tucked her chin into the collar of her white turtleneck and reached into the back of the SUV for her medic bag.

Police cruisers filled the Aquarian's parking lot. A rectangle of yellow crime-scene tape flapped in the icy wind, quarantining a single motel room. Camera flashes pulsed behind the ratty orange curtains, signaling the collection of evidence. All signs pointed to whatever had happened not being good.

Ana got out of the Jeep and walked with her head down toward room 11.

The wind made her brown eyes water. She was halfway through the crowd when the door opened and Sergeant Mike Richardson stepped out into the cold. His face was blotchy red, and he appeared to have been crying. He sniffled, wiped the tip of his slightly crooked nose, and headed toward the rental office.

"Mike, wait." Ana waved her hand in the air. Mike seemed too lost in thought to hear her. "Mike, hey."

Jim Moore, Ana's shift supervisor, rushed out of an ambulance parked on the outskirts and headed straight for her. "Ana, stop!" His frantic shouting caught both her and Mike's attention. "Mike, stop her." A pair of emergency shears hung from a loop on his uniform and flapped against his leg as he ran. Tufts of sandy blond hair stuck out from beneath his knit cap, and his expression held a mix of urgency and sadness.

Mike doubled back toward the motel room.

Ana began to suspect that her not getting the call was intentional. Her heartbeat raced, and her palms grew damp inside her gloves as she waited for either Mike or Jim to explain their panic. When neither did, she said, "What's wrong?"

Jim grabbed her right bicep hard enough that she couldn't easily pull free. "You shouldn't have come here."

"Let her go." Mike pushed Jim's hand away. "Let me handle this, *please.*" He steered Ana down the crumbling sidewalk toward the snowy parking lot. "I told Jim not to call you."

"He didn't," Ana said. "I saw the cruisers and the ambulance, and since nothing else was happening, I came to help. What's wrong? Why won't anyone answer me?"

Mike steadied his quivering bottom lip. "You have to leave. I'll explain everything as soon as I can, but you can't be here now."

Ana's inner voice insisted that *here* was exactly where she belonged. She looked around the parking lot at the cars, the ambulance, and the approaching coroner's van. A camera crew struggled to set up its shot in the heavy snow. Terri Tate, *Capital News 9*'s lead reporter, powdered her face by the van's dome light. The Aquarian's sign flickered in Ana's periphery and drew her attention. There, in the shadows of an overflowing Dumpster, was her sister's metal-flake blue Honda Civic. A lump rose in her throat, and tears streamed down her wind-burned cheeks.

"Sydney!" Ana broke for the motel room door, elbowing her way through the crowd and catching Mike off guard enough to get a small lead on him. He rushed after her, but she was through the motel room door before he caught up.

"Ana, stop!" Mike shouted for Coop to grab her, but the encroaching mob, including the persistent Terri Tate, kept him from doing so.

Time moved in slow motion as Ana took everything in, ignoring the chatter of those in the crowd outside as they tested the limits of the crime-scene tape.

Labeled plastic bags held pieces of evidence: an empty vodka bottle and some kind of prescription. Black fingerprinting dust covered every surface, and two investigators worked at collecting samples. A third snapped pictures of a folded piece of paper on the weathered nightstand, its finish bearing ring watermarks from decades of glasses left to sweat upon it.

Across the room, Julian Blake, a seasoned investigator, jotted down items in a small notebook. He wore jeans, a department sweatshirt, and a navy blue jacket with the name "Blake" embroidered on the right side. His black hair sprouted in patches along the back of his head, and his hazel eyes, red from lack of sleep, indicated he'd been called in from home.

Elsa Russell, Julian's new partner and the only female investigator with the Marion PD, looked up when the wind blew her curly red hair. She lunged to grab Ana's arm but quickly lost her grip. "Ana, you can't be in here."

Ana collapsed to her knees, interlaced her fingers, and started chest compressions. "No. No. God, no." Rainwater tears blurred her vision. "Sydney, come on."

"You're contaminating the scene, Ana. Stop." Julian tried to pull her back, and Ana threw her elbow as hard as she could into him.

Everything she knew about crime-scene processing, and about death, was gone from her mind.

"Get out of my way." Mike shoved past Julian and wrestled Ana into a cross-legged sit. She fought him, squirming and screaming, but he didn't let go. He pulled her arms across her chest and used his body like a straitjacket to hold her. "Ana, stop it. Please, she's *gone*. Sydney is gone." He was crying, too.

"Let me help her," Ana wailed. "It's not too late."

Mike set his stubbled cheek against the top of her head and rocked her.

"Please, let me go," she whispered.

Julian mumbled something under his breath as he assessed the compromised scene. "Mike, I'm sorry. You have to get her out of here."

Mike dragged Ana from the stench-filled room into the frigid morning.

Julian slammed the door, and Ana fixed her eyes on the eleven, the room number irrevocably burned into her memory.

Jim knelt in front of her, and she stared right through him. "Ana, listen to me. You need to go home." He looked at Mike. "She can't drive, and I can't have her back on shift. I need the Jeep keys."

"Give me a damn minute, Jim, would you?"

The crowd parted for the coroner who wheeled a gurney through a fresh inch of snow, an empty body bag secured under the strap.

He knocked on the door, and Julian let him in.

"Ana, can you hear me?" Mike brushed the hair back from her face. "Can you give me your keys, honey? I'm going to take you home."

Ana fished the keys out of her pocket and handed them to Mike who, in turn, handed them to Jim.

The heavy, wet snow soaked through Ana's clothes, and though she knew she should be freezing, she was physically and emotionally numb.

Mike hooked his arms under hers and lifted her. She shuffled her feet in the direction he pulled her, eluded by an act as simple as walking. Had Mike not taken her away, she wasn't sure she would have ever left.

The whispering crowd silenced as the coroner emerged from the motel room. Two young men forced the gurney's wheels through the accumulating snow, loaded Sydney's body into the back of the ambulance, and tapped the rear door, signaling it was all clear to go.

Ana watched the ambulance drive away.

Shock substituted someone else as the victim: some faceless, nameless person Ana didn't have to grieve for.

Anyone other than her sister.

CHAPTER 3

Colby Monroe stared at her reflection in her dressing table mirror and brushed her reddish-blond hair over her shoulders. She leaned forward and gently stretched the skin around her spring-green eyes. In the sunlight, she saw the faint lines beginning to work their way out from the corners. Despite the constant compliments, she was seeing the signs that every day of her thirty-six years was starting to catch up with her.

The sound of tires on the driveway drew her to the bedroom window where she shivered in her black negligee, watching her husband Jared's silver BMW 6 Series disappear into the garage. She closed the blinds, self-conscious of her minor flaws, and dabbed on a fresh coat of vanilla-flavored lip gloss.

The front door opened, then closed, and Jared stomped off his boots. He set his keys on the entranceway table and turned on the water in the kitchen sink. A bar stool slid across the hardwood floor, and the smell of coffee crept upstairs.

Colby grabbed a stick-lighter off the dresser, lit several candles, and turned down the bed. She climbed beneath the comforter and stared at the time on the alarm clock: 8:02 a.m.

Jared was getting home later by the day.

Fifteen minutes passed, and as Colby was about to give up on her plan to romance him, Jared appeared in the doorway. He ran his hands through his dark brown hair, cut close at the sides and left longer on top in a style resembling one worn by George Clooney.

"Hey," she said.

Red lines shot through the whites of his dark eyes. "Hey. Are you just waking up?"

She hadn't slept past six in the morning since leaving her job as an OR nurse at County Memorial almost four months earlier, and he knew it.

"No," she said, softening her hard tone. "I was waiting for *you*." She pulled the comforter aside, leaned up on her elbow, and smiled.

Jared let out a sigh, and, for a long moment, didn't say anything. He didn't have to. She could see his disinterest, and it hit her in the place where her fear of aging festered, hurting her more, she guessed, than he had intended.

"I'm sorry." Jared shook his head. "It's been a long night." He went into the en suite bathroom and shut the door.

Tears burned behind Colby's eyelids, and she closed her eyes until she was sure she could contain them. The hurt was visceral, and she refused to let Jared see that. She blew out the candles, put on her silk bathrobe, and knocked on the bathroom door.

"Jared, open up." The shower turned on, and she reached for the door handle, finding it locked. "Come on. Unlock the door."

Jared answered, wearing a white towel wrapped around his waist. He held his hand high on the doorjamb and stretched in a way that caused his chest and biceps to flex. Country club racquet ball kept him in impeccable shape, and, at age thirty-nine, he didn't have a gray hair on him, a fact that secretly annoyed her.

Steam from the shower rolled into the bedroom.

"We need to talk."

"I'm exhausted, Colby. I don't have another fight in me right now."

She pushed past him and turned off the water. "I said *talk*, not *fight*."

"There's no difference with you. One day you're telling me that you want a divorce, and the next, I come home to find you half-naked in bed." He held up his hands as if asking her what she expected. "At least this time you were alone."

Talking went quickly out the window.

"Is that what this is about? It's been four months, Jared, and you haven't so much as looked at me. Do you know how much that hurts, or what it feels like to always be the least important thing to you? I quit my nursing job for you. I gave up my independence to sit here, alone in this house, indentured to you for taking care of me."

"You quit nursing for *me*?" Jared scoffed. "You're always the victim, aren't you? Well, let me refresh your somewhat-jaded memory. You quit that job because you slept with Simon Walker, chief of medicine at the hospital we both worked at. Everyone knows about it, and if you hadn't quit, he sure as hell would've found a way to fire you to stop the chatter. I have to walk on eggshells at that place to save my own ass. Sure, I could take a job somewhere else, but I worked my way up to department head. Those jobs just don't exist out there, and I'm not starting over. Do you have *any* idea how hard it is to sit across a meeting room table and talk about Emergency Department funding with a guy who slept with my wife?"

Colby slapped him hard enough across the cheek that her palm stung afterward.

Jared's head whipped to the side, and a red handprint surfaced on his cheek. He drew a deep breath in through his nose and clenched his teeth. "I think we're done here," he said, and closed the bathroom door.

The lock clicked, and Colby stood for a moment in disbelief of what she'd done. No matter how much time passed or how many times she apologized, Jared would never forgive her. She wasn't even sure she wanted him to.

CHAPTER 4

Dr. Dorian Carmichael hung his lab coat over the back of his office chair and stared out the second-floor window of his Oakland Street office. He ruffled his wavy, dark blond hair, and rubbed a stray eyelash from the corner of his caramel-brown eyes.

A mound of snow slid from the roof of the detached garage and piled on the construction trash next to it. Tearing down the old building was the last step in converting the 1900s home he had bought with his first bit of grant money into a welcoming obstetrical surgical practice. Nestled in a primarily residential neighborhood, the office was close to County Memorial Hospital where his pioneering of a uterine transplantation procedure had him quickly ascending the ranks.

Before his research, women born without a uterus, or those who had lost theirs to disease, were limited to surrogacy and adoption if they wanted to have a family. Dorian's procedure gave them the ability to experience childbirth firsthand. The response was overwhelming. Like anything new, the procedure wasn't without complications, not the least of which was the unwillingness and general lack of donors, but he'd forged past that, and had operated on his first human, a woman named Stephanie Martin.

Four blocks away, a grieving family held his second patient's fate in its hands. Thirty-six-year-old Janice Harmon remained alive on life support after a car crash had left her clinically brain dead. A perfect donor match for Emily Warren, a twenty-eight-year-old who had lost her uterus to fibroids, Janice, who had never had children of her own, and whose family would never see a penny from agreeing to the donation, was the key to a high six-figure paycheck that helped keep things, especially with County's CEO, Mitchell Altman, lubricated.

A knock came at the door, and Dorian turned to see his nurse, Noreen Pafford, at the threshold, holding a sandwich.

Noreen was a young thirty: slim and fit, with a beautiful softness about her. Her highlighted brown hair was cut into a short bob style that ended just past her earlobes. A cascade of purple star earrings glistened against her ivory neck. Wispy bangs across her forehead gave her a pixie look that, if he was being honest, enchanted him in a one-night-stand kind of way. Besides being a genuinely caring person, Noreen was a more dedicated employee than Dorian had a right to expect her to be. She kept his long hours and never once complained. She filed his research paperwork, worked on grants, and eased tensions with his more-anxious patients in a way only another female could. Dorian wouldn't be where he was without her, a fact she reminded him of on late nights when a couple of glasses of off-duty wine colored the otherwise dry, clinical conversations. Those nights were like walking a tightrope. Dorian knew better than to bring his sex life into the workplace again.

Noreen slipped the stethoscope from around her neck and dropped it into her lab coat pocket. "You really should eat something." Her voice was sweet honey.

Dorian smiled and nodded. "You're always taking care of me." He sank into the leather office chair behind his desk and sighed. "Any word from County?"

Noreen set the turkey sandwich—light mayonnaise, no crust— in front of him, and leaned against his desk. Her jacket fell open and beneath it, a fitted blue dress revealed the delicate curves of her hourglass figure. "I went over there this morning and spoke with Janice Harmon's family." She pulled a piece of paper from her pocket and handed it to him. "Harvest team convenes at six a.m. Emily Warren's transplant is scheduled for eight."

"You got them to sign?"

She smiled. "There's not much I don't do for you."

"What about Prusak? Have you talked to Mitchell about him?"

Mitchell Altman, County Memorial's CEO and a man motivated more by power and money than ethics, had promised to take care of Marco Prusak, the pathologist who had staged a protest complete with blood and baby dolls. His position was that the transplant posed a risk to the fetus. At first blush, one would've thought he was protesting abortion.

"Mitchell gave him two weeks' leave," Noreen said.

"That's *it*?"

"Guess so."

Kristin Newman, the receptionist, appeared in the doorway. Her thin brown hair was pulled back from her plain, if not homely face. She wore a wrinkled cotton dress and Birkenstock sandals, which were entirely out of season. "Dr. Carmichael, your first afternoon patient is here."

Dorian swallowed a bite of his sandwich. "I'll be right down. See if she wants some water or tea while she waits."

Kristin muttered something as she walked away about not being a waitress. Her flip-flop footsteps echoed on the hardwood.

Dorian waited until she was downstairs to comment. "Tell me again why we hired her?"

"She's smart, efficient, and good with computers. Do you need her to be beautiful, too?"

"I guess I can't have everything."

Noreen guided his hands to her hips, beneath her lab coat, and smirked. "You can if you ask nicely."

CHAPTER 5

Ana dragged a brush through her tangled, wet hair. The shower, meant to revive her, only made her more tired. She inhaled deeply, the warm steam easing the congestion from hours of crying, but doing nothing to quell the overwhelming sadness. Depression surrounded her, crushing her with its weight.

She walked to the master bedroom and sat, slumped over, on the edge of the bed, holding her throbbing head between her hands. The light made her headache worse, and she closed her eyes, immediately recalling the image of Sydney's lifeless body on the filthy motel-room floor. For the rest of her life, that was what she'd see first when she remembered her sister.

She stood, a simple act made difficult by unrelenting grief, and haphazardly toweled off, leaving her back and shoulders damp.

The phone rang for at least the tenth time that night, and Ana checked the caller ID before answering. Word of Sydney's death spread quickly, in no small part due to Terri Tate's news report. If Ana heard another person say they were sorry, she'd scream. She stepped into a pair of black underwear, gray yoga pants, and a sweatshirt, and answered the phone on the fifth ring.

"Hello?"

It was Mike.

"Hey, I just wanted to make sure you were awake."

"I am," she said. "Why?"

"Can we talk?"

A car door slammed, and Ana looked out the window to see Mike's blue Dodge parked in her driveway. She hung her towel on a hook in the bathroom, headed downstairs, and stood, arms akimbo, in the open front door. The cold breeze froze her damp hair and chilled her scalp.

"Is there any news?"

Mike closed his cell phone and forced a tight-lipped grin. "Unfortunately, no." He moved to step inside, but Ana blocked him.

"I'm not feeling up to company."

"Ana, don't be mad."

"Don't be mad? Like it's that easy? You should've called. We're family, right? Isn't that what you always told us? The minute you realized it was Sydney, you should've said something."

"I didn't want you to see her that way, Ana. There was nothing you could do."

"You honestly believe that?"

A plow truck cleared the road in front of her house, adding to the already enormous banks and filling the tense silence with its loud scraping.

Mike wiped his gloved hand down the side of his face and sighed. "Yes"—he looked directly into her eyes—"I do. Can I please come inside? It's freezing out here."

Ana kept her distance, avoiding their usual greeting hug and feeling a little uncomfortable because of it. "If you have no answers, why are you here?"

"Other than being concerned about you, I thought you might want your car. I can give you a ride to the station." Mike took her keys out of his pocket.

With everything that had happened, Ana barely remembered handing them over.

"You should be investigating, not driving a taxi."

"I've done all I can do for tonight. I have Julian and Elsa on it, people with a different perspective and fewer attachments. You know, you screwed us with evidence. We're going to have to disclose that ambush of yours."

At the time, Ana knew she was crossing a line, storming the crime scene, but she was too panic- and grief-stricken to care. "Jim seem angry about what happened?"

"A bit, but right now he's more worried about you than protocol."

Ana rummaged the coat closet for something warm to wear, settling on a down-lined parka and pulling the hood up over her wet hair. "He probably should be."

Mike flashed a concerned look.

"I didn't mean it the way it came out," she said. "I just meant that after all the years I've known him, he should be more concerned about me than disciplinary action."

Mike pressed the button on his remote start, and the late-model Ram sprang to life. A cloud of white smoke poured from the tailpipe, and the wipers made a pass across the windshield. Mike opened the passenger's side door and helped Ana inside.

A Willie Nelson song played quietly on the radio. It was barely audible over the sound of the blasting heat, but it brought back better times. Mike had sung that song to her and Sydney when she was young.

Though most people didn't know it, Mike was pretty good at campfire guitar.

"Look, I'm sorry," Ana said. "I know you thought you were doing the right thing. Anger's one of the first steps, right?" Mike nodded. "So what do Elsa and Julian think happened?"

———

"Suicide?" Ana's eyes went wide with disbelief.

Even with four-wheel drive and the roads clear, Mike kept his speed under thirty. "Elsa found a note on the nightstand. I know what you're thinking."

"I don't think you do." On a scale of one to ten, four being how pissed off she was at him when he arrived, and ten being a swarm of angry hornets, she hit a solid twenty. "Suicide, Mike? Does that make *any* sense to you?" Mike shrugged. "The woman fought for her life, enrolled in school to be a grief counselor, to help other depressed people, and you think it's even plausible she killed herself?"

"It's been a tough year. Maybe a lot of what Sydney was doing was self-help. Between separating from Anthony, the surgery, and the cancer, I don't know what to believe. Less has broken stronger people."

"No one was stronger than Syd, and you know it."

"I'm not taking anything at face value, but given the scene, nothing looks out of place."

"Sydney, at the Aquarian—out of place." Ana ticked off her argument on her fingers. "Pills and vodka—out of place." Another finger. "The note—out of place. There wasn't one goddamned warning sign, Mike, not *one*. She wasn't withdrawn, or upset. She was even making peace with what Anthony did to her, the cheating piece of shit. Do you know how hard that is for a woman to overlook?"

"I know it was hard for her, but she wasn't one to complain, especially where you were concerned."

"And what is *that* supposed to mean?"

"It just means that Sydney was always strong around you. Ever since your parents' accident, she only ever wanted to be your rock. She wanted children, Ana, and you know damned well that was a big part of the problem between her and Anthony. When she had the hysterectomy," Mike said with a sigh, "it was all over from there. I'm not condoning or condemning what Anthony did. I'm just saying Sydney suffered silently. It was her way. The note is with a forensic handwriting specialist. If anything's suspicious, he'll find it. We fingerprinted the room, but a place like the Aquarian, it's got a jaded history. We're getting hits off the prints left and right. Every drug dealer, ex-con, prostitute, pimp, and john who has ever been in that room left at least his fingerprints behind, most of them more." Ana cringed at the visual. "Is there any reason to believe Sydney would be tied up with anyone with a criminal past?"

"Really, Mike?" Ana pulled a face.

"I had to ask." Mike rolled up to the stoplight and blasted the defroster. "Some things stay between sisters."

"If there was something like that, don't you think I'd have mentioned it?"

"I'd hope so, but I'm looking for anything to rule out some of these prints."

A moment of silence passed between them.

"Any chance you found Anthony's?"

Mike turned and looked at her. "Why do you ask?"

Ana pointed ahead when the light turned green. "Things got out of hand with the divorce. Sydney wasn't exactly honest with Anthony, and he's hurt, enough that he tried laying claim to half of her house."

"The house your parents left to both of you."

"Yes, but you know I'd never take the place away from her. She loved it. She had a lot more memories with our parents there than I did."

"They're your memories, too."

Fresh tears spilled down Ana's cheeks. "I know, but after giving up everything to stay with me, Sydney deserved to keep her home."

"What did you mean Sydney wasn't honest with Anthony? About what?"

Revealing Sydney's secrets had Ana feeling like a traitor, though she knew it was only a matter of time before Anthony told his version. She needed Mike to understand why Sydney did what she did. "It's no secret that Anthony wanted a stay-at-home wife and a large family. It's the life he came from. One of nine children, I mean, what can you expect? Sydney just finished taking care of me. She wasn't ready for children. She wanted them, yes, but Anthony had been hounding her since their honeymoon. Sydney wanted to get her degree. After what she'd been through, Mike, it wasn't just the cancer that pushed her toward grief counseling. She said no one understood a crisis like people who had faced and beat one. Anthony didn't agree. He told her to leave the past in the past, and she tried. He actually made her feel bad about her struggle. In a moment of weakness, she agreed to try to get pregnant, well, I mean, agreed to him, but she knew she had made a mistake as soon as she said it. Months went by without her conceiving, and she convinced him that something was wrong. He agreed to let her enroll in school, to be supportive of what she wanted to do, if she'd agree to see a fertility specialist. She did, but found a dozen reasons not to keep her appointments. When Anthony found her birth control pills, it was the beginning of the end."

"She was taking them the whole time?"

"Yep. She said Anthony was suspicious. I told her she was being paranoid."

"And that's when Misty came into the picture?"

Ana rolled her eyes.

Misty Harper, a twenty-five-year-old waitress at the R&M Diner on North Main, couldn't have been more Sydney's opposite.

Misty was too old to get off the dead-end path she was on, and she knew it. She flirted with anyone in uniform, married or not, and saw Anthony as a way out of her situation. Anthony wanted a stay-at-home type, and Misty wanted to be taken care of. He was an easy target.

"You know Misty attacked Sydney at the preliminary divorce hearing, don't you?"

Mike shook his head. "When did you two stop telling me things?"

The EMS station came into view. Ana's white Jetta was buried under a foot of fresh snow, but someone, Ethan if she had to guess, had been nice enough to lift her wipers.

"We didn't stop telling you everything—only the stuff we figured you didn't want to hear. The rest of that story was that Syd slapped Misty across the face and got hauled off by a bailiff. It took some amount of pleading to keep him from telling you."

Mike parked next to Ana's car. "And then what happened?"

"Sydney laughed and said, 'Bitch had that coming.'" Ana smiled and reached across the seat to give Mike the hug she'd earlier avoided.

He hugged her back and chuckled. "She wasn't wrong there."

CHAPTER 6

Anthony Dowling hadn't been too hard to find. He answered the door of Misty Harper's one-bedroom apartment, wearing only a pair of nylon shorts and holding a mostly empty bottle of beer. Dark curls covered his broad chest, and hair stuck up in sparse tufts along the back of his toned shoulders. His dark hair had been cut short enough that his scalp was visible, a drastic change from the wavy, gelled-back look Mike was used to seeing on him. Candles flickered in the background, and for as close a friendship as Anthony and Mike once had, the expression on Anthony's face was anything but welcoming.

Mike cleared his throat and peered into the dismal apartment. "Am I interrupting something?"

Anthony glanced over his shoulder. "I'd say it's pretty obvious, *Detective.*"

"Sergeant," Mike corrected, "but I'm not on duty." He pointed to his street clothes. "Can we talk?"

"Look, Mike, whatever Sydney told you, I haven't done anything wrong. From now on, our lawyers do the talking."

At six foot three, Anthony had a good five inches on Mike, who had to crane his neck to make eye contact. It had to be worse for Misty. She stood only to his chest. She was ten years his junior, so Misty and Anthony looked more like father and daughter, or uncle and niece, than a couple.

Misty appeared behind him, wearing a pair of sweatpants with the legs rolled up and an oversized T-shirt. Her green eyes had the half-dazed look of someone who just woke up, but the bags beneath them said she was exhausted. Faint red marks dotted the skin around her mouth, and she looked frail, as if she'd recently lost weight.

"Oh God. What *now*?" She scowled at Mike, keeping her head turned to the side in a posture he'd seen with domestic abuse victims hiding a shiner.

Anthony wasn't the type, but Mike angled for a better look anyway.

"You really don't know?" For as fast as word normally traveled in Marion, somehow, it seemed, neither Anthony nor Misty had heard what happened to Sydney. He hadn't planned on being the one to break the news.

"Don't know what?" Anthony said.

"It's better if we sit down. May I come in? I just want to ask you a few questions."

Misty shook her head. "You don't have to let him in, Tony. Tell him to get lost." No one had ever called Anthony "Tony." He hated the nickname, and everyone who *really* knew him, knew it.

Anthony backed away from the door and gestured for Mike to come in. "Let me grab a shirt, would you?" He blew out the candles and headed toward the bedroom.

Mike paced the cramped galley kitchen, taking stock of the bleak surroundings and wondering how Anthony could've ever thought this was a better situation.

A pile of laundry overflowed from a plastic hamper in the corner, and the room reeked of smoke. Mike had heard about a big fire in the warehouse district a week earlier, but it seemed a long time to have not done the laundry. Dishes were piled in the kitchen sink, and a dirty apron hung from a nail in the wall. The yellowed name tag heralded too many years spent serving fryer grease-soaked food.

Misty, who hadn't said a word since Anthony let Mike in, must have noticed him staring. She huffed out a breath, rolled the apron into a ball, and threw it in the trash.

"Aren't you going to need that for work?" Mike said.

"She doesn't work anymore." Anthony came out of the cluttered bedroom, wearing a firehouse sweatshirt, shorts, and a pair of dingy socks with the pink-red hue of having been washed with mixed laundry. He pulled out one of four mismatched chairs at a vintage kitchen table and offered Mike a seat.

Mike brushed the crumbs off the chair and sat down.

Misty turned her head into the light and blew a thick curl from in front of her face.

Mike noticed what looked like scratch marks down her cheek. "What happened there?"

"She broke up a fight at the diner," Anthony answered before Misty had a chance to. "You know how it gets in that place late at night when the bars close."

Misty uncrossed her arms and tousled her hair. "It wasn't a big deal."

"Big enough deal that you quit, though, right?" Mike said.

Again, Anthony spoke for her. "She was going to quit anyway, weren't you, babe?"

"Yeah, sure." Misty brushed her hair back from her forehead, and Mike caught the glimmer of a diamond solitaire on her left ring finger.

"Looks like congratulations are in order."

"Not if this divorce isn't finalized." Anthony sighed. "You said you had some questions, so shoot. I know this isn't a social call."

"Okay, does Sydney know about the engagement?"

Anthony shrugged. "If she does, I didn't tell her. It's been hard enough trying to reach a divorce agreement without pissing her off worse. Misty and I have been trying to keep things quiet, but, you know how it is."

Misty set a pot on the cluttered counter, a mix of clean and dirty dishes, and it slid, knocking a spatula into a pile of crumbs on the dirty linoleum floor. She picked it up and, without so much as brushing it off, put it into a drawer.

Mike tried not to think about how many times she'd done similar things at the diner he frequented. "I do 'know how it is,'" he said. "Divorces get nasty, even between the most agreeable couples. Is that why you were going after half of Sydney's house?"

Anthony looked over his shoulder at Misty and lowered his voice. "I don't want the house, Mike. Sydney should know that. It's a bargaining chip to get the things that *do* matter to me. She's not giving an inch. Maybe you can talk to her for me? At this point, I just need this to be over with."

There was something going on with Misty that Anthony wasn't comfortable talking about.

Mike drew his bottom lip between his teeth and let it out before asking the big question. "Anthony, where were you last night?"

The color drained from Anthony's face.

Misty turned around at the sink, her hands dripping soapy water on the floor. "He was here, with me. Why?"

"Has something happened to Sydney?" Anthony's mouth bent into a frown.

Mike drew a breath and nodded with tears in his eyes. "I'm afraid so. She's . . . dead."

Misty dried her hands on her pants and set them on Anthony's shoulders.

He quickly pushed her away.

"Just give me a goddamn minute, would you?" Anthony started to cry, the kind of genuine tears Mike, himself, had cried for hours after finding Sydney's body. "What happened?"

Misty all but threw the rest of the dishes into the cabinets. She'd gone from empathetic to angry in a matter of seconds, as if somehow Anthony's mourning the loss of his wife said more about his feelings for Sydney than those he had for her.

"I'm not in a position to share details right now. I'm sorry," Mike said. "Can you think of anyone who would want to hurt her?"

"Hurt Sydney?" Anthony cast a glance at Misty. "You're kidding me, right?"

"I wish I were. The first thing to come into question is usually motive."

"What are you getting at, Mike? You think I'm the closest thing Sydney had to an enemy?"

"I wouldn't classify you as an *enemy*, Anthony. I don't think Sydney would have, either." Mike turned to Misty. "What can you tell me about the fight at the courthouse?"

Misty threw her hands up and launched the dish towel across the counter. "All right. That's it. I've had enough." She flung the apartment door open. "You have to leave. Now."

Mike raised his eyebrows at Anthony.

"Sydney called Misty a whore and a home wrecker. There was a slap-fight and raised voices, but nothing out of the ordinary, considering." Anthony wiped the tears from his cheeks. "We were here last night, *both* of us, and neither out of the other's sight. Misty and Sydney had their history, but a minor scuffle doesn't equal murder, Mike. Not by a long shot."

Mike pushed in his chair and pulled a business card out of his shirt pocket. "If you think of anything at all that might help with the case, call me."

"I will," Anthony said, following Mike into the hallway and out of Misty's earshot. "Look, I'm sorry about how we reacted. This divorce has things here on edge. I loved Sydney, Mike. You know that. Even after the separation, I tried putting things back together, but sometimes life puts people on different paths, you know?" Mike nodded, at ease that this was the Anthony he'd known and trusted for years. Anthony reached out and shook Mike's hand. "You'll tell me as soon as you know something?"

"I will, thanks, and sorry for ruining your night."

Anthony shrugged. "It was ruined before you got here, trust me." He went back inside and closed the door.

Misty's shouting came as soon as the deadbolt latched.

Mike eavesdropped, and finding no useful information in their argument, headed back into the cold to track down the medical examiner.

CHAPTER 7

Ana walked up the flagstone path to her former childhood home, a craftsman-style bungalow on a postage-stamp lot where her parents once lived and where, in their absence, her sister, Sydney, had raised her.

Snow collected in the nooks and crannies of the stone columns holding the main roof over the expansive front porch. Ice coated the remains of the robin's nest that she and Sydney had kept a close eye on the previous spring. Two eggs had hatched, and, eventually, the young birds flew safely away. Sydney left the nest intact, hoping some bird might take up residence again the next year.

There was no indication, even in the throes of a messy divorce, that Sydney wouldn't be there to see it.

The porch swing creaked in the wind, and Ana closed her eyes, imagining her father's arms around her and her mother's sweet voice singing. They rocked, with Ana between them, the night before they left for the twentieth anniversary celebration from which they'd never returned. Sixteen people had died in the plane crash, but to seven-year-old Ana, this loss was the whole world.

She lingered at the threshold for a moment of silence before salvaging the spare key from under the snow-crusted welcome mat. She turned the lock and opened the front door, nervous to face the memories.

In twenty years, nothing had changed.

The living room was arranged exactly the same way their mother had left it. The plaid sofa and love seat, unraveling at the seams, had been repaired more than once. Her father's afghan hung folded over the back of her mother's rocking chair where Sydney had read J. M. Barrie's *Peter Pan* to Ana every night until she moved past the fact their mother had never finished the story. It had taken more than a year, and they read the book a dozen times before she was ready for something else. Ana could still recite her favorite passages.

Fresh tears ran down her cheeks. She let them fall, unable to stifle her grief.

She couldn't imagine how Sydney had lived with the memories, or how she would live with them, now that the house was hers.

She walked up the stairs to the tiny spare bedroom that had served as Sydney's office and sat down in the chair behind the desk. A half-empty cup of coffee on top of a coaster bore a faint pink ridge of Sydney's lipstick. Ana brushed her fingertips along the handle and powered up the computer.

If there was any explanation of why Sydney had gone to the Aquarian, Ana was determined to find it.

The blue log-in screen appeared, and Ana typed her full name, "Anneliese," the only password Sydney had ever used. She double-clicked the envelope icon and, as the messages poured in, looked over her shoulder. Being caught snooping was an irrational fear, but the reality that Sydney was gone hadn't fully set in, and Ana felt like an intruder. The in-box quickly filled with credit card offers and messages about unclaimed foreign inheritances.

Ana deleted the spam and printed bills she knew would have to be paid sooner than later. She reviewed the list of folders in the sidebar and opened one called "Divorce." Sydney had red flagged an e-mail from Anthony, dated a week earlier. Ana clicked on it. An arrow icon announced that the message had been forwarded to Sydney's attorney. Ana shook her head, unable to believe how far out of hand the divorce had gotten. Anthony made more of the usual threats, claims about taking the house and things that belonged to their parents if Sydney didn't cooperate, but by the end, it seemed his temper had burned itself out. He agreed to walk away with nothing if Sydney would settle in the next couple of weeks. Ana wondered what the hurry was. Anthony had e-mailed Sydney almost daily, but whereas the others sounded humble and like he needed forgiveness, this one demanded Sydney's cooperation and the last line was weighted with threat:

This is my last offer. Agree to it. Let this all be over. Give me what I want or I'll take it.

E-mails continued to load, and Ana sorted them by sender.

A dozen replies appeared from someone named Kristin Newman. Quick inspection of the electronic signature identified her as Dr. Dorian Carmichael's secretary from the Oakland Street office where Sydney had been a patient.

The uterine cancer diagnosis had hit Sydney hard, and she believed that the hysterectomy, that losing the ability to have children, was some kind of karmic punishment for secretly taking birth control. Ana told her that just wasn't the way things worked, but she couldn't make her sister believe it. She sifted through Kristin's e-mails. It seemed that Sydney had contacted Dr. Carmichael's office numerous times in recent weeks for copies of her pathology reports. Every request was met with an excuse as to why the office couldn't provide one. Kristin's most recent reply said for Sydney to speak with Dr. Carmichael directly.

Ana printed the message and added it to the growing stack. She grabbed a scrap of paper from the cube on the corner of the desk and reached into the side drawer, feeling around for a pen. Her nail caught on a small, hard edge, and she recoiled with a yelp, sucking the tip of her middle finger, which was now dark with blood. She held pressure on the cut and searched for the culprit. An ivory business card with raised black lettering that read, "Dr. Alan Sanders, Obstetrics, Gynecology, and Fertility Specialist," was stuck in the seam of the drawer.

Sydney never mentioned seeing another doctor.

CHAPTER 8

Mike entered the glass vestibule outside of the medical examiner's office and stomped his boots. He dusted the snow from his hair and jacket and silenced his cell phone. The wet soles of his shoes squeaked against the tile floor as he made his way past a dozen quiet offices to the autopsy suite.

Dr. Kimberly Taylor waited at the door, wearing a white lab coat and holding an electronic voice recorder. The hem of her purple dress rested just above her knees, and a gold cross necklace hung around her neck. Her short hair, the color of dark honey, was styled to emphasize her hazel eyes. Kim was only two years younger than Mike, and he'd known her almost her entire life. They'd gone through school together with only a grade between them. Kim had started early, while he had started late. She'd come a long way from the pigtailed girl he had adored from afar, and he still found her breathtaking even at her current age fifty. She smiled and reached out to hug him.

"How are you holding up?"

He lingered in the comfort of her warm embrace a minute before answering. "As well as can be expected. I didn't see this coming."

Kim held her hand on his shoulder. "Are you sure you want to do this right now?"

He didn't, but postponing hearing her findings for hours, a day at most, wasn't going to change that. "I need to know what happened."

Three self-draining, stainless steel tables cast long shadows across the dimly lit room. There were showerhead-type attachments in each of the sinks for washing down the bodies and scales for weighing organs. Several wheeled gurneys lined the side of the room opposite the refrigerated storage drawers.

A white sheet concealed Sydney's body at the center of it all.

Mike swallowed the lump in his throat and moved toward her.

Kim pulled on a pair of rubber gloves, turned on an overhead light, and with Mike's permission, folded the sheet back to Sydney's shoulders.

Her blond-on-brown highlighted hair had been freshly washed and brushed, and her eyes were closed. Kim had taken obvious extra care in preparing her.

Mike did his best not to focus on the crude stitching that seamed Sydney's head closed.

"The coffin pillow will hide that," Kim said, repositioning Sydney's hair. She lifted an evidence bag from the cart next to the table and showed Mike the label. "The bottle you found at the scene was a prescription for zopiclone, a sleep aid that is lethal in high doses, especially when mixed with alcohol."

"We found an empty bottle of vodka in the room."

Kim nodded. "I've gone over the case notes. The label says the prescription was filled the day before Sydney's death, making it a reasonable guess that there were thirty pills in the bottle when she checked in at the Aquarian."

"Would that be enough?"

Kim understood what he meant without his saying it. "It would, but . . ." She drew her lips together and tilted her head.

"But what?"

Kim pulled Sydney's right hand out from under the sheet. The rose-pink polish was chipped on two of her nails. Kim called attention to Sydney's index finger. "She was brought in with dried vomit around her mouth." Mike remembered that from the Aquarian. "See here, where her nail is broken? There were traces of vomit, like she had tried to make herself throw up the pills."

"Why would she do that? Second thoughts?" Mike operated under the assumption of suicide, whether or not he wanted to believe it.

Kim shook her head. "I don't think so. There are a couple of things that make determining death by overdose difficult. One is tolerance level. What is lethal to some is normal for others. It makes it hard to standardize a fatal level. There's also the possibility of postmortem distribution." Mike shrugged and held out his hands. "Drugs contained in fatty tissue are released into bodily fluids after death. The postmortem result might have been skewed."

"So you don't know how much was in her system?"

"I have an idea. In a fatal acute overdose, one would expect to see zopiclone levels in the 0.4–3.9 milligrams per liter range. Sydney's were at ninety *micro*grams per liter, which is less than the usual therapeutic dose. If she *did* take thirty pills, she got them out of her system before she digested them." Kim set Sydney's arm back under the white sheet. "Take a look at this." She lifted Sydney's eyelids to show him the smattering of tiny red and purple spots in the whites of her eyes. "Same as here." She pointed them out in the skin around Sydney's mouth. "Petechial hemorrhaging around the mouth could be caused by forceful vomiting, but I'm not sure that's the case here. Her heart was significantly enlarged, and there was foam in her airway from mucus in her lungs mixing with air as she struggled to breathe. Cause of death is asphyxiation, not drug overdose. Sydney suffocated."

Mike took a moment to absorb what he was hearing. Ana had been right. Someone staged Sydney's death to look like a suicide. His mind went immediately to the scratches on Misty's face. "Anything come back on her nail scrapings?"

Kim pulled the sheet up. "I don't see anything in the reports, but I'll check with the crime lab." She peeled off her gloves and threw them into the garbage. "Do you have any idea who would want Sydney dead?"

Mike shook his head. "It's a very short list."

CHAPTER 9

Marco Prusak rolled up the sleeves of his collared shirt and scrubbed his stained hands at the bathroom sink of his modest, one-bedroom apartment. No matter what he used to clean them, the dye from his protest refused to come off. The fake blood faded to a shade of pink not easily noticed against his olive skin, but the guilt of what he'd done had him unable to ignore it. He'd gone too far, and being suspended at a time when he was so close to his goal had him anxious to get back to his lab.

He splashed a handful of water on his face and stared at his reflection.

Dark circles formed beneath his near-black eyes. His recent, extreme weight loss caused his skin to sag and made his age lines more visible. Fifty-seven hard years, most spent preaching the word of Jehovah door to door and walking for hours in the sun, had him looking at least fifteen years older.

Grief compounded his advanced aging.

His life seemed an endless timeline, each milestone punctuated by tragedy; losing his infant daughter, Jasmine, had been the worst of it.

At six weeks premature, Jasmine's first days were filled with complications. She weighed only four and a half pounds and was slow to gain weight with only a feeding tube nourishing her. Days turned to weeks, and a list of new symptoms heralded something worse.

The color of her skin deepened in its yellow tone, her urine became dark, and her belly swelled. Doctors put her on phototherapy for jaundice, but when her condition didn't improve, a battery of tests confirmed their suspicions. Jasmine was diagnosed with complete biliary atresia, a congenital, and if untreated, fatal, abnormality in the opening of her bile ducts.

Marco and his young wife, Faith, prayed for Jasmine's improvement, spending all of their time in the Neonatal Intensive Care Unit, and suffering reprimand from Witness elders because of it. Preaching time, while independently reported, was monitored, and the dropping off of Marco and Faith's efforts made them look weak in their devotion. Congregation pressure broke Faith first, leaving him alone, emotionally distraught, and conflicted about his beliefs.

Jasmine continued her slow decline, and a consulting surgeon at County laid out a terminal prognosis. Without Marco and Faith's consent to a liver transplant, Jasmine would die.

To Faith, the news had been Jasmine's death sentence.

Organ transplants were discouraged, and downright frowned upon in their faith, unless they could be done without any blood transference. Bloodless transplants could not be done at County, or at any hospital within a five-hundred-mile radius.

Marco pleaded with Faith, and with the elders, but ultimately, their religious beliefs won out. The transplant was denied.

Faith wasn't at the hospital when Jasmine passed. Despite Faith's postpartum weakness, she was out distributing tracts, preaching of Armageddon.

Marco couldn't forgive her for not being there when Jasmine breathed her last breath. The nurse lifted Jasmine's lifeless body out of the bassinette and, for the first time, Marco was able to hold her without the tubes and catheters in place. Her stomach had blown up and her liver hardened, like a stone in her side. She was the color of saffron, an image that, fifteen years later, Marco still couldn't get out of his head.

Medical school was an act of defiance against the congregation and the beginning of a decades-long revenge plan already well under way.

Marco checked the time on his watch and paced his minimally furnished living room. *Watchtower* tracts and magazines covered the secondhand coffee table between an inexpensive sofa and a small tube television with no cable feed. He had no need of material things, only to finish what he had started. He picked up the handset on his cordless phone and dialed County Memorial's switchboard for the third time that morning.

"County Memorial operator, how may I help you?"

"May I speak with Mitchell Altman, please?" Marco had left several messages for the CEO, but all of his calls had gone unreturned.

Hold music broke the tension of the momentary silence, and Mitchell's secretary, Pam, came on the line. "Mitchell Altman's office."

"Pam, it's Marco Prusak. Is Mitchell available?"

"Hold on just a minute while I check." Normally Pam would chat, but this morning she was all business. A minute passed, maybe two, before she returned on the line. "I'm sorry, Mitchell isn't in his office. Can I take a message?"

Pam was a terrible liar.

"No, thank you. I'll deliver the message myself."

CHAPTER 10

County Memorial's Emergency Department hit a midafternoon lull after the early-morning rush of flu that had Marion's people coming in by the dozen.

Jared washed his hands, sat down at one of several computers behind the nurses' station, and sorted through the morning's lab results. Two of his patients were ready for discharge. One would have to be admitted. Open beds were scarce, and if he was lucky, monitoring that admission would keep him late enough to excuse his sleeping in the on-call room rather than going home to Colby, whom he hadn't spoken to since their most recent argument.

He typed in a series of orders and signed off on the discharge paperwork for his least sick patient, a young boy with an ear infection that could have easily been treated by his pediatrician.

Wilson Quinn, one of the department's physician assistants, appeared in front of him. Six foot three and with a full beard, Wilson had the appearance of someone more suited to the woods than long hours in a hospital emergency room. Those who didn't know him feared his meaty hands coming at them with needles and IVs, but despite his coarse exterior, Wilson had the best bedside manner in the unit, and the second steadiest hands Jared had ever seen. Ana Ashmore, a medic he'd worked with over the past couple of years, had the first.

Wilson leaned into the counter, his round belly straining the elastic waist of the green scrubs not intended for someone so large. "Ambulance is on its way in. You ready?"

Jared waved for Heather, one of the unit nurses, to take the papers. "Make sure you go over the instructions with the mom." He scribbled out a prescription and handed it to her. "This is for his antibiotic."

Heather nodded, took the paperwork, and headed to the room where the boy with the ear infection had been for hours.

Jared looked up at Wilson. "What do we know?"

Wilson read a scrap of paper in his hands. "The patient's name is Stephanie Martin. A neighbor found her unconscious on her kitchen floor."

"Symptoms?"

"Fever, delirium, and in quite a bit of pain. Jim says she's too dehydrated for him to get the IV in." Wilson rolled his eyes. "He says that a lot."

Jared searched the patient's name in the computer, and finding several Stephanie Martins, selected the most recent one. "Ana couldn't get it?"

Wilson smirked, his expression amused and all-knowing. "Jim didn't mention her."

Jared tried to hide his disappointment as he scrolled through a list of reports. "Shit." He pulled up Stephanie's operative note dated four months earlier.

Wilson chuckled at Jared's unusual use of profanity. "Something the matter?"

Jared nodded. "I knew I recognized the name. Stephanie Martin is Dorian's transplant patient."

"That isn't going to make Mitchell happy."

Stephanie Martin was the new transplant program's second incident of bad publicity, and Jared wanted no part of it. "This is a malpractice suit waiting to happen." He picked up the phone and dialed the operator.

"Switchboard, how can I help you?"

"This is Dr. Monroe in the Emergency Department. Can you get me Dr. Dorian Carmichael's office, please?"

Hold music played, and then the phone rang twice.

"Oakland Street Obstetrics and Gynecology, this is Kristin."

"Good morning, Kristin. This is Dr. Jared Monroe at County Memorial. I have an emergency for Dr. Carmichael. Can you connect us?"

"Just a minute, please."

Jared tapped his fingers on the counter, waiting impatiently for Dorian to pick up. If he could get away with not having his name anywhere on Stephanie's file, he'd be thrilled. He had only ever been named in one malpractice suit, a case on which he had performed only a brief, initial assessment. The patient's cardiologist was heavily investigated, and though everyone was eventually exonerated, they'd spent an awful lot of time together in meetings with legal. Jared couldn't imagine spending that kind of time with Dorian. Aside from the fact that his transplant program ate a good portion of the funds Jared desperately needed for the ER, Dorian had had a *thing* for Colby for as long as she had worked there.

"I'm sorry for the hold. This is Noreen. How can I help you?"

"Noreen, I need to talk to Dorian."

"I'm sorry, but he's in surgery today. I can get ahold of him—"

"Is he operating at County?"

"Yes, but—"

"Thanks, I'll find him."

The ambulance siren silenced as Jim, a seasoned EMS veteran and supervisor, backed into the receiving bay. The automatic doors slid open, and Jared headed over to meet him.

Jim hopped down from the driver's seat and rushed to open the back door. His eyes were glossed over, and he yawned.

"Long night?" Jared looked around him, hoping to catch a glimpse of Ana and finding Ethan Kerr instead.

Ethan, an EMT in his early twenties, with his precision haircut, chiseled facial features, and vivid blue eyes, stepped out of the ambulance as if walking out of a magazine.

"Fever's climbing," Ethan said. "We couldn't get a line, but she's stable."

Wilson waited until they unloaded Stephanie to have a look at her right hand and arm. "You stuck her, what, four times?"

"Five, by my count," said Jared, shaking his head. "Set her up in room one. Get an IV in her other arm and I'll be right there." Monica, one of several unit clerks, rushed past him, and he called out to her. "I need an overhead page. Call for Dr. Carmichael. I need him here, *stat*."

"You got it." Monica jogged to the nearest phone and placed the call.

Wilson and Ethan wheeled Stephanie away.

Jim rubbed his eyes and handed Jared his copy of the prehospital care report. "Her husband should be here any minute. His name is"—Jim flipped the sheet on the clipboard—"Riley Martin."

Jared reviewed the list of Stephanie's symptoms—fever, malaise, abdominal pain—and formulated a list of differential diagnoses from infection to organ rejection.

The latter spelled disaster.

Jim's radio announced another call, and he waved for Ethan to join him. "No rest for the weary, right? Pulling a double shift after two days of visitation with Kayla, I'm beat. Who would have thought a three-year-old could be so draining? After what happened, though, I mean, I had to cover Ana's shifts."

"What do you mean, 'what happened'? Is she all right?"

Wilson called from the doorway of room 1. "Line's in."

Ethan rolled his eyes as he pushed the empty gurney toward the ambulance.

"Jim, is Ana okay?" Jared ignored Wilson's repeated attempts to get his attention.

"She is, but her sister was found dead at the Aquarian last night."

Jared didn't know Sydney well, but he had met her at a couple of medical community functions and knew she and Ana were very close.

Wilson grabbed Jared by the sleeve and all but dragged him toward Stephanie's room. "I said *we're ready.*"

The overhead page called Dorian to the ER for the third time.

Monica shrugged and shook her head, a sign that he wasn't answering.

"Keep trying." Jared turned at the sound of fast-approaching, high-heeled footsteps.

Noreen Pafford, wearing a white lab coat over a fitted, blue dress, hurried toward him. A section of folded newspaper stuck up from her pocket and left a dark smudge where the melted snow smeared the ink. She ran her hand through her short hair and narrowed her eyes with obvious anger. "Where's Dorian?"

Jared, already on edge, fired back. "That's a good question, and one I've been trying to have answered for the past ten minutes."

Noreen checked her watch. "His case got out a half hour ago." She tapped away at the keys on her cell phone.

Jared started a triage sheet and went into Stephanie's room, noticing her increased heart rate on the vitals monitor.

"Stephanie, my name is Dr. Monroe. Can you hear me?"

The ebony-haired woman rolled her head toward him and groaned in pain. The fever had her sweating, and her hair clung to her flushed face. She appeared thin, too thin, and barely lucid.

Noreen stormed into the room and interrupted. "Why didn't you tell me that Stephanie Martin was the emergency?"

"Because *you're* not a doctor." Jared pulled a penlight from his pocket and continued his examination. He'd dealt with Noreen enough to know that she didn't believe in limitations. "Wilson, get her out of here."

Noreen stood her ground. "I'm not leaving until Dorian gets here."

"And I'm not going to ask again." Jared turned to Wilson. "Count to three, and if she still isn't out of here, call Security. I have a patient to treat."

CHAPTER 11

Dorian slipped off his surgical cap and rubbed his tired eyes. Hours under the intense operating room lights, of staring through the magnifying loupe, had a drying effect that no drops could quench.

PACU nurses moved fluidly around the recovery room, answering the alarms of the monitors connected to a row of patients coming out of anesthesia. Emily Warren remained sedated among them.

Dorian headed to the waiting room where Derrick, Emily's husband, sat in the corner, reading, or rather staring, at a magazine. He never turned the page. His short, brown hair was flattened on one side from leaning against his hand, and his green eyes, visible through his glasses, were bloodshot. The table next to him was covered in empty coffee cups, and his leg bounced up and down.

"Mr. Warren?" Dorian called out to him.

Derrick all but leapt out of his seat. "Is Emily all right? How did everything go?"

"Why don't you join me in the hallway?" Dorian smiled to ease Derrick's nerves. "Emily's surgery went well. You'll be able to see her in about an hour or so, as soon as she wakes up."

"'Well,'" Derrick said, wringing his thin hands, "as in, we'll be able to have a baby?"

"There are no guarantees. Everything looks great so far, but we have to start Emily on medication to stop her body from rejecting the new uterus. Once she is healed and her body has fully accepted the transplant, we can talk about pregnancy. It'll be at least three months, but it could take longer."

The overhead speaker crackled, and a monotone voice paged him.

"They keep calling you," Derrick said, a hint of annoyance in his tone.

"Excuse me a minute, would you?" Dorian was headed for the wall phone when Noreen burst through the door to the second-floor stairwell, red faced and snarling. Dorian rushed toward her. "What the hell are you doing here?" He steered her away from Derrick, who flashed a concerned look in their direction.

Noreen pulled her arm free and set her hand on her hip. "I've been trying to get ahold of you for the last half hour, paging you, calling you . . ."

"The overhead page doesn't come to the operating room, for one, and my phone is in my locker. I've been in surgery all morning. What's so important?"

Noreen thrust the folded newspaper against his chest.

He caught the local news section as it was about to fall. A page-two article told of an investigation into the death of Sydney Dowling, one of his more recent patients. He looked over his shoulder at Derrick Warren, pacing the floor and casting occasional glances in their direction.

"This doesn't say anything about us," Dorian said. "Or about her surgery."

"She's been calling the office nonstop. You don't think they're going to wonder what she was so concerned about?"

"Let them wonder. Have you talked to Mitchell?"

Noreen shook her head. "Not yet, but I'm sure he's seen the news. And that's not the worst of it. Stephanie Martin's in the emergency room with Jared Monroe."

Dorian wiped his hands over his face. "What happened?"

"She came in by ambulance. I couldn't get much more information than that. Jared called the office to talk to you, and Kristin transferred him to me. What if it's organ rejection, Dorian? It's all the evidence anyone needs, if they're smart."

"But they're not *smart*. Only three of us know what happened, and there's no reason to suspect otherwise. I can't talk about this right now. Not here."

Dorian opened the door to the waiting room and called the attention of the secretary behind the check-in desk whose name he didn't know. "Hey, excuse me." He waved, and she looked up from her monitor. "Please take Mr. Warren to the recovery room and have him set up someplace quiet with his wife."

Derrick, who Dorian could tell had been listening, knitted his eyebrows together. "I thought I had to wait an hour."

"I moved it up." Dorian waited until the PACU door opened before heading back to Noreen, standing with her arms folded. "Could this day get any worse?"

"It's about to. You know who I saw on my way in?"

Dorian sighed. "No, who?"

"Marco Prusak."

CHAPTER 12

Pamela Lewis sat cramped behind a small desk in the outer waiting area of Mitchell Altman's office. Her mousy brown hair was wound into a tight twist, shellacked in place with a glistening coat of hair spray.

Marco walked in from the hallway and caught her off guard.

"Marco, you scared me half to death. I told you, Mitchell isn't here."

Marco hung his coat on the hook behind the door. "I know what you told me, Pam, but it's important that I see him. I'll wait until he gets back."

Pam pushed her chair back from the desk and grunted as she heaved her considerable weight forward. The fabric of her snug blue-and-white dress pulled tight across her backside and hips, and Marco, though he would never tell her, could see the pattern of her underwear through it. Pam lumbered toward Mitchell's door and blocked Marco's view.

"I'm not sure when he's going to be back, but I'll make sure he gets your messages," she said loudly.

Marco sat on one of two chairs next to a round table topped with a vase of white lilies. "Maybe you could have him overhead paged for me?" He matched her in volume, guessing Mitchell was listening. "He's in there, isn't he?" he whispered, and pointed at the door.

Pam nodded. "I'm sorry, but Mitchell insists on not being interrupted today."

Marco pulled his left ankle on top of his right knee and slapped his checkbook down on the table. "I'm sure he'd make an exception."

The door opened behind Pam, and she moved to the side. Mitchell, four inches shorter and probably a hundred pounds thinner, stepped into view.

"What do you want, Marco?"

Pam lowered her head. "I told him you weren't available."

"I heard."

Marco picked up his checkbook. "We need to talk."

"Seems I have no choice. Come in." Mitchell slammed the door behind them. "I swear that woman can't do anything right," he said of his secretary, who had really tried her best to keep Marco away. It was no secret that Mitchell preferred the younger, prettier secretaries, like Amber, the twenty-four-year-old who worked for the CFO, one office away, and to whom he could almost always be found talking. Pam didn't stand a chance, and Mitchell took out on her the fact that he felt stuck. "What can I do for you?" He unbuttoned his expensive, navy blue suit jacket and poured himself a cup of coffee without offering one to Marco.

"None of this is Pam's fault," Marco said, waiting to be asked to be seated.

Mitchell hung his jacket neatly over the back of his chair, exposing a monogrammed dress shirt and a Rolex watch that cost more than all of Marco's material possessions combined. "Are you waiting for a written invitation? Have a seat."

Marco sat, checkbook in hand, and after pondering the hundred ways to say what he had come to, settled on the simplest. "I want to come back to work." He didn't intend to explain why.

Mitchell rubbed his hand along the back of his head where the faintest hint of horseshoe-shaped razor stubble peeked through his pale skin. "The suspension sticks, Marco. Do you realize what you could've done to the transplant program with that stunt of yours?"

Marco clicked his pen, wrote out a check to the County Memorial Foundation in the amount of fifty thousand dollars, and slid it across the desk. "Whatever disruption I might have caused, this should cover the damages."

Mitchell hesitated to pick up the check and took off his wire-rimmed glasses. "What am I supposed to do here? How do I explain why you did what you did without looking like a fool? Help me out. What possessed you?" His eyes fixed on Marco's stained hands.

"I can't explain how where I come from makes me who I am."

"How hard can it be?" Mitchell settled back in his chair. "I started off as a shop floor manager in a tape company, working to pay for a college education my family was too poor to afford. I spent five years there and had replaced a man who, after forty years of service, was forced to take a job greeting customers at Walmart to subsidize his retirement. I swore I wouldn't be that person. I'm money motivated. That's why I do what I do."

Marco considered the story and drafted a second payment. He folded the fifty-thousand-dollar check, made out directly to Mitchell, along the perforations and slid it across the desk. "What about now?" He needed to get back to his lab before someone discovered the evidence.

Mitchell leaned forward, a satisfied grin spreading across his face. "Add a personal apology to Dorian and we have a deal."

"I can start back to work immediately?"

"As soon as you'd like." Mitchell folded and pocketed the check. "It could probably go without saying, but this is a confidential arrangement."

"Of course. Everything around here is."

CHAPTER 13

Mike pulled into the Aquarian parking lot and shook his head. A day after Sydney's murder, Samuel had already put room 11 back into service. The yellow crime-scene tape had been torn down, but the knots that had held it in place remained, warning anyone who didn't know that something bad had recently happened there. Mike zippered his jacket and stepped out of his patrol car into an ankle-deep snowbank. Other than the section where residents had haphazardly shoveled, the lot was under a solid half foot of snow. He trudged to the rental office, stomped the snow off his boots and pant legs, and stared through the window.

Samuel slept behind the cluttered check-in desk, wearing the same clothes as the last time Mike saw him. He banged on the door before walking in.

"Hey, Sam, wake up." Sam startled and nearly tipped out of his chair. His foul body odor, a mix of onions and chicken soup, filled the room, and had Mike wanting to go back into the cold. "You're looking pretty rough there, Sam."

Sam sat up, the pointed bones of his shoulders melting into his skin. "S-s-something I can do for you, S-s-sergeant? I already gave my s-s-statement, twice."

"I have a few new questions to ask." Mike noted Sam to be more clear and present than the day before. "Anyone give you the okay to open that room back up?"

Sam took a sip from a cup of coffee old enough to have a creamer ring around the fill line. "Officer Blake d-d-did. I told him I ain't got that many rooms to r-r-rent to leave that one closed up."

Mike made a mental note to give Julian hell when he saw him next. "Tell me about when the woman, Sydney, checked in. What did she have with her? How did she pay? Did you notice anything unusual? Was anyone else there?"

Sam shrugged. "I—I—I didn't see her." He pointed at a metal lockbox and a tattered logbook on the counter. The handwritten sign read, "Honor system $10 an hour $30 a night. Ring bell for kredit card. Must sign in." The punctuation was minimal, and "credit" had been misspelled. "M-m-most people pay cash."

Mike turned the log so he could read it, noting three signatures for the room that night, none of which belonged to Sydney. "Is this the only register?"

"Yep. B-b-but the room was paid for. I ch-ch-checked the cash."

"The victim's name's not on here."

"W-w-we're not much for real names."

Mike nodded, figuring neither Marilyn Monroe nor Harvey Keitel had been the last to check in. "What about the security tapes? You never handed any over."

"Th-th-that's because there ain't any to give you."

A dull ache formed behind Mike's eyes. "What do you mean there *aren't* any?" Annoyance had him giving out unsolicited English lessons.

Sam opened the top desk drawer, pulled an off-brand cigarette from the pack, and tried to light it with his shaking hand.

The lighter flame danced, and eventually the tip of the cigarette caught. "The cameras ain't r-r-real. Some of the people that lived here wanted s-s-something done about"—he looked up as he considered his words—"the people who've b-b-been away awhile."

"You mean ex-convicts?"

Sam's bloodshot eyes darted between Mike and the door as if being caught talking to the police would adversely affect his business. "W-we all got problems in life. I don't judge. I put fake cameras in to s-s-stop the complaining."

"And I assume the hourly regulars and traffickers know they're not real?"

Samuel exhaled a cloud of smoke, having sucked down half a cigarette in only a few drags. "I—I—I don't know what you mean." He crushed out the butt in an overfull ashtray and opened the door. "If there ain't anything else, I—I—I have cleaning to take care of."

Mike, believing Sam's evasiveness stemmed more from being strung out and preserving his economy than knowing anything about what happened to Sydney, headed out into the cold. The crisp breeze carried away the terrible smell he couldn't believe he'd almost gotten used to. "I'll be in touch," he said, heading toward his cruiser.

"L-l-looking forward to it." Sam pulled down a ripped shade with another red-marker note that said, "Back in 5 minutes."

Mike was about to get into his car, when a door opened behind him.

An overweight woman, wearing a flannel nightgown and robe, called out to him. "Hey, you have a light?" She shook a cigarette from the soft pack in her hand and pinched it between her lips.

"No, I'm sorry. I don't."

The woman reached into the deep pocket of her blue terry cloth bathrobe and produced a lighter. "How about a minute?"

Mike felt a bit dense for missing the signal. "Yeah, I have a minute." He trudged back through the snowy lot toward room 13.

A curl of smoke mixed with the woman's coffee-soaked breath. "This is an off-the-record conversation, yes?"

"Sure," Mike reluctantly agreed.

"No names, no signatures?"

"If that's what you need." Mike knew he could bargain later if the woman knew anything valuable.

"It is. This isn't the kind of place you want to live running your mouth. You knew that girl from last night, didn't you?" The woman had the unique talent of simultaneously talking and exhaling smoke.

"I did, yes."

"I knew you did because I saw you crying." Mike lowered his gaze, a bit embarrassed. "Got a daughter, myself," the woman said, taking another drag. "That's why I go outside to smoke. It's no good for her. Gotta keep my baby girl safe, you know?" Inside, the young girl in the cutoff footie pajamas napped on the couch. Mike put her at four years old, not quite old enough for school. The wind kicked up, and the woman pulled the door the rest of the way shut. "Sam tell you the cameras are fake?" Suspecting a trap, Mike didn't immediately answer. "It's okay. He thinks we're all as stupid as he is. I saw him put them up. Know what gave it away?" Mike shrugged, unsure of where the conversation was headed. "No wires." The woman, who had clearly never heard of wireless cameras, was nonetheless right about these. She looked across the parking lot and down the row of rooms. "Know what else?" She continued without being answered. "I saw someone leave that room that night." She pointed at room 11. "I heard raised voices, a woman's voice, I guess, but I was right at the part in my program where the CSIs were going to figure out who did it, so I waited to hear. You ever watch that program?" Mike shook his head. "Probably get enough of that at work, I guess. Anyway, by the time I lowered the TV, the fight was over. I got up in time to see someone walking away."

"Walking away" and "walking out of the room where Sydney's body was found" were two different things. "You saw someone leave *that* room, specifically?" Mike pointed at room 11.

"No. I heard *that* door, specifically, slam." She turned his words around on him. "I know it was *that* door because it shook my place. I've been living here three years. I know what it feels like to have the next door shut." She lit a second cigarette off the end of the first. "Some nights, I hear it on the hour."

Mike considered telling the woman that a by-the-hour motel wasn't the best place to raise a young child, but he supposed she already knew that. It wasn't his place to pass judgment, and, most likely, there wasn't anything she could do about her circumstances. "Did you get a look at the person? See a car, maybe? Can you tell me anything in particular? Did the person have a tattoo? Or walk with a limp? Anything?"

The woman shrugged. "Black coat, black hat, black boots, and between the bitch of a snowstorm and the fact Sam still hasn't fixed the motion lights, that's all I got. Person might as well have been a shadow."

A sound, like a roll-up shade, caught their attention.

Sam appeared in the office doorway, sipping from the old coffee mug.

His presence shut the woman right up. She crushed out half a cigarette after smoking the first one to the filter. "I have to go."

Mike couldn't stand to lose a lead, no matter how vague. "Can you tell me anything else about the voices you heard, or maybe how tall the person you saw leaving was? Anything at all?"

"Been about all the help I can be," the woman said.

"How about height and weight?"

The woman lowered her voice. "I'm no good at sizing people up, but I'd guess they were no taller than five foot five, five foot six, maybe, and they were skinny."

"Like a woman?" Misty moved quickly to the head of the suspect line.

"Maybe, I don't know. I'm sorry I can't be more help." The woman glanced at Samuel and hurried inside.

CHAPTER 14

The fractured light of the stained glass lamp cast shadows across Ana's living room where she sat, crying, holding Dr. Alan Sanders's business card in one hand and a bottle of Xanax in the other. Making the funeral arrangements thrust her so deep into mourning that she considered chasing all thirty pills with the bottle of vodka on the coffee table in front of her. Sydney's death was finally real, and the loneliness, the sadness that came with it, would either strengthen Ana, or break her. The choice was hers. She threw the sedatives as hard as she could against the wall, the voice of her conscience sounding an awful lot like Sydney's, and dialed Dr. Sanders's office.

The phone rang, and when the switchboard operator answered, Ana sniffled.

"Dr. Alan Sanders's office, how many I help you?" Heavy static crackled on the line.

"I'd like to speak with Dr. Sanders, please."

"I'm sorry, we have a bad connection. Is this a medical emergency?"

"No, but—"

"This number is for medical emergencies only. The office reopens at nine a.m. You can try back then, or I can relay a message."

"It's important he gets back to me. My name is Ana Ashmore. My sister is a patient of his. Her name is Sydney Dowling." She wasn't yet ready to speak in the past tense.

The static became louder. "I'm sorry," the operator said. "Can you repeat that name for me?"

"Dowling. D-O-W-L-I-N-G." Ana overenunciated as she shouted Sydney's name. "Have him call me at 518-222-1515." The crackling disappeared. "Hello?" Ana pulled the phone away from her ear. Tears blurred the small screen. "Hello?"

The line went dead.

"Dammit."

Ana slammed the phone down and picked up the vodka. She rolled the chilled bottle between her hands, her body heat melting a band around the middle, and took a long swig. The fiery liquid burned down her throat, and worse than the taste, was the smell. It reminded her of the vomit on Sydney's lips as she performed CPR, too late to save her. Ana poured the rest of the bottle down the kitchen-sink drain, and turned to see Ethan standing outside the front door. She smoothed her hair behind her ears and dried her eyes before answering it. Mascara didn't so easily wipe off, and she was sure she looked a mess.

"What're you doing here?"

"I was in the neighborhood. I thought you could use some company, and maybe one of these." Ethan held one of two coffee cups out to her. "Banana bread latte, right?"

She inhaled the sweet cinnamon and banana smell and waved Ethan in. "I'm sorry. I don't mean to be a jerk. I just feel like a wreck right now."

"Well, you look beautiful." Ethan hugged her and made himself at home.

Theirs was a casual friendship, with the added benefit of sex when either of them was unattached. Ethan, Ana had noticed, remained not only single, but unavailable to anyone but her. She sat on the couch and tucked a pillow under her arm.

Ethan picked up the pill bottle. The cap was broken, and the pills had spilled on the floor. "Since when do you take Xanax?"

"Since I stopped sleeping."

"They're not going to do you much good on the floor." Ethan sat next to her and eased her socked feet onto his lap. "You want to talk about it?" He gently massaged the arch of her right foot, and she could see he knew what she was thinking.

"Not really."

"You're not alone, Ana. I know how close you and Sydney were."

"I said I didn't want to talk about it."

Ethan's hands worked their way up her calves. "I know, I'm just saying. People are worried about you. They love you. I—"

She stopped him before he could say it. "We said no attachments, Ethan."

"I just want to make sure you know I'm here. I care about what you're going through." He looked over at the pill bottle he set on the coffee table. "I don't want you doing anything stupid."

She'd have done about anything to get him to stop talking.

"I don't want to think about any of it right now," she said, pulling him toward her. "Help me forget?"

The vodka blocked out the voice in the back of her head shouting not to lead him on.

"Are you sure?" Ethan knelt between her legs and lowered himself on top of her until his soft lips met hers.

"Positive," she whispered.

He smiled, and his bottomless, blue eyes swallowed her whole. His warm breath played on her skin as he crushed her with kisses.

"I love you," he said, and she moaned in response, arching and digging her fingertips into his back as he slid her pants over her hips.

Each movement took her farther away from her pain.

Ethan pulled his shirt over his head, and Ana stroked the sparse, soft hairs on his muscular chest, tracing the long lines of his abs until she felt the top of his jeans and unbuttoned them.

"I want you." She sat up and lifted her arms for Ethan to take off her shirt and bra.

Their practiced movements were rhythmic, and neither missed a beat as they finished undressing each other, their bodies becoming one.

Ana's mind went blank, primal urge overtaking logic and sadness.

Tomorrow, she'd deal with the fallout, but tonight, making love to Ethan wasn't a mistake; it was an escape.

CHAPTER 15

Mike walked into the Barfly Tavern wearing jeans, a hooded sweat-shirt, and a dual-layer Columbia jacket more suited to a winter trek up a mountainside than an overheated bar. The smell of urinal cakes mixed with the stench of stale beer to make the kind of odor only someone who had smelled decomposition at a crime scene could get used to.

The rustic pub, located on the outskirts of Marion, served as a second home to a primarily male roster of cops and firemen. It was the kind of place one went to let off steam, which was exactly what Anthony Dowling appeared to be doing four seats down the bar.

Mike peeled off his gloves, debating whether to sit, or turn around and walk out.

"Mike, old man. Good to see you. It's been a while." Nestor Rodriguez, the dark-skinned barkeep, who was as wide as he was tall, waved Mike in, enticing him with a frosted glass of Sam Adams. The hard white light of the compact fluorescent bulbs that were a recent, if not gaudy, addition to the bar's mismatched motif, emphasized the deep craters in Nestor's face. He wiped down the scratched and faded bar with a formerly white bar mop, and collected Anthony's empties.

Anthony looked up from his beer.

Mike, seeing no choice in the matter, took the seat next to him.

"Twice this week. Mike, we've got to stop meeting like this." Anthony's breath smelled of whiskey, beer, and peanuts. The half-empty bowl in front of him and the pile of shells on the floor at his feet said he'd been there for some time.

Nestor set Mike's beer down, and moved casually out of earshot.

Mike took a sip. "Believe it or not, I wasn't looking for you." He looked at the open, empty ring box next to Anthony's beer-soaked coaster. "But since you're here . . ."

"I don't know how things got this far." Anthony turned the box over a few times in his hands. "It feels like one minute I'm being seduced, the next minute I'm getting divorced, and then I can't take back any of it."

"You don't know what you've got until it's gone, right?" Mike could offer nothing more than clichéd wisdom.

"I guess. Knowing I can't apologize puts things into perspective. Have you seen Ana? I was going to call her, or stop by her house, but what can I say to her? I'm probably the last person she wants to see."

Mike nodded. "Probably. I can tell her you asked about her. Let her come to you if she wants to, but I wouldn't hold my breath." He waved for the bartender's attention. "Nestor, another beer for Anthony, please."

"You don't have to do that."

"I owe you one for the ruckus I caused the other night, don't you think?"

"You mean Misty? She's got a temper, but she's harmless. The mention of Sydney's name throws her over the edge. Alpha female nonsense, or something."

"If I lived to be two hundred years old, I'd never figure women out. Speaking of figuring things out, something's been bothering me since I left Misty's place."

"The scratches, right?" Mike hadn't expected Anthony to be so forthcoming. "The story I told you about the fight at the diner was true, mostly. She didn't break up a fight—she was in one." Anthony closed the ring box and set it on the counter. "It was the damned ring. I told Misty we should wait until the divorce was final to get engaged, but you know how women are." Mike shrugged, having relatively little experience in the matter. "Misty cried, I felt bad, and even though I knew better, I gave in and proposed. I wasn't even sure I wanted to . . . but . . ."

Mike sensed Anthony's withholding. "But?"

"Two nights ago, Misty was working the night shift at the diner, when Patricia Dentmore shows up, more than a bit tipsy. You know Trish, right? She's been a friend of Sydney's since grade school." Mike nodded. "Anyway, she sees the ring I gave Misty and goes off. She's screaming and yelling, calling Misty a home wrecker and God knows what else. Butch—he owns the diner—comes from around the counter and tries to get the two of them outside. He's telling Misty to calm down and take it easy." Anthony shook his head. "That woman's anything but calm, or easy. Misty slapped Trish, and the two of them literally ended up rolling around on the floor, scratching and pulling hair. Butch pried them apart, but he fired Misty on the spot."

Mike let out a low whistle. "You weren't kidding about her temper. So, she didn't quit?"

Anthony shook his head. "No."

"Where did Misty go after the fight?"

"I know what you're thinking, Mike, but Misty's not a killer. A hothead and an occasional pain in the ass, but she had nothing to do with what happened to Sydney."

Mike held his hand open, palms facing up, and shrugged. "You can see how I'd wonder. Listen, you didn't even have to tell me as much as you did, but right now, I either have to have something solid about where Misty was that night, or I'll have to formally exclude her." The implication was anything but subtle: cooperate, or I'll haul her in.

Pool balls clicked together on the table a few feet behind them, and the bar was otherwise silent. Mike hadn't realized how loudly they'd been speaking, but the men who had been going about their business had stopped to listen.

Anthony looked over his broad shoulder and sighed. "Nestor." He patted the bar in front of him. Two shots, please. The usual."

Nestor grabbed a bottle of rye, two shot glasses, and turned up the radio loud enough that everyone went back to what they were doing. He set the glasses in front of Anthony and filled them to the rim.

Anthony slid one to Mike and lifted his glass. "To life events."

Mike pounded his shot, unsure of what, exactly, they were toasting.

Anthony wiped the rye from his lips and held the glass up for a refill. "What you're asking for is an alibi, and we both have one. Butch called me down to the diner after the fight. He had Misty in the back room with an ice pack on her face. Trish was long gone. Misty was crying when I got there, and not 'lost my job' tears, something much worse. She must've told Butch before she told me what was wrong, or he wouldn't have been catering to her the way he was. She started spotting. You know what I mean?" Mike shrugged. "Bleeding?" Anthony said, as if that made his point clearer. Mike still had no idea. "We spent the night in the County Memorial emergency room. Mike, Misty's pregnant. With the fight, she was afraid the bleeding meant she was having a miscarriage. We were at the hospital from the time I picked her up at the diner until three the next morning. You can verify with the hospital. I never left her room."

If Anthony was telling the truth, and Mike's instinct said he was, there was no way either he or Misty could've had anything to do with Sydney's murder.

Mike didn't know what to say, and he let Anthony fill the void with his apologetic rambling.

"I'm sick over what happened, Mike. Sydney and I were fighting, but it's what people do during a divorce. They hurt each other." Anthony eyes glossed over. "I never meant a single threat. I'm just so *stuck*. I've got Misty all over me about the baby, and Sydney, you know how headstrong she is. She wouldn't give an inch."

"Was," Mike corrected. "How headstrong Sydney *was*. And the pregnancy?"

"The baby's fine." Anthony said.

"And I guess that's a blessing, but it's not what I mean. Did Sydney know about the baby?"

"Oh God. No. It would kill her."

Mike could see Anthony regretted his choice of words as soon as he said them, and he held up his hand to avoid another awkward apology. "I know what you meant." He laid a fifty-dollar bill on the bar. "Nestor, we're all set here. Can you call Anthony a cab for me?"

"Will do."

Anthony kept his head down, sulking over his beer.

"You've got quite a mess to clean up." Mike patted him on the shoulder. "I can't say I envy you." He fished his keys out of his pocket, and grumbled all the way out the door.

The news, shocking as it was, put him in the worst possible situation. Not only did he lose the single lead in Sydney's case; he now had to break the news of Misty's pregnancy to Ana.

CHAPTER 16

The snow crunched under the tires of Dorian's Land Rover, the color of which—Baltic Blue it was called—appeared black except in sunlight. He pulled into the empty driveway of his Oakland Street office, exhausted, achy, and annoyed that his overpriced plow service hadn't yet done its job.

Twelve hours of surgery, the news about Sydney's death, and avoiding the repercussions of Stephanie Martin's complications had him run ragged. He'd had too many close calls, evading both Riley, Stephanie's husband, and Mitchell Altman, who was, no doubt, more concerned about potential legal action than Stephanie's well-being.

Dorian unlocked the side door and went up the back stairs that divided the examination and waiting rooms from the staff offices. The stale air smelled of heat and construction dust, the aged ventilation in desperate need of cleaning now that the remodeling was finished. Dorian opened the window an inch to let in the cold breeze. His office had been straightened. The charts he needed to review were stacked neatly in the center of his desk. On top of them, a copy of the next day's schedule was marked with red ink.

He picked up the paper, rolled his eyes, and grunted. His first hour had been blocked, his patients rescheduled, and Noreen had written *Meeting with Mitchell* in their place. He collapsed in his chair and buried his face in his hands.

"Everything okay?"

He nearly shot out of his chair at the sound of Noreen's voice. "Jesus, Noreen. Announce yourself or something, would you?"

Fresh snowflakes clung to her wispy bangs, and she wore a loose, baby doll dress instead of the scrubs he'd seen her in earlier.

"Aren't you freezing?"

"I'm comfortable enough." She lifted her arm to show him the wool trench coat draped over it. "I was on my way home and saw your car parked out back. I figured I'd better make amends. I'm sorry I lost my temper earlier. It was unprofessional, and it won't happen again." She hung her coat on the empty chair across from him and leaned forward, giving him a look down the wide neck of her dress. Her nipples were visibly erect beneath the black lace, demi-cup bra.

"Noreen, I really have to get these charts done. I'm exhausted."

She smiled when he stared longer than he should have.

"Let's see if I can help with that." She stood behind him, kneading the tension from his shoulders.

The massaging felt so good that Dorian lowered his head and closed his eyes.

"You're really knotted up. What happened today?"

"Where to start?" he whispered, the question punctuated with a soft moan.

"How about with Stephanie Martin?"

The mention of her name drew Dorian immediately back. He pushed Noreen's hands away and opened one of the charts on his desk. "Did you get her the private ICU room I asked for?"

"I did."

"Then you know what happened."

"I know you had to reverse the transplant. What went wrong?"

"Clotting. She would've died if I waited. First surgery is an official failure."

Noreen reached across his lap and pulled open his top desk drawer, brushing his groin with her hand. "Maybe this will make you feel better?" She handed him an envelope with the flap tucked inside. "I delivered Mitchell his, too."

Dorian examined the watermarked bank check in the amount of one hundred thousand dollars.

"Derrick had it couriered over first thing this morning."

"Think this'll help with tomorrow's meeting?" Money always eased things with Mitchell.

Noreen shrugged. "Can't hurt, right? I talked to the nursing staff in the ICU, and they understand that Emily Warren never transfers to the surgical floor. I don't see any reason to risk the Martins and Warrens crossing paths, especially not while we're keeping the news about Stephanie quiet."

"That's all I need, Riley talking to Derrick. The guy's nervous enough as it is."

Noreen set her hand back on Dorian's shoulder. "Riley Martin is upset, but there were no guarantees. We have every legal waiver and consent, signed, in Stephanie's chart."

"That's not the problem, and you know it."

"We're covered, Dorian. Relax. There's no paper trail, nothing to tie Stephanie Martin to Sydney Dowling. You took care of your end, right?"

Dorian nodded, starting to see the light at the other end of this.

"Then there's nothing to worry about." Noreen pushed his chair back from the desk and stood in front of him. "You need to let this go," she said, putting his hands on her hips.

Dorian buried his face in the thin fabric covering her stomach and closed his eyes. The delicate smell of lavender radiated off her skin, seducing him and bringing him closer to the ever-shrinking line between them. His hands smoothed over the gentle slope of her toned buttocks, and he lifted the hem of her minidress.

"I can't do this," he said, without pulling away.

"Yes, you can." Noreen pressed her parted lips to his, opening her mouth slightly and touching the tip of her tongue to his.

"Stop. We can't." This time, he moved back. Sex with Noreen, which he had so far avoided, spelled eventual disaster.

"You know I can keep a secret," she said, as though issuing a reminder.

With as much as Noreen knew about him, he had to tread lightly. "It's not that. It's not you."

Noreen rolled her tear-filled eyes. "It's not you; it's me," she mocked. "That's just great. You can sleep with half of Marion, but I shouldn't take it personally that you find me repulsive."

"Don't say that. You're beautiful, Noreen, and brilliant." He reached for her hand. "I *am* attracted to you, *very attracted*, but I can't give you what you want."

"And what, exactly, do you think that is? I'm not looking for a marriage proposal. I just thought we could have some fun is all."

Suddenly, sleeping with her seemed the easier option.

"You deserve more than that," Dorian said in a tone as sincere as he could muster. "You're too important to me to be a one-night stand."

The hard lines of anger melted from her face, and her lips curled slightly upward. "You mean it?"

"Sure do," he said, to which she smiled.

He'd won her over. He just didn't know for how long.

CHAPTER 17

Dr. Clara Lynch, a pathologist from Saint Matthew's Hospital who worked per diem for County since before Marco was hired, had filled the brief gap of his three-day suspension. Clara was a stellar clinician, but controlling and pigheaded enough to believe that hers was the better way. Most people wouldn't move so much as another person's pen, especially not for a few days' work. Clara wasn't most people.

Marco couldn't find even a pack of slides without a scavenger hunt, and he wondered how she moved so much so quickly. He looked up at the clock, impatient for his last delivery.

Brenna Wiese, his lab assistant, put the day's pathology reports in envelopes for mailing. She hummed out of tune, listening to music through a pair of skull and crossbones earbuds.

The noise annoyed Marco, but history taught him little would come from his complaining. Brenna was smart, conscientious, and premed, on course to be a forensic pathologist. Mitchell had seen to it that she was hired as a favor to her father, one of his country club cronies, and he'd reminded Marco more than once that Brenna's appearance didn't matter in a lab.

Brenna pulled her dyed black hair back into a rubber band, exposing a set of gauges so large that a highlighter could pass through her thin earlobes. Her nails, also painted black, had been chewed back to the skin, and she was spinning something around in her mouth that Marco was afraid was a piece of fingernail.

He waved to get her attention.

The usual thick tension of two diametric opposites working in close quarters was made worse by his brief absence.

"Brenna." Marco slapped his hand against the counter, and she jumped.

"I'm sorry, what?" She took the bud out of her right ear.

"Do we have the final schedule?"

Brenna looked around the desk and shook her head. "I didn't get an update this afternoon. I'll call over and have one sent."

She picked up the phone and was about to dial, when a young man, early twenties, with long hair spilling out from underneath a surgical cap, rushed through the door, pushing a specimen cart.

"I'm sorry, I'm sorry. It's crazy back there." The man slapped a piece of paper in front of Brenna and haphazardly unloaded his haul.

Marco watched as the young man, whose tattoos peeked from the edge of his scrubs shirt, tried to get Brenna's attention. A disaster, on several levels, unfolded. The disorganized new hire was at least partly to blame for the schedule getting so far off track.

"I don't believe we've met. I'm Dr. Marco Prusak." Marco's extended hand met one slick and clammy.

"Matt Hogan," the young man said, keeping his eyes on Brenna.

"First day on the job?" Marco lifted a specimen container of intestine and searched, unsuccessfully, for a patient label.

"Second." Matt peeled the half-stuck label off another specimen jar and affixed it to the side of the container still in Marco's hands. "These things stick to everything."

Marco raised his eyebrows.

"Look, it's right." Matt pointed at the list in front of Brenna. "Hemicolectomy, patient 224789. It's the only intestine on the schedule."

Brenna smiled.

"I'll see you later." Matt patted Brenna's desk before leaving.

"Can't wait." Marco straightened the label, still not completely stuck to the plastic. "Brenna, we're going to have to match the specimens to the list to make sure we have everything."

"I can do it. It'll only take a minute." Brenna grabbed a red, felt-tip marker and set to reconciling the list. "We *are* missing one, the add-on case, Stephanie Martin."

The name registered immediately.

"Let me see that." Marco snatched the schedule from her hand, unable to believe what he was reading.

Dorian's transplant had failed.

Brenna picked up the phone to call for the missing specimen.

Marco stopped her. "Don't call. I'll go."

Brenna wrinkled her forehead as she hung up the handset. "Ohhh-kay."

"What operating room was the surgery done in?"

Brenna called up the schedule on her computer. "OR three, which is up next for cleaning."

"Thanks," Marco said, and hurried out the door.

CHAPTER 18

Ana arrived at the Parker and Sons Funeral Home, suited in head-to-toe black, a half hour before viewing hours were scheduled to start. Her feet ached from the high heels she only ever wore to funerals, and she had a dull headache from the tightly wound bun of hair tugging at her temples.

John Parker, the youngest, possibly strangest of the Parker sons, with whom she went to high school, met her at the door, wearing an ill-fitting, navy blue suit and a silver-gray, clip-on tie. His pale skin glowed white in the harsh, natural light flooding in through the expansive floor-to-ceiling windows. Other than his thinning brown hair, John hadn't changed a bit from the shy outcast others had made fun of.

Ana's stomach flip-flopped as he offered her his arm and led her down the long aisle toward Sydney's coffin.

The heavy smells of white lilies and embalming fluid reminded her of her parents' funeral held in this exact room. Nothing had changed, not even the carpet, and she was unprepared to be the little girl standing coffin-side, tracing the lace edge of her mother's pink blouse, only this time with her sister.

She pulled a tissue from the pocket of her fitted suit jacket and wiped her running nose as Sydney came into view.

John slid the kneeling bench in front of the mahogany coffin.

The white satin liner sharply contrasted with Sydney's black dress and blended with her fair skin. Her hands had been folded, and unlike the knotted, wrinkled hands Ana recalled from funerals past, celebrations of long lives well lived and lost only to old age, Sydney's were young hands, beautifully positioned to hold the ornate rosary beads that had been their mother's. Her nails had been painted a cotton-candy pink to match the gloss on her lips. Her long hair had been washed and styled in a way that covered the heavy autopsy stitching, and a cascade of curls framed her expressionless face.

A flood of memories nearly made Ana collapse.

John caught her just as her knees started to buckle, and he ushered her to a seat in the front row.

"Are you all right?" he said. "Should I get you a glass of water?"

Ana crumbled, crying so hard she couldn't answer.

A pair of strong arms wrapped around her and pulled her close. A low shushing accompanied the patting of her back and the familiar, musky smell of Mike's cologne. She leaned into him, and he rocked her, not speaking or offering condolences, but letting her grieve, in the same way she could tell from the hitch in his breath, that he was grieving.

Minutes passed before Ana felt cried out, the dry, momentary spent feeling easily mistaken for mustered strength. She pulled back from Mike's firm hold and held his hand.

"I can't do this," she whispered. "I can't be alone."

"You're not alone." He said it in a way that made her almost believe him. "You just have to get through the next couple of hours."

The clock struck eight, and the first wave of visitors arrived. Ana wondered if she had the strength in her to face them.

A row of police officers and investigators, some still in uniform, made their way up the aisle.

Coop offered Ana a warm smile and bent down to hug her. Always the lightest spirit in the room, Coop emanated goodness. "If there's anything you need, Ana, I'm here."

Ronald Graham, Julian Blake, and Elsa Russell formed an impenetrable barrier that backed the growing line of mourners down the aisle and into the overcrowded waiting area. Each extended their sincerest condolences, and the words "I'm sorry for your loss" opened Ana up a little more each time she heard them.

Ron straightened his uniform shirt, taut over his round belly, and offered Elsa his arm. The two walked silently forward. Elsa never looked directly into the coffin and pulled Ron away after little more than a moment of silence.

Ana excused herself, focusing her attention on anything that would give her a reprieve from the inundating apologies. She turned a fresh page in the signature book and read the cards on the floral arrangements.

Mike stayed close behind her.

Several large arrangements blanketed the funeral parlor walls. Most had been sent by either police or emergency medical services. Smaller arrangements, plants, and baskets made a double half circle around the casket. Ana read the tags, unfamiliar with a handful of the senders. One of the larger bouquets, three dozen or so dark red roses at the foot of the casket, caught her attention.

"Who's that one from?" she asked Mike, who was standing closest to it.

Mike carefully picked through the buds and shrugged. "I don't see a card."

Ana checked the floor to see if it had fallen, but she found nothing. "Maybe the florist made a mistake."

With only one local florist—one very busy local florist, based on the number of arrangements—it seemed possible.

Ethan made his way across the room. His royal blue tie emphasized his sapphire eyes, and Ana could see his sadness was less to do with Sydney than with her. He pulled her into an awkward embrace she only half accepted and asked her how she was holding up.

She answered with a shrug, their night together an unwelcome intruder between them.

"Listen, I'm sorry I had to run out this morning, I . . ." Ethan's whispers caught Mike's attention.

"I really can't talk about that right now."

Mike flashed a puzzled look that quickly disappeared when the front door opened and the funeral home filled with the sound of a woman shouting.

"You don't belong here. *Leave.*"

Ana recognized the irate voice as Patricia Dentmore's and went to see what was happening. She nudged her way through the crowd and found Trish, crying on the porch with an empty Styrofoam cup at her feet.

Anthony stood on the sidewalk, dripping with coffee.

"I tried to make him leave," Trish said.

"Get out!" Ana shoved Anthony as hard as she could, but he barely moved.

Mike, Coop, and Ron Graham, who was in uniform, hurried outside.

"I mean it, Anthony. Get the hell out of here." Ana pounded her small fists into his chest, and tears rolled down her cheeks.

Anthony stumbled back a step, but he didn't fight her or try to protect himself.

"Mike, should I do something about this?" Ron reached around the back of his belt for his handcuffs.

"Let me handle it. Anthony, what are you doing here?"

"I have every right to say good-bye, Mike. I'd never forgive myself if I didn't."

Ana kept punching and pushing him. "You have no right, you cheating piece of shit."

Faces pressed against the funeral home's windows.

"Mike, please. Talk to her."

"Ana, stop it." Mike pulled Ana back and steered her toward Ethan. "Take her inside."

"I'm not going anywhere until he leaves." She marched back to Anthony. "Go, get out of here."

Mike blocked her from hitting him again. "Ana, that's enough."

"Enough? My sister is lying in a coffin, and you say 'enough'? This is his fault." She pointed her finger at Anthony and quoted his e-mail. "'Give me what I want or I'll take it.' Isn't that right, *murderer*?"

"Ana, it's not what it sounds like."

Mike handed Anthony a wad of tissues, and he patted the coffee from his face. "Ana, go inside. We'll talk about this later."

"You haven't told her yet, have you?" Anthony asked Mike.

"Told me *what*?"

Ethan reached out to Ana, and she slapped his hand away.

"Told me *what*?" Ana repeated.

"That you're engaged to a home-wrecking *whore*. Is that the big secret?" Trish said. Mascara tears rolled down her cheeks, and the faint green-yellow of a shiner peeked through her makeup.

"No," Anthony said, staring directly at Ana. "It's that Misty's pregnant. Before you go making any more accusations, ask Mike about my alibi."

CHAPTER 19

Dorian waited outside of Mitchell's office, watching the suited woman from Finance, whose name he couldn't remember, gather her things and leave in a huff. He ran his hand through his wavy, blond hair and sighed to vent the stress.

A large vein pulsed in Mitchell's forehead, and the tone of his previous meeting set Dorian even more on edge.

"Get in here." Mitchell peeled off his pin-striped suit jacket, two large circles of sweat drenching the armpits of his monogrammed, white dress shirt. "And close the door."

"Absolutely." Dorian paced the length of the office, too nervous to sit. "Look, Mitchell, I know I should've come and talked to you last night."

Mitchell flopped in his chair and leaned back in a way that emphasized the curve of his belly. "Listen, I've had a real bad couple of days. Riley Martin's threatening to sue, the ethics committee called an emergency meeting, and I have to sit with a panel of attorneys after lunch. I'm annoyed that you avoided me yesterday." He mopped his bald head with a white handkerchief. "But I'm even more pissed off about the timing. Will you please sit down?

You're making me nuts." Dorian pulled a chair back from Mitchell's desk and sat. "We expect a huge turnout for tonight's fund-raising event—*your* fund-raising event, to which Cynthia Davis has purchased a seat."

Cynthia Davis had entered the research stage for uterine transplantation a year before Dorian, and a paper she'd written, though Dorian would never admit it, was the genesis of his early work. She was smart, but lacked ambition, and treaded lightly where Dorian went full speed ahead.

"Cynthia's not half the surgeon she thinks she is," Dorian said, "or this would be *her* fund-raiser."

Mitchell smirked. "But you realize that what happened with Stephanie Martin bolsters her points that you're too eager and reckless. Cynthia's smart, not like the other fanatical protesters, and she has facts. She can turn people against you if word leaks far enough, so I'd be careful about her. There are going to be at least a dozen high rollers there tonight, checkbooks in hand. I've managed to keep Stephanie's case somewhat quiet, but I need to know what, exactly, happened."

"Exactly?" It was an answer Dorian didn't have. "There was extensive clotting, bad enough that I had no choice but to remove the uterus. Cynthia made no point about that in her speculation, and her trials are so far behind, she'll never be competition. No one could've seen this coming. As for Riley Martin, let him threaten. You think we didn't have every waiver and release signed before we went ahead with the surgery? The Martins knew what they were getting into."

"But did they, really? I hate to even bring this up, but you know you're going to have to work with Marco to give me something more definitive about what went wrong, right? How are you going to handle this?"

The mention of Marco made Dorian's hands shake. "I'm doing everything I can," he said, not yet willing to admit more than he absolutely had to. "The Martins and the Warrens are on separate units, totally opposite ends of the hospital. Emily should be discharged in the next twenty-four hours, which should give us a little breathing room. I'll get you your answers, with or without Marco."

"You'd better. Bill Warren is one of those checkbooks I was talking about. Fail again and you'll tank your whole project."

"That's not going to happen," Dorian said. "I'll send Emily home with a visiting nurse, on us, to make sure nothing goes wrong. It's the closest thing to a guarantee I can give you."

"On *us*, or on County Memorial? Your program is expensive, Dorian, and a goddamned hornet's nest. That last meeting was to talk about your budget, and believe me, there's no room for absorbing any more costs."

"You'd really rather risk a repeat of what happened with Stephanie Martin to save a couple grand? Really?"

Mitchell wiped his hands down his face and grunted. "I knew this was going to happen. You told me you had this perfected and tested."

"In rats, Mitchell, *in rats*. This is one complication. Put it in perspective."

"One hundred percent failure, that's my perspective."

"Fifty," Dorian corrected. "Emily's case will be different."

"It better be, or consider me at the front of the growing line of people calling for your head."

CHAPTER 20

"How long did you know?" Ana stood in the entranceway of Mike's ranch home, her anger as pure as the moment she first heard Misty was pregnant.

Mike ran his hands through his wet hair, a cloud of menthol and cologne surrounding him and his face half-coated with shaving cream. "I didn't want you to find out that way."

"How long?"

"Less than forty-eight hours," Mike said. "And Anthony wouldn't have even told me if it wasn't part of his alibi."

"Sydney knew, didn't she?" Ana started to cry. "I thought there was no way she would commit suicide, but she wanted children so badly. This would've killed her. It *did* kill her, didn't it?"

Mike grabbed a dish towel off the counter and wiped the shaving cream from his face. "Sydney didn't commit suicide."

The affirmation was both a shock and a relief. For the past twenty-four hours, since finding out about Misty's pregnancy, Ana wondered. "What about the suicide note?"

"I'm looking into that, but it seems the crime scene was staged." Mike cleared his throat. "Kim confirmed cause of death." Ana had met Kimberly Taylor, the county medical examiner, on several occasions and knew she and Mike were close. "There were traces of zopiclone in Sydney's system, but not enough to have killed her. Kim says she suffocated."

Ana took a minute to process the grim fact. "And you went to Anthony for an alibi?"

Mike nodded. "We both know Anthony's no murderer, but I had to ask. No matter what happened between him and Sydney, he loved her, and anything he said otherwise was out of anger because of the divorce."

"And Misty?" Ana ran down the short list of suspects.

"No way either of them had anything to do with what happened. Misty and Anthony were at County Memorial the night Sydney was murdered. Misty had some minor complications after a fight with Trish Dentmore over the engagement."

Ana wiped her eyes, already red and raw from crying.

"I'm going to find who did this," Mike said.

"How?" Ana needed to know he had a plan.

"Julian is searching Sydney's house for leads. He has the best investigators with him, and we've called in a computer forensics expert. If anyone's contacted Sydney online, even if she deleted the message, he'll find it. I need you to promise me you won't go anywhere near her house until I give you the all-clear. Something that seems unimportant might be exactly what we're looking for. I can't have anything moved. You understand me?"

Ana considered telling him she'd already been there, but his paternal tone changed her mind. All she'd taken was a business card, anyway.

CHAPTER 21

One sin didn't wash away another. Marco knew that, and yet, somehow he was sure he'd be forgiven for dealing with Dorian Carmichael. Others saw Dorian's transplant procedure as a gift to women who wouldn't otherwise be able to have children, but Marco knew that Dorian was a God-playing egotist the first time an unexplained request for cross-matching hit his desk. Today was the day he would finalize the proof.

The lab was, as usual, quiet.

Brenna sorted reports, registered the morning's specimens, and straightened the stack of paper on her desk.

"I'm going to lunch." She took the black vinyl clutch from her desk drawer. "I'll be back in a half hour."

"I need you to make a run to the mail room, too," Marco said, buying himself time. "I didn't get there this morning."

Brenna huffed. She'd normally be expected to cut her lunch short for such errands.

"Take as much time as you need." Marco worked at a smile, but the look on Brenna's face said it came across as something else, something that made her uncomfortable. She leered at him as she emptied the mail room outbox, and left.

Marco waited until she disappeared from view before retrieving his file, the one thing Clara Lynch hadn't moved, from the locked cabinet drawer. He withdrew a red biohazard bag from cold storage, pulled on a pair of latex gloves, and untied the knot holding the plastic sack closed.

The remains of OR 3, more specifically the Stephanie Martin case, were mixed together inside. Blood-soaked gauze and disposable surgical pads obscured the recently removed uterus. Marco shifted the bag, reached in, and retrieved the discarded sample.

The organ was in terrible shape, much of the tissue necrotic and clotted, but it worked for his purposes: proving the donor's identity.

Marco sifted through several reports of the patients Dorian had operated on over the past seven months. There were more than a handful of ablations, a couple of D&Cs, and enough of a surge in hysterectomies to have raised Marco's suspicion. Each of the women underwent extensive and, given the nature of their procedures, unnecessary testing, including tissue typing and antibody screens—the types of tests necessary to match a donor to a transplant recipient. One of them was a match to this organ, which should've been sent to him instead of thrown out. Marco had barely beaten the operating room cleanup crew to it, and he had to pick it out of the trash. Had he not verified the surgical schedule, he might have never found the one thing that implicated Dorian in his wrongdoing.

CHAPTER 22

The ballroom of the Dakota Creek Country Club bustled with loud music and laughter. County Memorial staff mixed with an affluent guest list—young, new-money types who would respond to the good time everyone seemed to be having.

For Dorian, the night couldn't be over soon enough. He waited for the call to the podium and hoped to slip out unnoticed after his speech.

Noreen swept her bangs across her forehead and engaged him in the kind of light conversation he dreaded.

"Can I get you another drink?" she said, leaning over too far and standing too close.

"No, I'm good for now." Three gin and tonics landed Dorian with a faint but comfortable buzz, and he was starting to suspect that getting him drunk was part of Noreen's grand plan to get him into bed.

"Are you *sure*?"

He held his glass to his lips, the drink now little more than ice and a slice of lime, and glanced over the rim at Jared and Colby, just arriving.

Colby looked amazing and, for a minute, Dorian stared. The black, floor-length gown fit her perfectly. The low-cut bodice cradled her full breasts, and the slit over her shapely right leg extended midway up her thigh.

"On second thought, I will take another." Dorian handed Noreen his empty glass and smiled.

A growing line of partygoers backed up at the bar, and Noreen struggled to get the bartender's attention.

Dorian kept his eyes on the Monroes.

Jared disappeared into the crowd, and Colby remained at the ballroom's threshold, her body language and the expression on her face saying she'd rather be anywhere else. There was an obvious disconnect between her and Jared, and a glance around the room told Dorian he wasn't the only one who noticed. The women gossiped and rolled their eyes. Several men, including Simon Walker, made a few steps toward the door, drawn in by the siren's song of the most beautiful woman in the room. Dorian took that as his cue to move. He pushed in his chair and crossed the room, keeping his head down and doing his best not to be seen, except for by Simon, to whom he flashed a look that said, "Don't even think about it."

Dorian walked past Colby and pressed his back to the lobby wall next to the entrance where she was standing. She was close enough to touch, and he was sure she could hear him. "You haven't returned any of my calls."

"Dorian, I can't be seen with you here. Not tonight, *please*. I shouldn't even be here."

"Then why are you?" He took a step closer, so that their shoulders were nearly touching.

"You know Jared likes to keep up appearances."

"For what it's worth, I'm glad you came. We should talk."

"There's nothing to say. It's over."

"Is it?" Dorian closed his fingers around hers, knowing the answer, for him at least, was that it wasn't. "I should've told you 'I love you' back."

"Isn't that just like you? A little too little, a little too late." Colby's crimson lips bent into a frown, and she pulled her hand away, walking, teary eyed, toward the bar.

Common sense warned Dorian to leave her alone, but he followed her anyway.

"Colby, wait."

Colby pushed through the crowd at the end of the bar and held up her hand for the bartender. "Vodka and cranberry, please."

"Colby, come on, will you at least look at me?" Dorian's tone garnered its share of attention.

"Vodka and cranberry, *please*." Colby slapped her hand on the bar, and a man, Dr. Jennifer Oliver's husband, if Dorian's memory served, whistled for the bartender's attention.

"Can we get the lady a drink, please?" The six-foot statue of a man smiled at Colby as the bartender came down from the far end of the bar to serve her.

"What can I get you?"

"Vodka-cranberry, lime, no ice." Colby spoke softly, her cheeks blushed with embarrassment. "Thank you," she mouthed to the attractive man who had helped her.

The bartender set a short glass on the bar and poured a heavy-handed shot.

Colby waved for him to keep going.

"Colby, seriously?" Dorian stepped between her and the man undressing her with his eyes.

"You know what? Make it a double."

The bartender repeated the overpoured shot in a fresh glass, topped both off with just enough cranberry juice to tint the drinks pink, and dressed each glass with a slice of lime.

Colby slapped a twenty on the bar.

"You know drinks are free, right?" Dorian said.

The bartender leered at him.

"For the fast service." Colby shot the first drink back in one long gulp.

"Please, can we talk?"

"You don't give up, do you?" Colby shook her head, and a lock of reddish-gold hair fell from the twist, settling along her jawline. "This isn't the time or place."

"Then when?" Dorian set his hand on her forearm, and she pulled away, just as Noreen swept in from the other side of the bar.

"There you are." Noreen handed Dorian a gin and tonic, her hand lingering a long moment on his.

Colby flashed her daggers and recovered with an obviously fake smile. She chugged her second drink and ordered a third.

Dorian set his drink on the bar and turned to Noreen. "Think you can give me a minute?"

"A minute for *what*?"

Dorian could tell Noreen had no intention of leaving regardless of his answer.

"Excuse me." Colby stepped away from the bar, but she hadn't made it two steps before running into Jared.

"I've been looking for you," he said.

"There's a lot of that going around," Dorian said. As if Noreen weren't enough interference, Jared all but sealed his fate.

Colby smiled, enjoying the benefit of her two stiff drinks. "I was just coming to find you."

"Really?"

"Yes, *really*."

"How many does that make?" Jared pointed at Colby's drink with a look of heavy suspicion.

"Two. Why? Does it matter?"

It wasn't hard to see why Colby cheated. Jared treated her like an unwelcome child. Dorian couldn't imagine why she stayed.

Jared adjusted his bow tie and ordered a glass of cabernet. "It's been less than a half hour," he said condescendingly. "Maybe you should slow down."

"For you? *Anything.*"

Dorian knew if he didn't step in, Colby would leave in a cab if she had to. He took a long sip of his gin and clapped his hand on Jared's shoulder. "Jared, how are you?"

"Better than you, I'd imagine. Must be nerve-racking, worrying about the Stephanie Martin news getting out on a night like tonight. How does it feel to be such a failure?"

"Jared, stop it." Colby's eyes went wide.

"*Ah-ah-ah.*" Mitchell appeared behind them, wagging his finger. "We're supposed to be enjoying ourselves. Take the night off, would you?" he said to Jared. "Dorian, may I speak with you a minute, in private?"

"Excuse me." Dorian followed Mitchell to the outskirts of the ballroom, his heart lodged firmly in his throat and his eyes fixed on Colby.

"What the hell did I just walk into?" Mitchell said. Dorian couldn't decide if he was being rhetorical. He started to answer, and Mitchell held his hand up. "You know what? I don't even care. I don't want her name brought up again tonight."

Dorian stared off into the distance.

"Are you even listening to me?" Mitchell said.

"Yeah, I'm listening. It wasn't me who brought her up."

Mitchell checked his watch. "I don't care who it was. Don't let it happen again. You're on in thirty minutes, so get your head together." He snatched Dorian's drink from his hand. "I don't want you even *thinking* about Stephanie Martin right now. I've got three people looking to make large donations and two more considering it. You're going to talk this transplant procedure up as if you've answered the highest calling in the world, you hear me?" Dorian nodded. "And tell a cute story or something. People love stories about babies."

"I'll do what I can."

Colby teetered on her stilettos and stumbled into the ladies' lounge.

"Anything else?" Dorian asked.

Mitchell followed his sight line and shook his head. "Yeah, stay out of trouble."

Dorian smirked, checked on Jared and Noreen's positions, and finding them both embroiled in conversation, slipped through the crowd toward Colby. He pushed the ladies' room door and called through the slight opening, "Anyone in here?"

"Go away," Colby said.

"Are you *sure* you want me to leave?" A long silence followed. "Is anyone in there with you?"

"No."

"'No,' you don't want me to leave or 'no,' there's no one in there with you?"

"Both." Colby sniffled and answered the door, blotting her mascara.

An oversized chaise and mirrored vanity decorated the sitting room, which smelled of the dozens of roses in the crystal vases surrounding them. Dorian went inside and closed the door behind him.

"Are you all right? What happened?"

Colby forced a chuckle. "Do you know how long it's been since someone asked how I was?"

"I'm sorry . . ."

Colby held her well-manicured finger to his lips. "I don't need you to be." She kissed him, pressing her body against his and pushing him backward until he hit the door. Reaching behind him, she locked it.

Dorian returned her eager kisses with the aggression and passion that had always sent her over the edge. She reached down and slid her hand over the length of him until he couldn't stand it a minute longer. He turned her to face the full-length mirror and worked the slit of her dress up over her hips. He kissed the back of her neck, watching her willing expression as she moaned in response. Her hot breath steamed up the mirror, and he backed up, for only a second, to take her in.

Stiletto heels. Black silk panties. Thigh highs.

She was stunning.

"Tell me you want me." Dorian cupped his hand between her legs. Her wetness soaked through the silk and coated his fingers. She smelled like vanilla and sex, and her heat drove him crazy.

She arched to meet the curve of his hand. "I want you."

He all but tore off her underwear, and unzipped his pants.

A knock came at the door, and she begged him not to answer. He covered her mouth with his right hand and thrust into her, squeezing her left breast. She pressed her palms flat against the glass and met his driving pace.

Soft moans escaped through his splayed fingers and mixed with his own stifled cries, just loud enough to drown out the sound of his name being repeatedly called from the podium.

CHAPTER 23

Jared awoke the next morning, tangled in the sheets of the guest bedroom that had become his second home. His head ached from downing a fifth of vodka after the embarrassing night that had him wondering if he shouldn't just call County and quit.

Colby's fling with Simon had been bad, but this *thing* with Dorian was so much worse. Jared tried to block out the humiliation that resurfaced the minute he thought of the emcee calling Dorian's name and Dorian stumbling out of the ladies' room after Colby. Colby's hair had come loose from its pins, and the back of her gown was tucked into her underwear. Dorian's bow tie was crooked, and his pants were unzipped.

For as long as Jared lived, he'd never forgive her.

Finances aside, and there was a considerable amount of wealth and property to consider, Jared had been holding out hope that Colby would find the right thing to say to make him forgive her. There was no simple solution, but it was clear that he and Colby were through.

He opened the bedroom door and listened to the silence that had replaced the sound of repeated toilet flushing, most likely because the alcohol had made Colby sick.

Jared turned on his cell phone, which he had shut off after Mitchell's tenth message, and checked the time. His shift started in a little over an hour, and as much as he wanted to be anywhere other than in the same house with Colby, the thought of facing the medical staff made him cringe.

He staggered down the hall toward the master bedroom and found an awaiting disaster.

"What the hell?" He reached across a mound of his belongings and wiggled the locked door handle. "Colby, open up." He pounded the door with the heel of his hand, the jolting pressure sharpening his dull headache. "Colby, come on. I need my razor."

"It's out there," she said. "Leave me alone."

She didn't unlock the door, didn't apologize, or explain, and if there was an ounce of remorse in her, Jared couldn't find it. He sifted through the stack and gathered the things he'd need sooner than later. She'd emptied his underwear and sock drawers into a laundry basket and shoved his shaving kit and toothbrush into the corner.

"My toothbrush, really? How long do you plan on staying in there?"

The rhetorical question, as expected, went unanswered.

He piled his clothes, most of which were still on hangers, on top of the basket and relocated the load to the guest room in two cumbersome trips. In the breast pocket of a jacket headed for the dry cleaner was the business card he swore he'd never use: Wendell G. Cobb, attorney-at-law.

Wilson had given it to him, partially as a gag, but more as a passive offering of help after Jared intimated that his most recent fight with Colby had become physical.

"It's only a matter of time until you hit back," Wilson had said.

Jared would have never considered it even a remote possibility, but after what had happened with Dorian, and with the pure disgust he had felt, Wilson's was a fair warning.

Jared dialed the attorney's number, relieved, and a bit sad, that things had gone so far.

CHAPTER 24

Dorian kept his head down as he walked into County Memorial, the previous night's indiscretion radiating from him like a beacon as he hurried toward Emily Warren's room. Two of the unit secretaries, a middle-aged blonde and an older woman with pure white hair, exchanged hushed conversation as he passed. The older one's mouth fell open, and the younger one giggled, making Dorian self-conscious.

He'd gone too far this time, and he knew it.

He turned the corner into Emily's room and breathed a sigh of relief. He closed the door behind him and quietly grabbed her chart from the bin on the wall.

Emily was sitting up in bed, sipping a cup of water.

Derrick slept, slumped over, in the chair at her bedside. His laptop and several notebooks covered the portable table.

Emily wasn't what Dorian considered conventionally beautiful. Her nose was too pronounced and her lips a bit thin. A smattering of freckles, made obvious by her lack of makeup, dotted her fair skin and in some places blended together, making her appear much younger than her twenty-eight years. She pulled a brush through her unruly, light brown curls and tucked her frizzy hair behind her ears.

"Good morning," Dorian said. "How are you doing?"

Emily shrugged. "You tell me."

Derrick's eyes rolled open and went immediately to the wall clock. "What time is it?" He fumbled for his glasses, askew in the breast pocket of his blue dress shirt.

"It's six thirty."

Derrick looked at Dorian. "You're early. Is everything all right?" He pushed in the foot of the lounge chair and straightened himself up.

"Everything's fine. I'm starting office hours at eight and wanted to make sure that Emily's paperwork was in order for her discharge."

"I get to go home?"

"On one condition," Dorian said. "You have to agree to home care, which we will provide. We want to make sure you're healing and taking the necessary medications."

"Did you do that with your other patient?" Derrick said, now fully awake. "What was her name? Stephanie Martin?" The anxious pressure was like a half-ton weight on Dorian's chest, and he was unsure of what to say next. "I heard you talking after Emily's surgery and thought I should check into some things. You didn't tell us the procedure failed."

Emily's pale face flushed with concern. "You didn't tell me that."

"I wasn't sure it was true. Is it, Dr. Carmichael?"

"Our patients' treatments are confidential, Derrick. I'm afraid I can't discuss that with you."

"Then you should tell the nurses to be more careful when they talk. You can say I overheard it, though I won't repeat what we talk about. I understand things happen, but I want what's best for Emily. Perhaps that's Dr. Davis?"

Dorian interpreted the mention of his rival as a passive-aggressive threat. Seeing no option but to come clean, he answered. "I'm sorry, but you heard correctly." The words came out heavy and lifted the secret's substantial weight. Despite what he had done to keep the patients separate, staff always talked. "There were unforeseeable complications with Mrs. Martin, but there's no reason to expect the same will hold true for Emily. We're taking extra precautions and will follow her closely."

"You told us everything would be fine."

Dorian peeled back Emily's blanket and lifted her gown to examine her surgical wound. The wide cut, held closed by deep retention sutures, though fresh, appeared to be healing. He gently pressed around the distant margin. "Does that hurt?"

"No worse than usual," Emily said.

"Everything *is* going to be fine, isn't it?"

"Everything looks good." Dorian tried to sound as encouraging as possible without making promises. He pulled a card from his wallet and wrote his cell phone number down on the back. "If you have any questions or problems, call me directly, day or night. I don't want you to have to go through the office, or my answering service." He handed the card to Derrick. "The discharge nurse will be in around nine o'clock, and I'll have Noreen arrange your first home visit."

If she hasn't quit.

CHAPTER 25

"Thanks for letting me know." Ana hung up the phone and pulled into the EMS station, eager for the distraction of work.

Mike had called twice in the past twenty-four hours, both times to tell her that Julian hadn't found any new leads at Sydney's house. She didn't imagine he would, considering she'd taken the one thing worth having. She'd placed half a dozen calls to Dr. Sanders's office, getting the same runaround from him as Sydney had gotten from Dr. Carmichael, and the same gut feeling of guilt. The edges of his card had started to peel, and a corner had been torn off. Ana dialed the number, which she'd nearly committed to memory. The receptionist answered on the second ring.

"Dr. Sanders's office, how can I help you?"

"Good morning. This is Ana Ashmore calling to speak with Dr. Sanders, again, please."

"I've given him your messages, Ms. Ashmore. I'm sure he will return your call at his earliest convenience."

"And when do you think that'll be? It's urgent that I speak with him."

"I'm sorry. He's with patients and cannot be disturbed."

"You say that every time I call."

"Then maybe you should wait for him to call you," the receptionist said, and hung up.

Ana let out a frustrated growl and caught sight of a shadow in her periphery.

Ethan shivered, breathing into his cupped hands. His blue eyes stared back at her from beneath a pulled-up hood and, without his even saying a word, Ana sensed increased tension between them.

She turned off the engine and opened the door, pocketing the card and her phone.

"Hey," he said, "you're still not answering my calls."

"I've been busy looking into things. You know, stuff with Sydney." She figured that was the one thing he wouldn't give her crap for.

"I'm worried about you." Ethan wrapped his arm around her, and she backed away.

"Don't be," she said. "I'm fine." She locked the car and headed toward the front door with him at her heels.

Jim, with whom she'd briefly spoken only hours ago to get the all-clear to return to work, stood near the front door. "How're you doing?" He ran his hand through his sandy blond hair and huffed out a breath.

She moved around him, headed for her locker. "I'm fine." She was getting sick of answering that particular question. "And tell anyone else whose wondering."

Mattie, the young dispatcher, offered a tight-lipped smile. "If there's anything I can do."

"You can *do* your job," Ana said, cutting her off. "I'm not made of porcelain. If everyone wants to help"—she looked into the dining room where several others were nibbling at a group breakfast—"they can just act normal."

She stuffed her things into her locker, kicked off her shoes, and stepped into her jumpsuit.

"Listen," Ethan said quietly, "I was thinking, maybe I could stay at your place a few days. You've been through a lot, and I hate the idea of your being alone. I can make you those blueberry pancakes you like, bring you coffee in bed, you know, make sure you're taken care of."

"I'm all right, really. I just need time."

"What if I'm asking because I miss you?"

She sighed, feeling terrible for having led him on. "Then I need space."

He sat across from her at a table for two, and pushed a plate of breakfast and a cup of coffee in front of her. "How about one night, then? See where it goes? You said you wanted people to act normal. I want what we had before."

Ana slammed the mug hard enough on the table that the steaming coffee splashed out over her hand. "What we *had* was a fling, Ethan. God, don't you get it?"

Jim, who had been reading the paper a couple of tables away, got up from his chair, gestured for Ethan to take a walk, and handed Ana a wad of napkins.

"Listen, Jim, I'm sorry. I didn't mean to shout. The damned coffee spilled, and Ethan, God, he's relentless."

"Just stop a minute, would you? Stop and listen. I took a lot of heat for what happened at the Aquarian. By all accounts, you should be suspended, at the very least. I know what you're going through—at least I know it was hard enough to keep you from thinking clearly, which is out of character, and that's what I told everyone. You weren't yourself. The Ana I know would never risk an investigation or compromise a crime scene, especially at a call she wasn't supposed to go to in the first place. I let you come back, but I can't have you blowing up at people. Maybe it's just too soon."

"I'm good, really. I *need* to be here. If all I have to think about is Sydney in that room, if that's all I have in my life, I'll go crazy."

Ethan, who had remained close enough to eavesdrop, brought a box of tissues from the supply closet. "It was my fault," he said to Jim. "I overstepped my boundaries."

Ana peeled back the perforated seal and was blowing her nose when dispatch radioed a call at an address she recognized as one of her regulars.

"I'm fine, Jim. Really. What's it going to be?"

Jim sighed. "Go, both of you. Get out of here. But Ana, don't make me regret this."

CHAPTER 26

At County, leaked secrets spread quietly. They were whispered between doctors and nurses, housekeeping and transportation, and people hesitated to jump at rumors. It had taken the better part of a month for the story about Colby and Simon to make the rounds, and the source of the leak was never officially uncovered. Jared had been able to deny the affair when he had to.

What happened with Dorian at the fund-raiser hadn't been leaked. The broadcast had been public, and the evidence was there for all to draw the same conclusion that he had: Colby and Dorian had slept together, and probably not for the first time.

Fact was not gossip and, this time, people spoke openly and with conviction.

The looks of pity and quiet chatter started at the main desk and continued all the way to the on-call room, where Jared, who was as nervous about his foothold at County as he was ashamed of being made a fool of, found Wilson fast asleep on the couch. His round, expressionless face was the color of white paper, and there were a few bits of popcorn embedded in his thick beard. A pair of readers was folded neatly on the arm of the couch, and a medical journal lay open across his chest.

Jared shook him gently and waited for a response.

Wilson puffed out a sour breath and started to snore.

"Hey, Wilson, wake up. *Wilson.*"

Wilson jumped up and nearly smashed Jared's nose with his forehead. "What the hell? Are you trying to give me a heart attack?"

"Who knows what happened last night?"

Wilson was coming off a twenty-four-hour shift, one where he'd have spent time in more than just the ER. He didn't spread gossip, but he listened to it.

"Good morning to you, too." Wilson wiped the sleep from the corners of his eyes and yawned.

"I asked you a question, Wilson. *Who knows?*"

Wilson dog-eared a page of the medical journal, sat up, and straightened his shirt. "Who doesn't know?"

The pounding in Jared's head pulsed in pace with his heartbeat. He opened the community refrigerator, stocked with half-empty containers and unclaimed lunches, and grabbed a bottle of water from the door.

Wilson handed him two acetaminophens. "Don't worry about it. You didn't do anything wrong; she did. Besides, it'll be old news in no time."

"Easy for you to say. I have to look at Dorian every day, knowing what he did, to my *wife.*"

"Maybe not for long."

Jared choked down both tablets at once. "What do you mean?" He finished the water and threw the bottle in a recycling bin.

"You know I hear things." Jared nodded. It was the reason he went to him first, to assess the damage done. Wilson poured a cup of coffee from the dingy carafe. "I was down in Administration picking up a check for the retreat next month, and I overheard two of the secretaries talking. Apparently, Cynthia Davis, that surgeon from Saint Matthew's, was here yesterday."

"So?"

"So?" Wilson shook his head. "So she went straight to Mitchell's office, was in there for the better part of an hour, and left carrying a folder, the blue-and-white folders that HR hands out. It looks like Dorian's days might be numbered."

Jared, seeing a glimmer of hope, wondered what he could do to hasten Dorian's exit. He thought about leaking news of Stephanie Martin's failed surgery to the press, but considered the implications to his own career if he were found out.

Wilson smirked. "I know that look. What's next?"

"I meet with the lawyer whose card you gave me, I guess. I called this morning."

Wilson wiped the crumbs from his beard and leaned against the counter, slurping his bitter-smelling brew. "I'm not talking about what happens with Colby, and you know it."

"Then what?" Jared didn't want to put Wilson in the situation of knowing something he shouldn't if push came to shove.

"If it's true that Mitchell's looking to replace Dorian, this thing with Colby should be the nail in his coffin. If it's not true, and it might not be because I didn't see Cynthia here, personally, then there's at least a seed to be grown. Rumors don't materialize out of thin air. If I were looking to get Dorian out of here, I'd make friends with Marco Prusak. He's a strange guy, but I'd bet good money that if anyone is digging up dirt on Dorian, it's him. A lot of people think Marco's on some kind of religious crusade, and he might be, but the fact that he put himself so far out on the line with that protest of his, I'd wager that whatever his issue with Dorian is, it's personal."

CHAPTER 27

As soon as Dorian pulled into his office driveway, it was clear that something was wrong. Noreen was almost always the first to arrive, and he allowed her to share the off-street parking because they kept such similar hours. He looked around, assuming she'd parked on the street, but found no sign of her.

He unplugged his phone from the car charger and dialed her cell.

The call went immediately to voice mail. Rather than leave a message, he headed inside to see if she'd gotten a ride in.

Kristin sat behind the cluttered reception desk, engrossed in returning the long list of overnight calls that had come from the exchange. She barely looked up when Dorian walked in.

A middle-aged woman, wearing a turtleneck and a denim dress, thumbed through a *Good Housekeeping* magazine and tapped her foot nervously.

"How long has she been waiting?" Dorian said. Kristin responded with a confused look, balancing the phone between her shoulder and her ear. "The patient, in the waiting area. How long has she been there?"

Kristin capped her highlighter and squinted to see the clock on her monitor. "About a half hour."

"And Noreen hasn't put her in a room yet?" It was Dorian's subtle way of pretending not to have noticed her absence.

Kristin handed him a copy of his hectic schedule for the day. "I thought she was making rounds with you."

"No, I haven't heard from her. Call her at home. I need her to arrange home health care for Emily Warren, and there's no way I can handle this full a schedule without her. Tell her she needs to get here."

"What if she's sick?"

Dorian ignored the question, picking up his laptop and referencing the schedule for his first patient's name. "Melissa Montgomery?"

The patient set down the magazine and was about to clean up her coffee cup when Dorian stopped her.

"Kristin will take care of that. I'm sorry for the wait. We're going to go into this room right here." He opened the nearest door.

"Dr. Carmichael?" Kristin rushed around the desk, holding an unmarked mailing envelope.

Dorian turned on the exam room light and ushered his patient inside. There was fresh paper on the examination table and a gown on top of that. "You can go ahead and get changed. I'll knock before I come in."

The timid woman nodded and set her purse on an empty chair.

Dorian closed the door and took the envelope from Kristin. "What's this?" She shrugged. "Where did it come from?"

"I don't know. Someone slid it through the mail slot. I found it on the floor this morning."

An uneasy feeling came over him, the fear that this had something to do with Noreen, or Colby. He waited until Kristin was back at her desk to open it and couldn't believe what was inside.

"I'm ready." Melissa, his patient, peeked from behind the mostly closed door, shivering in only a gown and socks.

Dorian slid the paper inside the envelope and went into the exam room, his mind sorting a thousand grim possibilities. He started up his computer and opened the woman's electronic chart, finding letters from both her primary care physician and the oncologist who had referred her for a hysterectomy. Her case was complicated, and he was having a hard time concentrating.

Melissa swung her legs back and forth over the end of the table and flexed her feet, emphasizing her toned, thin calves. "I brought these from the imaging center. My oncologist thought you should have a look." She held out two disks encased in white paper envelopes.

Dorian loaded the first, full of CAT scan images, into his computer. His preoccupied mind refused to comprehend the complex, layered images.

"Are you all right?" Melissa said.

Dorian clicked his mouse and opened another file. Still, nothing made sense. He couldn't work like this.

"Actually, no," he said. "I'm sorry. I was notified of an emergency just before coming in here, and I'm afraid I'm going to have to reschedule. I'll make sure Kristin gets you back in any time this week that is convenient for you, if that's all right."

"That'll be fine."

Dorian felt terrible for first making Melissa wait, then rescheduling her, but a malpractice suit would be worse than a delay. He shook her sweat-slick hand, and after thanking her for her understanding, headed back to the reception desk to allow her time to change.

"Any luck getting through to Noreen?"

Kristin shook her head. "She's not answering her cell or her house phone."

"I have to go. Reschedule Ms. Montgomery for her earliest convenience. Double-book me, triple-book me, whatever. Just fit her in. Also, call and cancel my day. Tell the patients I had an emergency."

"Wait, what? You want me to cancel a full day at the last minute? Where are you going?"

"To find Noreen."

CHAPTER 28

Seventy-five-year-old Henry Coleman had had his first heart attack two years earlier, and had called Ana his "angel" ever since she first saved his life. The near-death call resulted in a triple bypass, but with a handful of lifestyle changes, Henry avoided a second incident.

Dorothy, his eighty-year-old wife of fifty-five years, had EMS on speed dial.

Ana recognized the address as soon as the call came in.

Ethan backed into the driveway of the small, cape-style house and reached for his bag. "Are we good?"

Ana zippered her coat and pulled on a fresh pair of gloves. "Yeah, we're good." She climbed out of the ambulance and went inside. "Hello, anybody home?"

She knocked as she opened the door, familiar enough with the couple to feel comfortable doing so. The house smelled of chicken soup, boiling away on the stove, and of strong, rose-scented perfume that reminded her of embalming fluid.

"We're in here, angel." Henry coughed and sounded short of breath.

Ana followed the scuff trail on the laminate floor left behind by the black rubber feet on Dorothy's walker. "Hello?"

Henry sat with his feet up in the living room recliner. He was a kind man—short and squat, with deep wrinkles that came from years of working on tugboats and smoking unfiltered cigarettes.

"My angel." He smiled, and his skin folded into itself, each wrinkle swallowing the next. His slate-blue eyes appeared clear, and if he was in pain, it wasn't obvious.

"Mr. Coleman, I'm starting to think you're just calling for company." Ana returned his smile and put her stethoscope in her ears.

Ethan walked into the room, and Mr. Coleman lifted his hand off the arm of the chair. "I'd say I was trying to take you away from all of this, but how can I compete with this handsome young man?"

Ana listened to Henry's heart and logged the first set of vitals. "Want to tell me what's going on?"

"I thought I was going to lose him." Dorothy shifted in the seat next to Henry's and reached for him with her shaking hand. She dabbed at her nose with a crumpled tissue and lifted her thick glasses to wipe her green eyes, which were fading beneath the haze of advanced cataracts.

"She always thinks I'm dying, angel. It's nothing, really."

Ethan ran down a list of meds with Henry, referencing the cornucopia of bottles next to him for dosages.

Henry pointed at a wad of crumpled-up foil. "I didn't tell Dorothy, because I didn't want to hear her yelling at me, but I overdid it. I ate a whole chocolate bar, and I got some pain."

Ana took his thin wrist in her hand and checked his pulse. "Can you describe the pain for me?"

Henry coughed again, and Ana handed him his glass of water. "Burning, I guess. Like heat in my throat and chest."

"Is there any pain anywhere else? Any tingling or numbness?"

Henry smacked his lips. "No, just a terrible taste in my mouth."

Dorothy shuffled over to the coffee table and handed Henry a peppermint from the bowl on the table.

Ethan, looking a bit smug, shook an empty medication bottle. "How long ago did you run out of your Aciphex, Mr. Coleman?"

"A week, maybe two."

Ana wrapped her stethoscope around her neck and stepped back. "It sounds to me like your reflux is acting up, but I can't be sure. It's up to you if you want me to take you in or if you want to see your regular doctor . . ."

"He needs to go to the hospital," Dorothy said. "He's being pig-headed. This isn't just today, and it's not from the candy bar he knows he's not supposed to eat. This has been going on for almost two weeks."

"She doesn't know two weeks from two hours anymore. Dotty, give it a rest."

Ana second-guessed herself, realizing she might only be getting half of the story. "You know, it doesn't hurt to get looked at."

"Please," Dorothy said, starting to cry, "I want to make sure."

"All right, I'll go," Henry said, "on one condition. You need to call Judith and have her bring you to the hospital. I don't want you stuck there all day without a ride. You know where we keep her phone number, right?"

"I know how to make a phone call, for Pete's sake."

Judith, Henry's grandniece whom Ana had met on several occasions, had been a godsend for the elderly, childless couple.

"Ethan, will you get the gurney?" Ana said.

"No. No. No. I'm not helpless." Henry reached over the side of the chair, pulled the lever to retract the footrest, and with some effort, managed to stand. He walked to the closet, his gait steady, but awkward, and opened the door. The smell of mothballs, once faint, filled the room. He put on a navy blue wool coat, one that appeared at least two sizes too big, and shrank under the coat's substantial weight. "Come on," he said. "Let's get this over with."

He picked up the cordless phone on the way to the front door and dialed Judith's number. "Here, Dotty. Phone's for you."

He handed Dorothy the phone and shuffled toward the ambulance.

Ana gestured for Ethan to help her and, between the two of them, they settled Henry in. Henry shivered, and Ana added a second blanket before tightening the straps that secured him to the gurney.

"All set?" Ethan said.

Ana nodded and sat on the bench seat.

The rear doors slammed, and Henry rolled his head toward her, reaching for her hand.

"Everything all right?" she said.

Henry drew a labored breath, looking noticeably worse in Dorothy's absence. Ana rechecked his vitals; his blood pressure had gone up.

"How come a pretty girl like you isn't married?" Henry asked.

"Who says I'm not?" She forced a smile, uncomfortable having this particular conversation, even with her favorite patient.

Henry's tired eyes settled on her left hand. "No ring."

"Ah."

"Dorothy and I have been married fifty-five years next month," Henry said, his eyes tearing up. "She knows things without me saying."

"She seemed upset. Is there something you're not telling me?"

Henry made a motion just short of a shrug. "No, not really. It's just that Dotty's starting to forget things."

"She remembers to call us." Ana tried to lighten the mood.

"I'm worried what happens when I'm not there to take care of her."

"We're not going to let that happen, are we?"

"No, no we aren't. Speaking of being taken care of . . ." He nodded toward the driver's seat. "What about that good-lookin' fella?"

Ana wrinkled her face. "Not so much."

"Fifty-five years, Dorothy and I have been together, for better or worse, and you know we only dated a couple of months before we got married? Maybe if you gave him a shot. He likes you, you know? He watches you when you aren't looking," Henry said with a wink. "I knew Dotty was the one the day I met her. Love at first sight. You believe in that?"

"Sure do," Ana said.

Unfortunately, the person she felt that way about was married.

CHAPTER 29

Noreen lived alone in a condo at Pemberton Trace, a well-maintained, twenty-unit community made up largely of single professionals who, like her, were more interested in their careers than in doing yard work. There wasn't a single car worth less than forty thousand in the lot, and Dorian was in a full-on sweat by the time he pulled into it. He parked in a space marked "Visitor," slid the envelope into his coat pocket, and stepped into the light snow.

"Good morning." One of a dozen young men clearing the sidewalk greeted Dorian as he walked past.

"Morning," Dorian said, and picked up the pace. He knocked on the door and waited for Noreen to answer, praying there was an answer to this envelope that didn't involve his going to jail.

"Noreen, it's Dorian. Open up." When she didn't answer, he knocked harder. "Noreen, come on. I know you're in there."

The large, twenty-something-year-old man stopped shoveling. "There a problem?"

"No, no problem." Dorian knocked more quietly until Noreen finally answered.

"What do you want?" Her terry cloth bathrobe was belted closed, and she stood with her arm stretched across the opening.

"Can I come in, please?" Dorian looked over his shoulder.

The man stared at them as though committing every detail to memory in case he was about to be some kind of witness.

"I have nothing to say to you."

"Please, it's freezing out here. Let me explain."

"I'm not interested in an explanation."

Dorian pushed past her. "Then I have some questions."

"Get out," Noreen shouted.

"I'm not leaving until we talk about what happened."

"Dorian, I mean it. I'll call the police."

The man started walking toward them, and Dorian slammed the door.

"What I did, it was stupid. It was a *mistake*."

Noreen's hazel eyes narrowed to two swollen slits. "You think I didn't know about you two? You think I haven't seen how she is with you?"

"What do you mean? What are you talking about?"

"Colby Monroe, Dorian. You've been screwing her for over a year and everyone, except for her husband, knew it." Noreen's near-accurate observation stunned him. "She used to call the office all the time, said she had cases to talk to you about, but wouldn't give me specifics. I'd come looking for you after rounds and neither of you were anywhere to be found. You're not nearly as good at hiding things as you think you are, and if Jared didn't know before last night what was going on between the two of you, it's because he didn't want to believe it."

Dorian wanted to tell Noreen she was wrong, but he knew better. If she put the envelope under the door, he had to placate, not argue with her. If she wasn't responsible, he had bigger problems.

"I'm sorry. I never meant to hurt you."

Noreen wiped a hand under each eye, smearing her makeup further. "I've tried everything, *everything* to get you to pay attention to me." Her breath hitched and she sniffled. "Tell me you don't love her."

"I don't love her," Dorian said automatically, even though he didn't mean it.

Noreen's demeanor shifted as she closed the gap between them, making Dorian suddenly aware of what was about to happen, of what *had* to happen to keep his secrets safe.

"Tell me you love *me*," she said, sliding his jacket from his shoulders.

"Noreen, we can't do this."

"Tell me." She pressed her lips to his and dug her nails into his shirt.

"I love you," he whispered.

Noreen dropped her bathrobe and stood naked in the sunlit room. "Now show me."

CHAPTER 30

The ambulance doors opened, and Ana looked past Ethan to see Jared Monroe standing on the other side of the ER doors. Just the sight of him made her jittery, and she fought to contain the emerging grin. Two years of tense conversations, of lingering too long, and of standing close together when all she wanted was for him to ravage her, had her mind working overtime on scenarios other than the one they were about to have.

"Ready?" Ethan said.

Ana made sure that Henry, who had briefly dozed off, was secure. "Ready." She helped Ethan lower the gurney, and sighed when she realized what she was walking into.

Jared managed the piteous smile Ana had come to know well in a short time, and she wondered who had told him.

The doors slid apart, breathing a wall of heat into the winter cold. Ana stood aside, and Ethan eased the gurney over the threshold.

Wilson Quinn, the physician assistant with whom Ana had interacted over the past couple of years, reached for the rail. "We're all set in room two."

"Dotty will be here soon," Ana said, coaxing Henry from his sleep.

"Mr. Coleman, how are we doing today?" said Wilson.

Henry grumbled something unintelligible, and Wilson started in with a list of the usual questions. Henry, who remained groggy, did his best to answer them.

Ethan followed Wilson into the exam room and helped transfer Henry into the hospital bed, all the while keeping an eye on Ana.

Ana tried to get out of having another conversation about what happened to Sydney, but she could tell from Jared's expression there was no avoiding it.

"Hey," he said. "Can we talk a minute?"

Ethan scowled.

"I'll be right back." Ana held up a finger, saying she'd only be a minute, and followed Jared to a quiet corner near the supply room.

She could have gotten lost in the darkness of his sad eyes.

"I heard about what happened. I'm so sorry for your loss. Is there anything I can do?"

Ana wiped a fresh tear from her cheek, his sympathy worsening her pain. "No, I . . ."

Jared set his hand on her shoulder, and when she didn't shy away, pulled her into a tentative embrace.

She stepped back, a bit dazed, and caught the reflection of the light off his wedding ring.

"Ana, I need a copy of this." Ethan, who was pushing the gurney back toward the ambulance bay, stopped and thrust a piece of paper at her.

Jared flashed him an angry look, and softened when he looked back at Ana. "If there's anything, please don't hesitate to ask."

She thanked him and took the paper Ethan had given her to the unit clerk, Cecelia, for copying.

Cecelia rubbed her round stomach and did a bit of a stretch. Ana had no idea how Cecelia managed a demanding career with four children and one on the way, but she did, and made it look effortless.

"Not much longer, huh?" Ana, desperate to focus on anything other than her own problems, struck up a conversation about Cecelia's pregnancy.

"Three weeks, and it can't come soon enough." She took the paper from Ana. "Just one copy?"

"Yeah, just one, thanks. Did you find out if you're having a boy or girl?"

Cecelia shook her head. "We don't want to know this time. Four girls, we're holding out for a son. I'm not sure my husband can handle any more pink." Her face lit up in a smile, and when it faded, the remaining awkward expression had Ana wondering if Cecelia, too, had heard about Sydney.

"You know, you guys are pretty cute together."

"Ethan? Oh God, we're not *together*."

Cecelia handed her the two sheets of paper and spoke softly. "I meant Jared. It's obvious you two like each other, and after what happened with his wife . . ." She rolled her eyes.

"What happened?" Ana said, not even bothering to refute her interest in Jared.

"She cheated."

"Who cheated?" Ethan came from out of nowhere.

Ana played stupid. "What're you talking about?"

"What're *you* talking about?" he said. "Mr. Coleman's all set. You have that copy or what?"

"Yeah, right here. I was just talking to Cecelia about her new addition." Ana handed him the papers. "Fingers crossed for a boy." She held up both hands with her fingers crossed and smirked.

Cecelia smiled. "Think about what I said."

Ethan congratulated Cecelia and ushered Ana toward the ambulance. "What was that about?"

"I told you, the baby," Ana said, looking over her shoulder to see Jared watching them leave.

CHAPTER 31

Dorian's postcoital nap took a quick and violent turn. The last thing he remembered was the sound of plow trucks clearing the parking lot, and the next thing he knew, doors were slamming and Noreen was shouting.

"What is this?" she said.

Dorian sat bolt upright, his mind taking a minute to catch up with what was happening. Sunlight poured through the space between the bedroom curtains and blinded him. He shielded his eyes with his hand. "What is it? What's the matter? What happened?"

Noreen stood at the foot of the bed, holding the envelope he'd carelessly left in his coat pocket.

"Where did you get that?" He hadn't planned on mentioning it, not after what happened between them.

"Where did *I* get them? Where did you?" Noreen threw the papers into the air, and they rained down around him, the corner of the envelope narrowly missing his head. "The envelope fell out of your pocket when I went to hang up your coat."

Dorian stammered and settled on telling her the truth because it came first to his sleepy mind. "Someone shoved it through the office mail slot. That's why I—"

"That's why you *what*? You thought I was *someone*? You thought *I* put these through the slot to what, *scare* you? Or maybe you brought these to scare me? Is this some kind of blackmail?"

"Wait, *what?*" Dorian felt around under the sheet for his underwear, and when he found his shorts, put them on. "What are you talking about?" The comforter caught on his foot, and he kicked it aside. "You're telling me you don't know where that came from?"

"I told you, from your pocket."

"Shit, Noreen. *Shit.*" He gathered up the hair at his temples in two clenched fistfuls.

"Wait." Her full lips bent into a twitching frown. "That's why you're here?" Tears glistened in her eyes, and her mouth fell open. "You came here to do this with me so I wouldn't say anything? You thought I was blackmailing *you* to get you to what, get you to make love to me?"

"No, that's not it." He stepped into his pants, pulled on his shirt, and left it unbuttoned. "You have to believe me." He took her hands in his. "That's not why I did this. It isn't like that."

"Tell me how it is. Tell me you love me now, Dorian."

He couldn't do it, not again.

She sucked in her cheeks and spat in his face. "That's what I thought. Get out of my house."

"Dammit, Noreen. Do you have any idea what this means?" He wiped the spit with his sleeve and picked up the sheets of paper from on the bed. One was a lab report, a copy of the testing he quietly ordered on Sydney Dowling, the other, a copy of the surgical schedule with Stephanie Martin's name, written in marker, circled, and highlighted. "Look at these." She waved her hand dismissively. "Noreen, look at these."

"I already did."

"And?"

"And what? What do you want me to tell you?"

Dorian, thinking he might have made the wrong inference, was desperate for a silver lining. "What do you think this is saying?"

"Are you serious right now? The two tied together like this, I think the answer is obvious. The question isn't *what they know*. It's *who knows what?* I can't believe you thought I'd do this to you."

Dorian searched his mind for anyone who would suspect his wrongdoing and have access to confidential patient information.

"Oh God." He felt sick at the realization. Noreen had been the obvious answer, the most likely to use what they did against him, but she wasn't the culprit. "It was Marco Prusak."

CHAPTER 32

A banner, tied between two pillars on the grand porch of Emily and Derrick's five-thousand-square-foot house, welcomed Emily home. A line of high-end cars—Porsches, BMWs, and Mercedes—stretched halfway down the block, heralding a crowd inside.

"You shouldn't have done all of this." Emily reached for the door handle, and Derrick stopped her.

"All of what? It's only family and a couple of close friends. They wanted to come to the hospital, but I asked them to help us keep this private. They'll only stay long enough to check on you, and then they'll leave. I promise."

Emily pulled down the visor and checked her drawn reflection in the mirror. Dark circles surrounded her eyes, and she hated how visible her freckles were without concealer. She hadn't taken a shower in days, and her frizzy, greasy hair stuck out of the elastic holding it back. "I just wish I knew to expect company is all." But it wasn't *all*. The news of Stephanie Martin's failed transplant weighed heavily, despite Dr. Carmichael's vague reassurances. "This was your father's idea, wasn't it?"

Derrick sighed. "He's excited."

"Does he know what happened to the other patient?"

"I told him, but we both think it best we don't tell Mom. It's all going to be fine." Derrick smiled and went around the passenger's side to help Emily out.

A flood of cold hit her as soon as the door was open, and she shivered, sparking new pain in her incision. She let out a groan and gently crossed her arms over her stomach.

"Easy does it."

"It's freezing out here." Emily swung her legs one at a time over the doorsill, and pulled her coat closed.

Derrick squatted in front of her and wrapped her arm around his neck.

"On the count of three. One, two . . ."

"Three." Emily braced herself for the pain that came when Derrick eased her onto her feet. She stood, frozen for a minute, and waited for the knifing pain to pass. She shuffled clear of the car door, which Derrick closed behind her.

The front door opened, and Mayor Bill Warren, Emily's father-in-law, greeted them, wearing a tentative grin and holding a glass of Merlot. "Anything I can do to help?" He wore a navy blue suit with a white dress shirt and an understated tie. He was an older version of Derrick, lean and bookish, but he wore contacts instead of glasses, and had the smug confidence of a used car salesman.

"No. I'll get there," Emily said, but with each painful, nausea-inducing step, she wondered. When she finally made it inside, her face was windburned and her nose runny.

Derrick unfolded the wheelchair tucked between an ornate, mahogany coat tree and the wall by the door. "Dr. Carmichael said it would be good to keep you off your feet for a while." He adjusted the footrests and pressed his lips to her forehead. A look of concern washed over him. "Are you feeling all right?"

"Fine enough," Emily said. "Let's get this over with."

Bill waited at the other end of the hall and opened the door to the first-floor master bedroom when they reached him.

The crowd erupted with shouts of "Surprise!"

Emily tried to smile, but something was wrong. The mix of heat and the smell of food made her nauseated. She swallowed the vomit rising in her throat and grimaced.

"You like it?" Derrick said.

In the short time Emily had been in the hospital, Derrick had converted the first-floor master to a children's playroom. The walls were painted a delicate yellow and decorated with a pastel Noah's ark mural.

"Isn't it amazing?" Margaret, Emily's redheaded mother-in-law, rushed over to her. Her long hair was piled into a high bun, and she wore too much blue eye makeup. "The ark was my idea."

"When you're up to it, I'll show you the nursery upstairs," Derrick said.

Emily clamped her hand over her mouth. She had tried to repress the sick feeling, but the smell of her mother-in-law's perfume was too much. She waved her hand at the garbage pail, and Derrick quickly grabbed it.

Emily buried her face so far in the pail that the crowd disappeared, and after several seconds of painful retching, she was too embarrassed to come out. "Take me to bed," she said, her voice echoing. She spat and waited. "Derrick, I need to go to bed."

"I'm sorry," he said. "Excuse us."

Emily crossed her arms over the edge of the can and didn't look up until she felt the wheelchair reenter the hallway. Several of the wives conjectured that their being there was a bad idea from the start. Bill, in his most mayoral tone, assured the visitors their presence lifted Emily's spirits.

Emily sighed, her breath hitching when the inhalation stretched her stomach.

Derrick steered her into the already prepared guest bedroom and set the brakes.

"Close the door." Emily withdrew her head from the sour-smelling container. The room spun, and she waited until she was sure she wasn't going to be sick again before trying to lift the footrest.

"I got it. Hang on a minute." Derrick moved them and took the can from her.

"Don't go too far with that." The nausea was already returning.

Derrick turned down the bed and eased Emily out of the chair. She took a couple of steps and felt the first bit of relief when her skin pressed against the cool cotton sheets.

Derrick had already filled her prescriptions, which were lined up on the nightstand. He opened a bottle of water and handed her two pills.

Margaret, not one to miss out on the action, knocked softly. "Derrick, everything all right?"

"Everything's fine, Mom. I'll be out in a minute."

"Emily, dear. Anything I can do?"

Emily waved her hand and swallowed the pain pill.

"No, Mom. We need a minute, please."

"Have we heard anything about when the nurse will be here?" Emily wasn't ready to admit to Derrick how much worse she felt since leaving the hospital.

"It's only been an hour. I'll call Dr. Carmichael this afternoon before his office closes if we don't hear anything by then."

"Maybe you should call now."

A knock came at the door.

Margaret, again.

"Mom, please." Derrick peered through the small opening, shielding Emily from view.

"Your father wants to talk with you," she whispered, loud enough for Emily to overhear.

"Tell him I'll be right there." Derrick closed the door and headed into the adjoining bathroom where he flushed the vomit down the toilet and rinsed the can. He dried it with a paper towel and set it on the nightstand next to the bed. "Why don't you see if you can get some sleep?" He placed a cool, wet washcloth on Emily's forehead. "I'll get everyone out of here. You're right. I shouldn't have let them come in the first place."

"Tell everyone that I'm sorry." She adjusted her pillow and turned on Food Network for noise while she slept.

"I'm sure they understand." Derrick pulled the room-darkening drapes and forced a smile. "Get some rest. I'll be back in to check on you as soon as they leave."

"Derrick," she called after him.

"Yeah?"

"I love you."

"I love you, too."

CHAPTER 33

"Nestor, a Corona and a mug of Sam Adams, please." Ana ignored the men's stares as she took her seat at the bar. "And crack that door open, would you? It stinks in here." As many times as she'd been to the Barfly, the acrid smell of urinal cakes was hard to get used to.

It was ten times worse with the heat on.

Nestor slid a lime wedge into the neck of the Corona bottle and poured a frosted mug of Sam Adams on draft. "Anything else?"

"Just that door."

The frosted mug started to sweat as soon as Nestor set it down.

"You got it." Nestor propped the door open with a rubber wedge, and a cool breeze blew across the bar.

Ana squeezed the lime into the bottle and took a sip. The sour juice coated her lips and stung where the chapped skin had split. She licked at the wound, and a man, one of the few she didn't know, nodded in her direction. She rolled her eyes and focused on the small television broadcasting the most recent headline news.

It had been a long, confusing day, and as Ana waited for Mike to arrive, she thought about all that had happened. She wouldn't call herself superstitious, but she did believe in signs. Henry Coleman had been the first, talking about someone to take care of her. The right person could have made the past week much easier, and if Cecelia was right—Ana considered her the second sign—the one person she imagined herself being with was becoming available.

"Is this seat taken?" Mike slid off his knit cap and set it on the bar.

"Thanks for coming," Ana said, and reached out for a hug.

Mike looked around the room, and she followed his eyes.

Two firemen from Anthony's station racked up a fresh game of pool. Ron and Coop sat at a booth in the corner and were three empty pitchers of beer into what looked to be the beginnings of a long night.

"Interesting choice of location."

"Beer's cheap and the company's trustworthy." Ana slid the defrosting mug over to him. "Any luck?"

Their meeting was to discuss leads in Sydney's case.

Mike scratched at the gray-and-white stubble on his chin and pulled a smart phone from his pocket. "Maybe." He called up a series of pictures, screen shots of criminal records that were nearly impossible to read given their small size. "Tell me if any of those names or faces rings a bell."

Ana sorted through a half-dozen suspects, four female and two male, zooming in on the screen to read their laundry lists of charges. "Robbery, prostitution, drug possession, and intent to sell. None of these are murderers, Mike. And no, none of their names or faces rings a bell, except for maybe this one." She held up the screen and showed him the picture of Lucinda Morales. "I think we brought her into County once for an overdose."

"Are you sure?" Mike sipped his beer.

"Positive. Where did this list even come from? What do any of these people have to do with Sydney?"

Mike shrugged. "I was hoping you could tell me. There were literally hundreds of fingerprints in that room, half of which belonged to people with priors. Julian and Elsa sorted the suspects by physical description."

"Description? Why, did somebody see something?"

Mike shrugged. "Yes and no. I went back to question Samuel and to get the surveillance tapes from the Aquarian."

"You have a tape?"

"No. The cameras are fakes. There wasn't any footage, but there's a possible eyewitness. She described a mid-five-foot, slender person, wearing a dark trench coat in the Aquarian parking lot the night of Sydney's murder."

"Like a woman?"

"Maybe, or a small man, or Sydney met someone there who had nothing to do with what happened. It's too vague a description and too loose an association for me to say anything definitive. The witness saw someone walking away, but not leaving room eleven. The person was wearing all black, it was dark, and snowing. Misty's alibi checked out. She was at County all night. The only reason I'm even looking into this is because the witness said she overheard a fight."

"Was there evidence of a struggle?"

"Sydney had a broken fingernail, but Kim says it's consistent with her shoving her finger down her throat to induce vomiting."

"Anything off the supposed suicide note?"

"No prints."

"And no pad, right? The note wasn't written there?"

Mike waved for Nestor to refill his beer. "Right. There wasn't a notepad in the room."

"Can I see it?"

Mike hesitated and looked down at the bar. "It's in evidence lockup."

"Mike, come on. You have all of those files on your phone to show me, but not the note?"

"It's not important."

"It's important to me. Please?"

Mike flipped through a handful of photos and handed her the phone when he reached the shot of the crumpled piece of paper.

Ana ordered another round before reading it.

You never really know what you want until you can't have it.
I will never have the family I deserve.
I will never be a mother. I will never be loved.
I've lost too much to keep going.
Anna, I'm sorry.
I just can't stand the pain.

Ana handed him back the phone. "They spelled my name wrong."

Mike wiped beer foam from his mustache. "What?"

"My name, look at it. I've never used a double 'n.' They spelled my name wrong," she repeated, pointing at the second-to-last line.

"Shit. How did I miss that?"

"And whoever it is, they know about the surgery, that Sydney can't have kids."

Mike nodded. "Most people know. It's not like it was a secret."

"And about our parents? That bit about loss says that whoever did this knew about our past."

"Again, not a big secret."

"It's not, no, but whoever wrote this knew about me. Not enough to spell my name right, but enough to call me Ana. They knew about our parents and about Sydney's surgery. Who would know all of that?"

"I don't know."

"Mike, stay with me here. Someone who took a medical history would have reviewed Sydney's family and social history as part of the intake process. What if whoever killed Sydney was part of her treatment?"

"It's a reach, Ana."

"A reach, maybe, but not an impossibility."

CHAPTER 34

The smell of marijuana drifted through a slightly open window as Noreen made her way through Windsor Towers, a low-end apartment complex that catered to petty criminals, the poverty-stricken, and for some reason, to Dr. Marco Prusak, whom she planned on holding accountable for Dorian's recent run of bad luck.

Marco lived in apartment 24, and Noreen surveyed for potential witnesses before confronting him about the envelope.

The blue light of a television flickered behind the blanket-covered window of the adjacent unit. Pounding bass shook the door across the hallway. The tenants screamed loudly inside, either in the midst of a heated argument, or caught up in a tryst rough enough to make a porn star blush.

Noreen lifted her bag onto her shoulder and held her gloved hand over the peephole while she knocked.

"Who is it?" Marco asked. Noreen answered with a second knock. "I said, 'Who is it?'" Marco cracked the door enough for him to peer out.

Noreen forced her way in, slamming the door behind her.

"What are you doing? Get out of my house!"

Noreen kicked him as hard as she could in his groin, and he doubled over with a loud, "Oof!"

"We need to talk." She uncapped the syringe she took from her coat pocket and held it to his throat. "Get up." Marco was on his knees, his arms wrapped tightly over his stomach. "Now."

Marco drew a breath and managed to get to his feet. He was hunched over and shuffled backward, nearly tripping over the bottom of his blue-and-white pajama pants, striped, to match his button-down shirt.

"Please, what do you want?"

"You know who I am, don't you?"

Marco nodded.

"Sit."

Marco backed into a kitchen chair and sat, as instructed.

"Give me your hands." Noreen set her bag on the table and held the syringe tight in her mouth. She didn't take her eyes off Marco for a second.

"Please, I don't want any trouble."

She grabbed his wrists and wrapped them in a band of duct tape. She cut with a kitchen knife and spat out the syringe. "Then why did you start it?" She wiped her mouth on the back of her hand.

"I don't know what you're talking about."

Noreen didn't have to know Marco well to know he was scared. "Where are the reports?" She flipped through the stacks of religious tracts piled on every horizontal surface.

"What reports?"

"The originals of the ones you delivered to Dr. Carmichael's office this morning."

"I don't know what you're talking about."

Noreen withdrew a vial from her bag and set it down, hard, on the table. "Since you're a doctor, I'm sure you're aware of the paralyzing effects of succinylcholine." She shook the syringe in her hand, indicating its contents.

Marco turned his dark eyes away from her. "Yes," he muttered.

"And insulin?" She showed him the IV setup and the insulin bag. Marco nodded. "You'll tell me what I want to know, or I'll put as many bags of it into you as it takes to kill you. Your blood sugar will drop, your brain will starve, and if you're lucky, you'll lapse into unconsciousness before you die, slowly. Is that what you want?"

"No, *please.*"

"Then cooperate." Noreen pulled a chair up in front of him. "Let's start with an easy question. It was you who delivered those reports to Dr. Carmichael's office, wasn't it?" She depressed the plunger until the needle tip glistened with liquid. "Wasn't it?" She moved it close enough to Marco to leave a wet spot on the thigh of his pants.

"Yes, yes it was me."

"How many copies are there?"

"Two," he said.

"Two including the ones you left for Dr. Carmichael?" Noreen made a show of thumbing the plunger.

"Yes."

"And where is the other set?"

"They're at my lab, at County." Marco was too scared to be an effective liar.

"*Where* in your lab?" Noreen figured she'd give him just enough rope to hang himself.

"In the locked file cabinet behind my desk."

"And who else have you told?"

"Told what?"

"Don't play dumb, Marco. Who have you told about the surgeries?"

"No, no one. I swear it."

Noreen pressed the needle tip to Marco's skin. "Why Dorian? You obviously have an endgame, but I haven't figured out what it is."

Marco's gaze settled past her, on his refrigerator and the photograph of an infant, the only thing hanging on it.

"I asked you a question." Noreen advanced the needle, but not the plunger. "You're out to ruin Dorian. What did he do to you?"

Sweat beaded on Marco's forehead, and his breathing bordered on panting.

"I'm only going to ask you nicely one more time, Marco. *Why Dorian?*"

Marco refused to answer.

It was clear that getting an answer was going to take more-drastic coaxing.

CHAPTER 35

Ten unanswered phone calls left Ana with no other option than to show up at Dr. Sanders's office and wait him out.

The receptionist, Shannon, to whom she'd spoken several times, finished the call she was on, glanced up from her computer screen, and hung up the handset on the receiver. She was younger than Ana expected, midtwenties, and dressed in a low-cut shirt more appropriate for a nightclub than a doctor's office. "Can I help you?"

"I'm here to speak with Dr. Sanders."

"Do you have an appointment?" The familiar, sharp tone quickly emerged.

"I don't, no, but—"

"Then you'll have to make one. He's double-booked through today and doesn't accept walk-ins."

"I've been calling for days. I need to speak with him about my sister."

"In that case, HIPAA requires you to have her permission."

Ana, well aware of privacy regulations, slammed her hands on the desk. The young woman jumped. "That's going to be a problem considering my sister is *dead*."

"Keep your voice down," Shannon said, shushing her.

A couple emerged from the examination room, beaming with pride. The husband, a dark-haired man in a tailored business suit, patted his wife's swollen belly.

The wife, a petite, older woman who looked like she'd been recently crying, reached out and shook the hand of a homely, but gentle-appearing man in his midfifties, with a comb-over hairstyle that attempted to hide his rather severe balding. "Thank you, Dr. Sanders."

"You're very welcome. Make sure she gets some rest," he said to the husband.

"Absolutely. I'll wait on her hand and foot." The husband kissed his wife's forehead and smiled.

"I'll see you back in a month after the amniocentesis. Shannon will call to set the appointments."

"So we're all set?" the wife said.

"For now. Congratulations, again."

Ana waited until the couple left to chase Dr. Sanders down the hallway. "Excuse me, Dr. Sanders."

Shannon, slow on her four-inch heels, tried to keep up. "Stop," she said. "You can't just go back there."

"Dr. Sanders, I need to speak with you."

There was an audible click as Dr. Sanders stopped his dictation and turned around. "Can I help you?"

Ana held up her hand. "I've been calling for days. Please, I need to talk to you about my sister, Sydney Dowling." She pulled his card from her jeans pocket. "I found this at her house. If you'll give me just a few minutes, I can explain."

"I tried to stop her," Shannon said.

Dr. Sanders swept aside the thin patch of hair sliding down his forehead. "I'm afraid I can't speak with you about another patient without her consent."

Ana's eyes welled up with tears. "And I'm afraid I can't get that because she was *murdered*."

The receptionist held out her cell phone and dialed. "Dr. Sanders, I have Security on the line. What do you want me to do?"

"Please, just a few questions," Ana begged.

Dr. Sanders turned to Shannon and sighed. "Tell them everything is all right, and let my next patient know I'm running a bit late." He looked at Ana. "Ten minutes. I'll give you ten minutes."

The receptionist shot Ana a dirty look, which Ana promptly returned with one of her own.

"Thank you. Really, thank you." Ana shook Dr. Sanders's freshly washed hand, and the smell of soap wafted off him.

"Follow me, please." He led Ana to his spacious, well-appointed office.

Two dozen similarly framed degrees hung behind a massive, cherry desk, displaying a variety of impressive credentials. A pair of cream-colored leather chairs sat facing them, the orange accent pillows complementing the orange-and-brown floor-to-ceiling drapes.

"I'm sorry for your loss." Dr. Sanders gestured for Ana to have a seat.

"I'm sorry for barging in. I didn't know what else to do."

"What is it you think I can help you with?" Dr. Sanders put on a pair of wire-rimmed glasses and smoothed his hair.

"I need to know why my sister came to you when she was seeing another surgeon."

Dr. Sanders leaned back and interlaced his fingers. "Sydney came to me for a second opinion after her hysterectomy. It's not uncommon for a woman who's lost the ability to have children to have an emotional reaction, but Sydney was desperate. She felt that maybe her surgeon had been too aggressive, or that she'd consented to an unnecessary procedure. She had done some research and I believe was considering a lawsuit."

"What kind of research?"

"There are alternatives to hysterectomies, at least temporary ones, for women of childbearing age. The goal is to keep the reproductive organs viable for birth if that is the patient's wish, and I believe it was Sydney's. Her main question was if her condition was severe enough to warrant an immediate procedure."

"And was it?"

Dr. Sanders massaged his temples. "I don't know. I asked Sydney for a copy of the pathology reports, but she was unable to get them. Her surgeon's office said they didn't have them, and County Memorial said they were 'lost.'" He made air quotes with his fingers.

"How can the reports be 'lost'? Everything at County is electronic."

Dr. Sanders shrugged, and his stethoscope slid down his shoulder. "I suppose accidents do happen. There could have been a registration mix-up, or the report could've been attached to a wrong account, but it seemed odd to me that Dr. Carmichael would've operated without having ever received the results."

Shannon appeared in the doorway. "Dr. Sanders, your next patient is here."

"I'll be right there. I'm sorry," he said to Ana, "I have to go."

She felt no closer to an answer. "Is there anything else?"

"Just this." Dr. Sanders pulled a manila folder from his desk drawer and handed it to her. "I ran a CA-125 and an LPA test. They're somewhat vague, and a bit unreliable, but as far as cancer antigen tests go, there should have been some abnormal result—a residual positive given how recently after Sydney's surgery the tests were taken. Sydney's symptoms didn't line up, clinically, with her diagnosis. She was never offered chemotherapy, or radiation, and both tests came back completely normal. There's a margin for error here, no doubt, but the fact of the matter is, Sydney showed no signs of ever having cancer."

CHAPTER 36

Dorian parked in the hospital's two-story garage, and his phone rang for the fifth time since leaving Noreen's.

"Damn it, Mitchell. Leave me alone." His voice echoed against the concrete structure.

The calls alternated between Mitchell Altman and Simon Walker, neither of whom he had any interest in talking to, at least not while he had no idea how much they knew about what he'd done.

What he would take back if he could.

Stephanie Martin's case came when he was desperate, not only for money, but for fame, and at a time when he needed to secure his foothold at County. Months had passed since the successful completion of his animal trials, and he was in limbo, waiting on a donor for the first human transplant. Unlike other organs, the possibility of getting a viable uterus was slim, the donation pool cut by more than half with the majority of recent donors being male. Of the female candidates with their reproductive organs intact, none was a match to Stephanie Martin, whose husband had donated a large sum of money to the hospital and paid another hundred thousand dollars to Dorian to ensure that Stephanie was at the top of the list.

He could say it was Noreen's idea, testing their patients for donor matches and convincing Sydney Dowling that she needed a hysterectomy, but he'd had a hand in coming up with the plan. Fear of death was a powerful motivator and all but forced Sydney's compliance. Dorian didn't foresee the transplant's failure, or others' interest in where the donated uterus came from.

Sydney Dowling had put the pieces together.

Marco Prusak had put the pieces together.

Dorian walked through the main entrance and hurried toward the bank of elevators.

The overhead page called him, almost immediately, to dial Mitchell's extension.

The secretary manning the front desk waved to get his attention. "Dr. Carmichael, you have a call." It was as if someone had put out an APB.

Dorian ignored her and pressed the elevator's call button.

"Dr. Carmichael." The woman spoke louder, and when he didn't answer, picked up her phone.

The doors opened and as soon as Dorian was inside, he pounded the button to close them.

One floor up, Mitchell Altman joined him. "Dorian, we've been looking for you."

"What do you want, Mitchell?"

The elevator ascended.

"Stephanie Martin took a turn for the worst. Simon's been calling you."

He and Simon had their own demons.

"Screw Simon."

"Like it or not, Dorian, you answer to him. This isn't personal. Whatever happened between you two, get over it. The Martins' attorney contacted me first thing this morning. We're in some serious shit here. No, correction. *You're* in some serious shit."

The elevator doors opened, and Mitchell followed Dorian all the way to Pathology.

"Did you hear me?" Mitchell kept up his badgering. "Simon says Stephanie's not going to make it, Dorian. She's septic."

"I don't have time for this right now. Tell Simon to call an Infectious Diseases consult to manage her antibiotics." Dorian threw open the doors to the lab and found Brenna, shuffling papers and nodding to the beat of her music.

Dorian stood in front of her, but she didn't immediately look up. "Where's Marco?"

"It's *your* job to call the consult," Mitchell said, "not Simon's."

Dorian pounded his fist on the desk. *"Where's Marco?"*

Brenna yanked out her right earbud. "Dr. Prusak? I don't know. I haven't seen him."

Dorian looked around the lab, at the neat stacks of files and specimens, and started sorting through them.

"What are you doing?" Mitchell asked.

Dorian ignored him, searching the cabinets and drawers for what he knew had to be there.

"Dorian, what are you doing?" Mitchell grabbed his arm, and Dorian shoved him hard enough to knock him off his footing.

Mitchell's jacket pocket caught on the edge of a file cabinet drawer, and the metal sliced his hand as he tried to break his fall. "Damn it." He held his injured hand to his chest. His bald head turned the bright red shade of sunburn. A purple vein throbbed at his temple. "Call Security," he said to Brenna, "now."

Brenna dialed, clearly shaken.

"You're finished here, Dorian." Mitchell wrapped his bleeding hand in a wad of paper towels.

Two security guards, David and Kurt, appeared in the doorway.

"Dr. Carmichael, I'm going to have to ask you to leave," David said.

"I'm *not* leaving without the paperwork."

"What paperwork? What are you talking about?" Mitchell said.

Dorian turned to Brenna. "Where's the paperwork on Stephanie Martin?"

Brenna shook her head. "Which? I don't know what you're talking about."

"Tissue typing, antibody screens, all of it."

"Dr. Carmichael," said Kurt, the larger of the two guards, as he moved in on him, "please, come with me."

"Not without the paperwork."

Brenna typed Stephanie's name into the computer and shrugged. "There's nothing."

Dorian scoffed. "You know what I'm looking for isn't there."

Kurt took another step closer and puffed out his chest. "Dr. Carmichael, I'm only going to ask once more."

"And I'm still not leaving." Dorian swiped his hand across the desk, sending a computer monitor crashing to the floor. Sparks flashed across the shattered screen.

Brenna screamed.

David dialed his cell phone. "This is County Memorial Hospital Security, requesting police backup."

Dorian couldn't give up. The proof was too damning, and it opened too many doors.

Stephanie Martin might die.

Sydney Dowling was already dead.

Even though he was facing arrest, leaving peacefully wasn't an option.

CHAPTER 37

Ana grabbed a beer from her refrigerator, pried off the top, and took a long sip. The cold malt replaced the moisture in her dry mouth, promising a comforting buzz. She turned on the living room lamp and grabbed her laptop off the end table. It was only 4:00 p.m., but for as dark as it got so early in winter, it might well have been eight. The computer screen emanated a blinding glow, the reflection of the dim lamp visible in the background. She opened an Internet browser, searched for Dr. Carmichael's office phone number, and called it.

"Oakland Street Obstetrics and Gynecology. This is Kristin. How may I help you?"

Ana invented a false identity to avoid the inevitable red tape. "Yes, Kristin, this is Susan Greene calling from County Memorial's Primary Care Center. How're you today?"

"Good, thank you. How can I help you?"

"Our computer system is down, and I have a patient here by the name of Sydney Dowling to see Dr. Shepherd. She's one of Dr. Carmichael's patients. I need to get a copy of her operative and pathology reports, please. Do you think you can send those to me?" Ana played the odds that the office hadn't yet been notified about Sydney's death.

"Dowling, you say? *Sydney* Dowling?" Ana could hear other lines ringing in the background. "I'm sorry, can you hold just a minute, please?"

"Sure, thank you." Ana's heart raced while she waited.

The hold music broke, and Kristin came back on the line. "I'm sorry for the delay. Are you there?"

"Yes. I'm here," Ana said.

"There must be some sort of mix-up. You say you have Sydney Dowling there for an appointment, correct?"

"Yes."

"The Sydney Dowling in our system is deceased."

They had been notified.

Ana, not sure of what to say, hung up the phone.

It was time to formulate plan B.

She needed an insider at County to look into things quietly.

County Memorial took HIPAA, the federal Health Insurance Portability and Accountability Act, to a whole new level and observed "need to know" with a vengeance. Computer access was heavily restricted. The few people Ana would even consider asking for help would only have access to demographics, insurance, and maybe orders. She needed someone with high-level access.

Her doorbell rang and she ran to answer it.

"Can I help you?"

A sizable arrangement of red roses, baby's breath, and lilies obscured the man on her doorstep. "Ana Ashmore?"

"Yes."

"These are for you."

Ana took the flowers, careful to avoid any thorns the florist might have missed.

The van parked behind her Jetta said the flowers were from Matrazzo's.

"Sign here, please."

"You've been busy," Ana said, and signed the delivery slip. "I hope this one has a card."

The driver, whose name tag read "Stan," drew his eyebrows together. "What do you mean?"

"I lost my sister about a week ago, unexpectedly. Matrazzo's delivered three dozen roses to Parker and Sons Funeral Home last Wednesday, but there was no card. If there's any way you can look into that for me, I'd really appreciate it. I'd like to thank the person who sent them."

"Absolutely. I'll look into it as soon as I get back to the shop. I'm sorry for your loss."

Ana thanked him and closed the door, eager to know who sent the flowers. She pulled the card and sighed:

I'm sorry for your loss. Anything I can do to help, I'm here. Jared.

The flowers were another in a growing line of signs. Not five minutes earlier she was considering whom she could trust at County, who had the high-level access she needed to look into Sydney's lab reports, and here, the man of her dreams was offering her a lifeline.

She just had to work up the courage to take it.

CHAPTER 38

Colby spent the morning placing phone calls to various prospective employers, doctors' offices, and even Saint Matthew's Hospital, preparing to be self-supporting for the first time in years. She was tired of feeling like a ghost, of fighting, of answering for things she wasn't sorry for, and of feeling indentured to Jared—who hadn't come home in two nights—for taking care of her.

She wandered into the guest bedroom where, up until a few days ago, Jared had been staying. The room smelled of his cologne, emanating off his laundry in the hamper. The queen-sized bed was neatly made, and the closet organized with several new garment bags from the dry cleaner.

Colby had always handled the dry cleaning, and regardless of what had happened between them, the fact that he didn't need her for everyday things stung.

She picked up the photo Jared laid facedown on the nightstand, the one of them in the Bahamas. Jared had surprised her that day and arranged for her to swim with the dolphins, something she'd wanted to do her whole life. He was considerate of her, once, almost doting. Their marriage, though always under some demand for split time or attention, had been otherwise perfect.

"Marriage takes work," her mother had said, and she remembered that every time things got bad.

They'd worked around the strain of Jared's demanding school schedule, staying up late and studying together when she enrolled in nursing school. They dealt with his being on-call and working long hours, and managed to sneak away for private time between shifts at County. He was the reason she applied to work there. But the more he was drawn into the bureaucracy, the harder he tried to ascend the ranks, the further he withdrew from her. He *became* the job, obsessed with statistics about patient outcomes and finances. He volunteered to head several quality committees, and their already meager time together vanished.

Dorian had been there. He listened to her complaints about being alone and made time for her when Jared stopped bothering to. Eventually the complaints disappeared, as did the thoughts of Jared altogether. Colby never meant to cheat, but Dorian made her feel like the most beautiful, intelligent, and desirable woman on Earth, and she needed to feel something other than ambivalence.

A knock came at the door, and she went downstairs to answer it.

"Hello?" Colby squinted, lifting her hand to block the bright sun breaking through the gray clouds.

A young, clean-cut man wearing khakis, a button-down shirt, and a heavy winter coat stood on the front porch. "Colby Monroe?"

"Yes."

"You've been served." He handed her a sealed envelope and was halfway back to his idling SUV before she could argue.

Colby ripped the tab and let out a frustrated growl.

The papers, prepared by one Wendell Cobb, attorney-at-law, said that Jared was filing for divorce on the grounds of infidelity.

"Dammit."

She flung the papers across the dining room table, and they fluttered to the floor in a storm. Her heart pounded, and a dull ache started at the base of her skull. She had offered Jared the option of mediation, a quiet, peaceful, agreeable divorce, and had been revisiting that idea for the past year.

He refused, every time.

She couldn't help wondering what made this time different.

She grabbed her cell phone from her purse and was about to call her lawyer, when a number she didn't recognize appeared on the display. Despite the turn her day had taken, she answered it.

"Hello," she said in a clipped tone.

"Colby?" Dorian's voice sounded defeated, not at all like him.

"Dorian?"

"Yeah, it's me. Listen, I need your help. Can you come get me?"

She grabbed her coat, purse, and keys. "Yeah, sure. Where are you?"

"I'm in jail."

CHAPTER 39

Ana's insides knotted as she walked into the ER, praying for a chance meeting with Jared and the strength to ask for his help.

"Ana, hey." Cecelia spotted her immediately.

"Hey, how's it going?" Cecelia looked like she'd gained several inches around the waist in the few days since Ana had last seen her.

Cecelia rubbed her stomach. "Good, but I don't think this one's waiting two more weeks. What are you doing here?" Ana stared off into the distance, listening to a voice she was almost sure was Jared's. "Ana? Earth to Ana. Hello?" Cecelia waved her hand back and forth.

"I'm sorry. What?"

"No uniform. You're not working. What's up?"

"Can you look up a patient's room number for me, please?"

"Sure, yeah. Is everything all right?" Cecelia waddled to her computer terminal.

"Everything's fine. The patient's name is Henry Coleman."

Cecelia typed his name. "Here we go. Henry Coleman, room two twenty-four B." Ana wrote down the room number on a scrap of paper. "He's here, you know, somewhere."

"Who's here? What do you mean?" Ana folded the paper in half.

"Jared. He's working."

"I wasn't looking . . ." Ana cracked a smile before she finished the lie.

"Yes, you were."

"Okay, I was."

"I hear he's been sleeping in the on-call room the past couple of nights. Maybe you have a better option? Ana's *Bed* and Breakfast?"

Ana's grin spread wider. "Stop it. That's not funny."

Cecelia held her thumb and index fingers an inch apart. "It's a little funny."

"I'm going to see my patient now."

Ana smiled all the way to 224B, only stopping when she saw Henry, withered in the bed.

His thinning, white hair was flattened against the pillow, his steely eyes half-open, and stubble covered his normally clean-shaven face. Ana turned to leave, but she stopped when Henry called out to her.

"Angel, is that you?"

"Yes, it's me, Mr. Coleman. How are you feeling?" She noticed an infusion pump at his bedside.

"Not bad. Not bad. You came here just to see me?"

"Well, you know, if I don't hear from Dorothy regularly, I get worried." Ana smiled. "Ready to go home yet?"

"I wish," he said. "It's bad news this time, angel. Cancer."

The word made her heart skip a beat.

Ana lifted Henry's slipping gown onto his bony shoulder. "Mr. Coleman, I'm so sorry."

"Don't be. I'm going to beat this for Dorothy," he said, his eyes damp with tears. "I can't leave her alone."

Ana nodded, though she knew that, at Henry's age, the odds were likely against him. "Is there anything I can get for you?"

Henry smacked his lips together and made a face. "There's a bowl of candies at the nurses' station. The pretty young girl who changes my sheets brings them to me for this awful taste in my mouth. Think you can grab me some?"

"Sure thing." Ana turned on her heels and froze when she saw Jared standing in the doorway.

"Cecelia told me you were here." He adjusted the stethoscope around his neck and slid his hands into the pockets of his pleated Khakis. He wore a button-down dress shirt, the top two buttons undone, and a T-shirt underneath. He looked even more handsome without a lab coat.

Ana didn't know what to say.

"Candy," Henry whispered.

"Oh right. Jeez. I'll be right back."

The deep folds of Henry's face retracted into a full smile. "No hurry."

Ana brushed Jared when she walked past him, and her skin erupted in gooseflesh.

"I'm sorry," she said.

"No problem at all." Jared's smirk made her feel like a clumsy, giddy schoolgirl.

"I was going to see if you were working, since I was here visiting. I wanted to thank you for the flowers. They're beautiful."

"You're very welcome," he said, "and my offer stands, if there's anything I can do."

Another sign.

People offered help once out of politeness, twice when they really meant it.

"Anything?"

Jared tilted his head to meet her gaze. "*Is* there something I can do?"

"I don't feel right asking."

"Well now . . . you have my curiosity piqued. What is it?"

She hesitated a moment before answering. "I've been trying to get a copy of my sister's lab reports, the pathology from her hysterectomy a little over four months ago, but her surgeon's office says they don't have them, and County says they're lost."

"It's a computerized system. How can they be lost?"

"That's what I said."

"And you need someone to do some digging?"

"I don't feel right asking you to jeopardize your job."

"Why do you need the reports now, if you don't mind my asking?"

Ana chewed her lower lip. "I'm not really comfortable talking about that."

"I see."

"It's not that I don't trust you." Ana reached out, needing for Jared to see that her interest in him was personal. "This whole issue, the thing I can't really talk about yet, involves someone here. I can't say more than that, but if I'm right, these records would prove wrongdoing on a criminal level. They would implicate a physician in ways I don't feel comfortable dragging you into."

"If it helps you figure out what happened to your sister, I'll do whatever it takes." Jared took Ana's hand, and her breath stopped for a single, exciting second. "Ana, I'm not going to pretend I don't have feelings for you. They've been there a long time, and now that I've filed for divorce, I can finally do something about them. I want to help you. I want to be friends and see where that leads. You can trust me, I swear it. I'll get what you need because I want to." The tenderness in his eyes had Ana falling in love. He pulled her closer, his face only inches from hers and said, "Tell me who the doctor is, and I'll find out what happened."

She leaned in, her lips nearly touching his ear, and whispered, "It's Dorian Carmichael."

CHAPTER 40

Dorian used the reflection off the precinct's personal-effects pickup window to straighten himself. The female officer on the other side—a frumpy, pear-shaped woman, wearing an androgynous uniform that did nothing to flatter her figure—double-checked her list and slid his things through the pass.

"Verify that this is everything you came in with, and sign here, please."

Dorian collected his watch, wallet, and keys, accounting for his credit cards and the twenty-three dollars he had on him when he was arrested, and signed the release form.

"Is that everything?"

"Yeah," he said. "I travel light."

Colby stood by the door with her arms crossed and a look on her face that could have been annoyance or anger, he wasn't sure which. Her reddish-blond hair was pulled back into a sloppy ponytail, and she had less makeup on than usual. Her normally bright green eyes were puffy, as if she had been crying, and she looked exhausted.

"I'm sorry," Dorian said, heading toward her with his arms outstretched.

Colby uncrossed her arms and took the keys from the pocket of her oversized parka. "Don't even . . . The day I've had."

Dorian took her incomplete sentences to mean he wasn't the only glitch in her day. He slipped his watch over his wrist and braced for the cold.

"Don't you have a jacket?"

He shook his head. "It's in my car."

"And where's your car?"

"My guess, the impound lot."

A few short hairs fell from her ponytail, and when she went to brush it back, Dorian stopped her. "Don't. It looks good."

"Ripped-up jeans, a T-shirt, and a ponytail. It doesn't take much to please you. All this time I was trying too hard."

He would never tell her, but she could make an outfit made of garbage bags look good. "You want to get out of here?"

"And go where?"

They walked down the steep steps toward Colby's car, parked a half block up.

"Do you trust me?" Dorian held out his hand.

"As much as I trust anyone these days." Colby handed him her keys and got in the passenger's side.

Dorian moved the driver's seat back and adjusted the mirrors. The car was still warm, and when he started it up, heat poured from the vents. He turned on his directional and merged into traffic, headed for the interstate.

"Want to talk about it?" He glanced over at Colby, who was fixing her hair in the vanity mirror.

She shrugged. "I got served with divorce papers this morning."

He smiled. "At least you didn't get arrested."

She dabbed a bit of pink lip gloss on her lips and put up the visor. "Want to talk about *that*?"

"No. Not really." Dorian reached across the center console to hold her hand. "I'd rather talk about this divorce."

"What's there to talk about?"

"What comes after?"

Colby's smile looked forced, almost fake. "That's a good question. I don't suppose you need a nurse for your office, do you?"

Dorian chuckled, thinking about Noreen, their fight, and how she threw him out of her house. The woman was a master of mixed signals. "I might, yeah. If I still have a medical license."

"That bad, huh?"

"I told you, I don't want to talk about it."

"So where are we headed? Can we talk about that?" Colby interlaced her fingers with his.

"I'd rather surprise you."

———

Dorian took I-490E toward the Bristol Mountain Ski Resort, an hour outside of town. Colby had gnawed her fingernails and then the inside of her cheek, when Dorian pulled her finger out of her mouth.

"That noise is driving me crazy. When did you start biting your nails?"

"In the second grade. Nervous habit." For as long as their affair had lasted, they were very much in the "dating" phase, hiding their flaws and bad habits.

"What's there to be nervous about?"

"Getting caught." Conceptually, Colby knew that being with "the other man" while about to face infidelity charges in divorce court was the worst course of action. Emotionally, she didn't care. She kept her eyes on the cars around them, noting one in particular, a silver Lexus, which seemed to be traveling their same route. Not wanting to seem paranoid, she let it go without mention.

Dorian turned onto NY-64, a much less populated road, and smoothed Colby's hand with his thumb. "Once we're past the ski resort, there won't be anyone for miles, trust me."

He was right.

The Lexus continued down the highway, reassuring Colby that she had, in fact, been paranoid.

Dorian turned onto Lakeside Lodges Road, a private road, which looked like it hadn't been plowed in some time. Colby was thankful for the Nissan's all-wheel drive as they made their way past the half-completed log cabins toward desolation.

Situated on a treed lot, acres from the nearest residence, Dorian's place had Adirondack-style charm and homelike warmth about it.

Dorian hopped out of the Rogue, punched the combination into the keypad, and drove into the garage. "Voilà, privacy. And no one knows you're even here."

"I'm sorry. I'm acting kind of nuts, right?"

"*Eh*, a little. Ready to put this day behind us?"

"Am I ever."

Dorian led her through a storage area and up the stairs to the main house. He pushed the door open and let her inside ahead of him. "After you."

He hit a switch on the wall and not one, but two fireplaces, at either end of a great room, roared to life, illuminating a masculine, well-appointed room, heavy with the smells of wood, leather, and pine.

The open-concept floor plan was breathtaking. Dark wooden beams spanned the length of a vaulted ceiling, which opened to a loft. The walls were a mix of rich cream and wood, the accents a hunter green. The built-in wine rack left of the kitchen was fully stocked, and an assortment of glasses hung from it, glistening in the soft glow of recessed lighting.

"Dorian, it's beautiful."

"Not as beautiful as the company." He gathered her in his arms and lowered his head to kiss her. "I assume this is okay, in here, where no one can see us?"

Colby slipped her arms around his neck. "It's better than okay," she said. "It's perfect."

CHAPTER 41

Dorian Carmichael.

Jared shook his head at the coincidence. Ana could be looking to implicate anyone else in wrongdoing, but that it happened to be his arch nemesis was almost a gift. Jared finished his shift around 12:30 a.m. and called home to tell Colby he was working late. The machine answered on the fourth ring. He checked his watch, noting the time, and decided Colby was either ignoring him, or asleep. He left a brief message and hung up.

Two nights in the hospital's on-call room and one at the Comfort Inn had him making mental notes of the things he wanted most from the house before he could no longer get in, or before Colby destroyed them in a fit of spiteful rage.

After almost twenty years of marriage, Colby knew what he valued most.

Jared knew *her* well enough to know those were the things she'd go after first.

Two unanswered calls to Wendell, his lawyer, left it unclear whether Colby had been served with divorce papers.

The fact that she hadn't called him, irate, indicated she most likely still had no clue.

"Dr. Monroe?" Cecelia lumbered toward the nurses' station, one hand on her low back and the other supporting her stomach.

"Cecelia, what are you still doing here?"

"Hurting, if we're being honest. I don't have too many of these shifts left in me. I need you to sign off on this last patient, and then I'm headed home."

Jared signed the discharge orders and handed them back to her. "Good idea. You should rest." She started to walk away, and he stopped her. "Hey, Cecelia. Quick question. Have you seen Dr. Prusak today?"

Cecelia shrugged. "No, I don't think he's here, or at least, he's probably not after what happened."

Of the ways to spread news at County, Cecelia was the most efficient.

"What happened?" he said.

"You didn't hear this from me."

Jared smirked. "Of course."

Cecelia leaned against the counter and stretched. "Dr. Carmichael was arrested earlier, taken out in handcuffs." Her eyes went wide when she said it. "He ransacked Dr. Prusak's lab and nearly attacked Brenna."

"Really? How did I miss this?"

"You were in Radiology reading the film on that little girl's broken arm. I bet it has something to do with that protest."

"Yeah, I'm sure," Jared said, though he knew better.

"Anyway, I'm going to get this patient home and get out of here. I have a feeling this is going to be a long night." Cecelia rubbed her stomach. "I'm either starting contractions, or I have the worst case of indigestion ever."

"Four kids and you're still not sure which?"

She smirked. "I'll blame the curry I ate for lunch until my water breaks. Good night, Dr. Monroe."

"'Night, Cecelia, and good luck."

"I'll need it."

Jared made sure he was alone before logging into the computer. He searched for Sydney Dowling by name, recalling her records, including her operative and lab reports, almost immediately.

He read the background information, gleaning from the brief history that Sydney's life before her operation was on the verge of falling apart. Social history mentioned a trial separation from her husband.

The procedure was a routine hysterectomy, but there was no mention of cancer, margins, or intraoperative biopsies to verify whether or not the disease had spread. Jared searched for pathology, filtering the labs by date, and rather than finding the usual gross and histology reports—documents that identified the type and extent of the cancer—he found tissue typing and antibody screens.

What the hell?

He checked the files, figuring maybe there had been a mistake, that the pathology reports were mislabeled, but they weren't. Nothing in Sydney's records indicated that she had cancer. Suddenly, he knew what Ana was onto.

There was only one way to be sure.

Physicians at County were assigned user IDs, and those IDs were associated with everything from transcription to lab results. The system was designed to streamline the administrative end, and Jared spent more than his share of time signing off on labs for his own patients.

Everything needed to be verified, meaning Dorian couldn't have acted alone. Someone higher up had turned a blind eye, at the very least.

The user ID was the first four letters of the physician's last name and the number "1." He typed "CARM1" into the orders section and searched for every test Dorian had ordered in the past five months.

There were dozens of attempts at matching donors to recipients; it was a fact that wouldn't normally raise suspicion, except that Sydney's name was on the list.

He printed off several reports linked to her account and tried to access the transplant files for the most-recent patients.

The records were locked.

He retyped his password and hit "Enter."

Still, nothing.

As far as he knew, his was unrestricted access. The most private portions of patient records, psychiatric evaluations and reports pertaining to HIV status, were critical when assessing ER patients. He would have thought transplant status was as well.

Someone was covering something up.

The question was who, and why.

CHAPTER 42

The reflection of the gas fireplaces' flames danced along the loft bedroom ceiling. An empty bottle of wine sat on the nightstand, along with two glasses.

Dorian propped himself up with his elbow, satisfied after not one, but two back-to-back lovemaking sessions. The first was purely animal, leaving Colby with a blouse full of popped buttons, and him with a back full of scratches. The second was softer, gentle and confirming, and afterward, they fell asleep in each other's arms. Dorian planned on sleeping until morning. Maybe going out to breakfast, or taking something in if Colby insisted on hiding, but when he saw that the alarm clock read 1:00 a.m., he knew she had other ideas.

"Something I can help you find?"

Colby slammed the dresser drawer and pulled a zippered sweatshirt over her blue lace bra. "I can't stay," she said, stepping into her jeans and checking her cell phone.

"What do you mean you can't stay? It's one in the morning." Dorian peeled back the comforter and patted the vacant spot next to him. "Come back to bed."

"I can't." Colby sat on the edge of the bed and put on her socks. "We have to go."

"Says who?" Dorian tried to pull her in, and she pushed him away.

"I'm not kidding. Jared left a message at the house. He says he's coming home."

"And?"

Colby picked Dorian's clothes up off the floor and all but threw them at him. "And I need to get home before he does."

"I thought you said he filed for divorce, and that it was over with him? Why does it matter if you're home or not?"

"Because I signed a goddamned prenup, that's why. The papers cite infidelity as his reason for divorcing me. I'll have nothing. I might be able to convince him the dinner was a one-time thing, throw myself at his mercy, but this . . ."

Dorian pulled up his plaid boxers. "Take it easy." He got out of bed and went to hold her. "Are you worried about money?" He laughed. "That's not a problem."

"Not yet it's not." She handed him his pants. "Put these on. We have to go."

"All right, all right. But so what if he knows about us? You know I'll take care of you."

"Maybe I'm tired of being taken care of." Colby hurried downstairs and flipped the switch, extinguishing the fireplaces and plunging Dorian into complete darkness.

"Hey, a little light up here, please." The bulbs in the gunmetal chandelier lit, bathing the loft in soft white light. "Thanks a lot." Dorian finished getting dressed and went down to meet her.

"I'm driving." Colby stood at the door, holding her keys tight.

"Are you sure that's a good idea?"

"I'm fine." Her hands shook, and her lower lip quivered.

Dorian folded her into his arms. "Come here a minute, would you?"

She protested at first, and then gave in, starting to cry. Her chest heaved against him, and she sniffled.

"It's going to be all right," he said. "We'll get back there, and you can tell Jared you were out at a bar, or something. No one knows we're here."

"What if *he* knows? What if he found out somehow?"

"It's impossible, Colby. You said yourself that he's working. It's going to be fine."

"I'll drop you at the impound lot on my way home," she said, pulling away from him. His Range Rover, which had been towed from County, had to be accounted for.

Dorian kissed her. "I don't want you to worry longer than you have to. Drop me by my place. I'll get a ride to the lot tomorrow. It's probably closed, anyway."

CHAPTER 43

"Jared. What are you doing here?" A cold breeze pierced Ana's T-shirt as she stood in the open doorway.

"I just got off work and saw your TV on. I thought I'd take a chance. Did I wake you?"

"No, God no. Come in." Sleep hadn't come easy, or without pills since Sydney's death.

Ana hung his coat and turned on the kitchen light. "Can I get you a cup of coffee, or a glass of wine?" She had never seen him in street clothes, but she very much liked the look of him in jeans and a sweater.

"A glass of wine sounds good, if you'll join me."

Ana set two stemless wineglasses on the counter, uncorked a bottle of Merlot, and poured it through the aerator. "Not that I'm not happy to see you, but what brings you by?"

Jared slid a manila folder across the breakfast counter. "Your sister didn't have cancer, did she?"

"I guess that's the question." Ana sat on the couch, and Jared sat next to her.

"She never told you about any of this?"

Ana shook her head. "She probably didn't tell me for the same reason I haven't told Mike—she wanted proof. Sydney was more like a mother to me than a sister. She kept her problems to herself, no matter how hard I tried to get her to talk. I'm guessing you have all the confirmation we need."

Jared nodded. "There's no pathology report from your sister's surgery because it wasn't done. Her hysterectomy was the same day as Dorian's first transplant, a woman named Stephanie Martin, who is currently in the ICU. There's no way that's a coincidence."

"He lied to Sydney, then?"

"Probably. Dorian does that."

"Why her?"

"Sydney was a match. I ran through Dorian's orders." Jared pointed to the file. "He tested over a dozen patients, running typing and antibody screens, looking for a compatible donor for Stephanie Martin."

"Who else would have known about the testing?"

"The pathologist, Marco Prusak, would've run the tests. I'm not sure that, out of context, anything would have looked suspicious, but it puts a new spin on his protest."

"Do you think he was in on it?"

Jared shook his head. "No way. He hates Dorian, though I have no idea why. Kind of gives him and me a common enemy, you know?"

Ana did know, but she hadn't said anything in order to spare Jared the humiliation. "I heard about what happened at the hospital benefit. I'm really sorry you had to go through that."

"No apologies necessary, and it's not the first time she's embarrassed me."

"I'm still sorry."

"I'm not," Jared said. "Not anymore." He set his hand on hers, testing the waters. Ana's heart raced, but she didn't pull away. "If it wasn't for that, I wouldn't be able to do this." He kissed her, and she wrapped her arms around his neck, kissing him back and tasting the wine on his lips.

Nothing ever felt more right, or wrong.

He ran his hand along her jaw, and she felt the ring, a reminder she shouldn't have needed.

"Wait." Ana backed away, her eyelids barely open, the thoughts of Misty destroying Sydney's marriage intruding on her and Jared's moment. "I don't want it to be like this."

Jared kissed her again, half-dazed. "Like what?"

"An obligation, or a fling. I'm not a home wrecker, and I don't want you to think that your gathering information about my sister is why I'm doing this."

"I can feel that it's not."

"Then I don't want anyone else to think it, either. I have to finish this thing with my sister, and you need to be divorced." A bit of distance between them and she was thinking more clearly. "Sydney figured this all out. She knew she didn't have cancer, and it got her killed."

"You think Dorian killed her?"

Ana shrugged. "What else fits?"

"Dorian's a lot of things. He's immoral, unethical, and greedy, but that doesn't make him a murderer. I'm not saying he's innocent. I'm just saying it doesn't seem like something he'd do, and I don't think he could've pulled this all off alone."

"Then I guess we have to figure out who else has something to lose."

CHAPTER 44

By the time Colby arrived home, she was sure she was sunk. Jared's message said he'd be late, but no later than one o'clock. Colby checked the time, drew a deep breath, and opened the garage door, relieved to find his parking space empty.

All of the explanations she'd worked up in her mind, the excuses about where she'd been and whose sweatshirt she was wearing, vanished with a sigh. She went inside the house and flicked the light switch, finding the bulb dead.

A sliver of moonlight crept from between the living room drapes, barely enough to illuminate a path three steps in front of her.

The hardwood floors radiated cold through her socks as she walked with her arms outstretched, her fingertips brushing along the walls.

"Hello?"

Her eyes slowly adjusted to the dim lighting and she squinted, staring at the spectral, gray outline in the distance.

"Jared? Is that you?"

A sharp pain tore through the sole of her foot. A shard of glass from the shattered light fixture embedded itself in her instep. She doubled over, limping for the next few steps until she could pull it out.

"Jared, this isn't funny. I'm hurt."

The entranceway lamp turned on, and a dark figure stood next to it, cloaked in head-to-toe black from ski mask to soaking-wet boots. The shadow wasn't Jared; it was someone else.

"Who are you? How did you get in here?" Her voice trembled.

The intruder wasn't much taller than Colby, and the person's body, though masked by heavy clothing, appeared slight. Colby looked around the room for anything she could use as a weapon and came up empty. Her mind shouted a thousand escape routes, the most direct being a straight line to the front door. She ran, but her assailant was faster. A gloved hand snagged a handful of her hair and yanked her backward, off her feet.

"Help!" Colby scrambled to get away, pulling until her hair felt as though it might come out at the roots. "Help, Jared!" She tried to crawl, digging her fingertips into the area rug. "Help me, please."

The assailant turned Colby over and climbed on top of her. New fears entered her racing mind, terrifying thoughts of being raped, or worse. She drove her knee into the person's groin and the attacker let out a loud, but absolutely feminine, "Oof!"

Her assailant was a woman.

The fact did nothing to help Colby's situation, but it gave her the glimmer of hope that she had a fighting chance—a level playing field. She balled up a fist and landed two solid punches to the right side of the woman's head.

"You shouldn't have done that." The woman produced a syringe from her pocket, and pulled the cap off with her teeth.

"Get off me," Colby shouted, and dealt another blow to the woman's face.

The syringe skidded across the hardwood, and the woman howled, holding her hand to her eye.

"You bitch!" The woman returned the jab, landing a solid, lip-splitting punch to Colby's mouth.

A warm, metallic film coated her tongue, and a second punch came, harder than the first. Colby's nose filled with blood, the smell of which made her sick to her stomach. She kicked her legs, desperate to get to her feet, and had started to gain ground when the woman pulled the wrought-iron lamp down on her head.

Colby howled, disoriented and in crippling pain. Her vision blurred, and she lay motionless, stunned by the impact and fighting unconsciousness.

The attacker clamped down on Colby's throat and pinned her to the ground. Colby pried at the woman's hands, but was unable to loosen her unbreakable hold. The blood in her nose made it hard to breathe. Her eye swelled, and her stomach churned. There was no recovering any kind of advantage.

This is it.

The woman reached for the wayward syringe and stabbed the needle into Colby's thigh, sending her drifting toward death.

CHAPTER 45

Emily lifted the hem of her nightgown, unable to get used to the look of the stitches, or how they felt tugging her burning skin. The redness had spread overnight, and the nurse who was supposed to have been arranged for still hadn't shown up.

Derrick had already left three messages for Dr. Carmichael, but so far, no one had called back.

Emily covered up and reached for the water and the bottle of painkillers on the nightstand. She swallowed two pills, and the water swishing in her empty stomach made the already terrible nausea worse.

"Dammit."

Something crashed in the kitchen.

"You okay?" Emily called out, a drugged slowness to her speech.

Derrick appeared in the bedroom doorway, dabbing at the faint brown splatter on his button-down dress shirt with a kitchen towel. "Yeah, I'm fine."

"What broke?"

"Coffee cup"—he looked at his watch—"and I'm late." He tugged at the knot in his tie and pulled it loose. "I'm going to have to change."

"Late for what? Where are you going?" For as much as Derrick loved her, and she knew he did, he was a slave to his work.

"I have to go to a client meeting, Em. My mom's coming to sit with you, and I'll be back in an hour, two tops. We have to keep money coming in for this baby."

As if money were ever a problem.

"Has the nurse called yet?"

"Not yet. I'll leave another message before I go." Derrick shook the prescription bottle of painkillers. "Is this supposed to be almost empty already?"

"It says four to six hours, as needed." Emily could see him doing the math. "I take them when I need to."

"Well, don't overdo it." He bent down and kissed her. "Mom will be here soon. Need anything?"

"No, I'm set." Emily settled in, shifting until she was comfortable and the tension was off her incision. The pills made it impossible to stay awake. She pulled the blankets up to her chin and drifted off to sleep.

CHAPTER 46

Marco's address had been easy enough to find. A quick Internet search directed Jared to Windsor Towers. He couldn't imagine why a pathologist making more than two hundred grand a year would live in such a low-rent complex on the outskirts of town.

The driveway had been only half plowed, and Jared parked in a void where a car had recently left. He reached for a piece of gum in his center console and chewed until he could no longer taste his own breath.

Despite the message he'd left telling Colby he'd be home late, he spent the night on Ana's couch, falling asleep after half a bottle of wine and intimate conversation that went on well into the morning. He had been infatuated with her up until that point, drawn to her sexually as much as anything else. Knowing her as he did now, how much pain and suffering she'd endured, he was convinced she deserved nothing less than true love, and he wanted to give it to her.

One night and he wanted to give her everything.

He was about to pull the key from the ignition when a bearded man blocked his door with a rusty, overflowing shopping cart.

Jared had no choice but to roll down the window. A distinct urine smell filled his car.

"Spare some change, sir?"

Even if it wasn't freezing out, he'd have been compelled to help the man. He reached into his back pocket and pulled a twenty from his wallet.

"Get yourself something hot to eat."

The man couldn't thank him enough. "Bless you, bless you, sir."

When the door was clear, Jared stepped out and locked his car twice, though he knew that a locked door didn't mean his car would be there when he got back.

He followed the signs to apartment 24, which couldn't have been farther from his parking spot, and knocked.

"Marco, it's Jared Monroe. Are you there?" Screams erupted in the apartment across the hall, and Jared knocked harder. "Marco? I need to speak with you. Please, open up." He wiggled the door-knob and found it unlocked.

A smell, like dirty dishes and mold, made him cough, and a terrible feeling took hold of him.

The sparsely furnished apartment had been tossed. Jehovah's Witness tracts littered the floor, and the end tables had been over-turned. The kitchen had been ransacked, the dishes shattered, and the cabinets left open. Jared kicked aside the broken ceramic and picked up a worn birth announcement for a little girl named Jasmine Prusak.

In their brief conversations, Marco had never once mentioned having a daughter.

"Marco?" Jared prayed that whoever trashed the apartment was gone, and that maybe Marco hadn't been there when it hap-pened. He moved slowly toward the closed bedroom door and turned the knob. A familiar odor eclipsed the rotten food smells coming from the kitchen. He cupped his hand over his nose to filter it.

Even without taking the scene in fully, he knew the stench of a decomposing body. He pulled his shirt over his face and suppressed the urge to throw up.

Sunlight poured through a set of dusty blinds and settled on a lump in the center of the bed. Tufts of dark hair and an off-colored forehead stuck out from under the green wool blanket. The single nightstand had been knocked over. The contents of its three drawers littered the floor.

From Jared's few minutes in the apartment, it was clear that Marco hadn't been robbed. The most valuable item in the place was an old, tube television, and it had been left behind. Someone, if instinct served, had been after information.

An audible click broke the tense silence, and the heat kicked on, magnifying the odor. Jared lifted the blinds and coughed as dust clouded around him. He opened a window to let in fresh air and pressed his face to the screen until he was able to face the smell again.

There was no sense checking for a pulse; the putrid smell guaranteed there wasn't one. Morbid curiosity had him pull back the blanket to make sure, though he was near positive, that the body was, in fact, Marco's. And it was. His olive complexion had taken on a pale, ashen tone. He had been stripped naked, and blood pooled along his backside, his buttocks and heels, appearing like one massive bruise. Lividity, the pooling of blood after death, indicated he had died in that bed, some time ago.

Jared flipped through the papers scattered on the floor and looked inside the toppled nightstand. He felt around the deep holes where the drawers would have been, and along the top and bottom edges for something taped or fastened to the wood. He looked inside the closet, and around the bed, noting a slight arc in the mattress and the sheet peeled slightly back.

"Bingo."

He slid his hand between the box spring and mattress, and his fingertips found the stiff leather binding of the book that had been hidden there.

New World Translation of the Bible.

Inside, two pieces of folded paper corroborated his and Ana's suspicions that Sydney's uterus had been implanted in Stephanie Martin. He put the book back where he found it, pocketed the reports, and called the police.

CHAPTER 47

Mike watched as Kim exchanged her soiled lab coat for a clean one. Her turquoise dress hung perfectly on her lean frame, emphasizing the slight curves of her athletic shape. A Navajo-style pendant dipped low into the "V" above her cleavage, and he tried not to stare. There were twenty-year-olds who didn't look as good as she did, but he figured telling her that would sound crass.

"You ready for this?"

"As I'll ever be." Mike focused on the ashen corpse flayed on the autopsy table.

"The victim's name is Dr. Marco Prusak. He's the pathologist at County Memorial Hospital."

Mike knew as much since he had been called to the scene by another of County's physicians, Dr. Jared Monroe, who came to check on the victim when he failed to show up at work. "Cause of death?"

Kim pulled on a fresh pair of latex gloves and rolled the victim's arm. "Educated guess? Insulin overdose."

Mike examined the tiny pinprick in the crease of the man's elbow. "Was he a diabetic?"

Kim shook her head. "No, and there's no record of a recent hospitalization. Residual trace shows insulin at the injection site, a spill when the needle was pulled. Whoever did this got sloppy. The tape residue indicates that the insulin was given intravenously. The level of knowledge and skill to administer this kind of treatment requires medical training."

"Training, like the kind a doctor would have?" Dorian Carmichael had been arrested for disturbing the peace at County Memorial in Marco's lab.

There was no way it was a coincidence.

"It could be a doctor, but it wouldn't have to be. It could be a nurse, or a paramedic." Kim swung a light over Marco's face, tilted his head back, and opened his mouth. "But it's definitely homicide."

Mike peered inside Marco's mouth and recoiled at the sight of a severed stub where his tongue had once been.

Kim closed Marco's mouth. "Whoever did this, it seems maybe they hadn't planned to. There are hesitation marks in the cutting. Compared with the almost impossible to prove, but suspected insulin overdose, this is very unskilled."

"And somewhat unoriginal." The crude glossectomy implied someone didn't want Marco saying something he knew. Mike made a mental note to look for a dull or serrated knife. "Tell me about the insulin. How does it work? What would the person feel? How long would it take to kill someone?"

Kim peeled off her gloves, threw them in the trash, and after rinsing her hands, sat down on a metal stool with her legs crossed at the ankles. "If the person knew what they were doing, it could take as long as the killer wanted for the person to die." Mike sat down in a chair across from her and jotted down notes while she spoke. "The brain needs sugar to function. The more insulin that is released into the blood, the lower the level becomes. An IV would allow for slow infusion, building to a fatal dose, or could release a fast fatal dose, depending on the rate of the drip."

"So, it's feasible that the killer would use this IV method to conduct prolonged questioning of the victim?"

Kim nodded. "Feasible, sure, if they could keep the victim conscious and lucid. Insulin is normally given subcutaneously with a small needle. An IV takes time. Lowering the blood sugar would cause discomfort. The victim would have headaches, shakiness, heart palpitations, and confusion. A deliberately slow infusion could cause panic, and if the victim was lucid, that might be a way to extort information. The long-term effect is unconsciousness, leading to eventual death."

"And the tongue? Was he still alive?"

"No. The lack of bleeding is consistent with a postmortem injury."

Mike sighed. "Thank God for small favors. I'm sure I know the answer to this, but was there any trace? How did the attacker manage to keep him still through all of this?"

"Adhesive on his wrists and ankles is consistent with binding using duct tape, and there's a needle-stick injury on his thigh. It's possible he was injected with something else to control him. There are a few things that wouldn't register on lab tests."

"What kinds of *things*?"

"Succinylcholine, for example. It'd keep him still long enough to tie him up if someone could keep him from suffocating."

Suffocating.

The word struck a chord.

"Mike, I'm sorry."

"It's okay. Were there any prints?"

"Not so far"—Kim brushed her sideswept bangs behind her ear—"but I'll keep looking."

CHAPTER 48

Colby's eyes rolled open and she drew a ragged breath. Her stomach growled and her head ached, either from the crushing impact of the lamp or from whatever she was injected with.

A faint crack of light found its way between the paper covering the windows of what appeared to be an old storage shed or a garage where she was being held. Sweat poured from her, even as she shivered from the near-freezing temperature. Duct tape held her in place, her right arm so that her hand bent over the curve of the armrest, and her left facing up with something running through an IV line into her vein.

She squinted and tried to make out the label on the bag.

In . . .

The bag was turned so that she couldn't read it. She pulled against the tape, finding no give, and bent herself as far in half as she could manage. Her back and neck burned as she leaned farther into position.

She rocked in the rickety chair, testing its strength. If she could break the frame, there was a chance she could slip her arms over the railing and get free. The crosshatched nylon webbing, frayed from years of age, creaked and groaned against the metal frame, but the construction was ironclad. She pressed her legs downward, against the tape holding her ankles, until her stocking feet hit the cold cement floor. She rocked back and forth, managing to move the swaying chair in a very slow circle until the IV line tugged and she was facing the pole.

Insulin.

Her worst fear was confirmed.

The woman who abducted her intended to kill her.

Colby scanned the room for something to cut herself free and spotted a pair of pruning shears on the corner of a utility shelf covered in gardening tools. She jerked her body forward, hopping with the chair and gaining forward motion. The IV line went taut, setting fire-like pain to her arm and reminding her she was pushing the limits of the end of her leash.

A row of damp, moldy bags filled with rotting compost blocked her way as she reached with her mouth for the pruners. Her teeth narrowly missed the handle and she scooted forward, pressing her knees into one of the moist bags and tearing it open. The smell became exponentially worse, and she coughed when the taste of mold coated her dry tongue. She knelt in the wet dirt and leaves, the chair on her back like a turtle shell, and closed her teeth around the textured handle.

A metallic taste filled her mouth as flakes of rust fell from the blades. A single lever held them shut, and she positioned them under her armpit, careful to make sure they didn't spring open and slash her. Dirt caked her lips and turned to coarse mud as she used her tongue and teeth to bite at the metal tab, which, once unseated, would give her something to cut the tubing with. Her front teeth ached to the point that she feared they would crack. The stiff metal released, but no matter how she positioned the handles, the shears didn't open. The blades were rusted shut.

CHAPTER 49

Jared's tires skidded on the fresh snow as he turned into his driveway and headed toward his house. He opened the garage door and tensed at the sight of Colby's car. There was no avoiding answering for the divorce paperwork, though the anticipation of her reaction was probably worse than the argument itself. He opened the door between the garage and the house, exhausted from the hours of questioning that accompanied finding Marco's body, and sighed.

"Colby?"

The house was unusually quiet.

"Colby, are you here?"

The hallway light had been shattered, the hardwood covered in tiny glass shards that crunched under his shoes. The visceral feeling that something was wrong, the same feeling he had when walking into Marco's apartment, resurfaced.

"Colby, answer me."

The hallway table was tilted at an awkward angle, and the metal lamp was unplugged, on its side on the floor.

Jared bent down, careful not to disturb the scene, and took a closer look. Droplets of blood clung to the lamp shade, spattered the floor, and dotted the beige wall. He consoled himself with there not being enough blood for Colby to have bled out, but guilt intruded on the moment, the feeling that if he'd just come home, rather than straying with Ana, Colby wouldn't have been alone.

Sunlight settled on a glass vial on the floor under the table. He pulled his sleeve over his hand and rolled it to read the label: "Succinylcholine."

Suddenly, bleeding wasn't the only cause of death on the table.

Succinylcholine wasn't something one could get their hands on easily, and he wondered what connected Colby to Marco Prusak. Two medical professionals and a hard-to-obtain drug? There had to be something that tied the two together, and he was afraid it would look like he was that tie. Coincidence or not, the evidence was damning, but wanting a divorce didn't mean he wanted Colby dead.

He ran up the stairs and checked each room, all of them turning up empty.

Colby was gone, vanished without a trace, and for the second time that day, Jared placed a call to the police.

———

Margaret fluffed her red curls and used the key Derrick had given her to let herself in to his and Emily's house. She was an hour late due to a nail appointment, but she was sure Derrick's asking her to come was unnecessary. The last three times she'd called the house, Derrick said Emily was sleeping. He was worried she'd been taking too much pain medicine, but Margaret told him there was no harm in her taking what she needed since she wasn't yet pregnant.

"Hello," she called out. "Emily, I'm here."

She picked up the remote control and turned on the end of her soap opera, making sure the volume was loud enough that she could hear it in the kitchen.

The kitchen was a bit of a mess, the sink full of cups and bowls. Margaret emptied and reloaded the dishwasher before filling the kettle with water and setting it on the burner.

"Emily, would you like some hot tea?" Margaret opened the door to the first-floor master and found Emily asleep. She opened the room-darkening drapes, filling the stale room with winter sunlight. "Honey, wake up."

Emily's hair was drenched, and the washcloth lying on her forehead was scorching hot. Her skin had taken on a waxy texture and was pale, even for her. Margaret shook her clammy hand, attempting to bring her around.

"Emily, honey, wake up."

Margaret pried Emily's eyelids apart, and her eyes rolled back so that all Margaret saw were the whites.

Gripped with panic, she dialed 9-1-1.

CHAPTER 50

Ana sat on the edge of an EMS station bunk, placing her sixth call to Jared since that morning and going directly to voice mail. Last she knew, he was headed to Marco Prusak's apartment, and she was eager to hear what happened.

"Hey, it's me. Sorry to be a pest, but I'm wondering how things went. Thanks, again, for last night. Hope to talk to you soon."

Insecurity bubbled to the surface; she feared that Jared, after hearing about her parents' accident, Sydney's life and death, and her feelings upon finding her sister's body, had decided she had too much baggage.

Ethan leaned against the doorjamb. "What happened last night?"

Ana nearly dropped her phone. "Ethan. Shit, you scared me."

"What. Happened. Last. Night?"

"Nothing. What do you mean?" Denial seemed the easiest route.

"You just said, 'Thanks for last night.' Who were you talking to?"

Ana held her hand on her hip. "I don't answer to you, Ethan. It's none of your business." She knew it was a lie even as she said it. He'd been there for her too many times for it not to be.

"Oh, right, but it's *my business* when you have no one else to talk to? I'm here every time you call, every time you need someone, but when I want to be there, when I try to be with you, you push me away. What do I have to do to get your attention?"

"Nothing, all right? There's nothing you can do. I just . . ." Ana weighed her words carefully. "I don't want to be with you." It hurt her to say it after how great he'd been and the time they'd spent together right after Sydney's death, but continuing to lead him on spelled eventual disaster.

"Because of someone else?" Ethan spread out across the doorway.

"We're at work. Let me out of here. I'm not kidding." Ana pushed past him, and he grabbed her arm. She whipped her head around and pried his fingers off her biceps. "Don't *ever* touch me again."

"It's Jared Monroe, isn't it?" The fact that he had noticed something between them left her speechless. "The guy's married, Ana. What the hell's the matter with you?"

"Nothing's *the matter* with me." Dispatch conveniently intervened with another call. "We have to go," she said, and unhooked the carabiner holding her keys to her belt loop.

There was no easy way to juggle a personal and professional relationship once things went bad. She couldn't make Ethan understand that her platonic love for him wasn't the same as her feelings for Jared, and she didn't want to hurt him more than she already had.

There was nothing to say that could make things right between them, and so they drove to pick up their patient in silence.

———

The patient's name was Emily Warren, daughter-in-law of Mayor Bill Warren, and Dorian Carmichael's second transplant recipient, as per the report of the call. Dispatch insisted that her treatment be as discreet as possible.

"Are you sure you should be here?" Ethan said.

"Is there some kind of conflict of interest I'm not aware of? I'm fine." Ana parked the ambulance and helped Ethan unload the gurney, thankful she hadn't told him more about Sydney's misdiagnosis.

A redheaded woman waved from the doorway of the elegant home, shouting for them to hurry.

Ethan rolled his eyes, and Ana smiled.

"She's this way." The woman, named Margaret, if Ana deciphered her panicked yammering correctly, led them to the bedroom where Emily lay unconscious and feverish, but breathing.

Ana immediately checked for a pulse.

"I'm Ana and this is Ethan," she said, hoping a first-name basis would allay some of Margaret's hysteria. "Can you tell us what happened?" She peeled back the comforter, finding Emily soaked through with sweat.

"My son asked me to stay with her because he had a meeting." Margaret's hands and voice were shaking. "I came in and she was asleep. I tried to wake her, but she wouldn't wake up."

Ana peeled the hot washcloth from Emily's forehead and took her temperature. "One oh three point six," she called out.

Ethan wrote down the number.

"Emily, can you hear me?" Ana noted Emily's elevated heart rate. "Emily, can you wake up for me?"

The answer was a clear and definite, though silent, "No."

Ethan started the IV.

"She's going to be all right, isn't she? She's going to be fine?" Margaret buzzed around the room, a whirlwind of red curls and lipstick, as she packed an overnight bag. "We need to tell Derrick what's happening. He isn't answering his cell phone. He said he had a meeting, but I don't know where, and I can't get ahold of his father."

"Margaret, calm down, please," Ana said. "Is there anything you can tell me about how Emily was feeling before this?"

"Derrick told me she's been taking a lot of pain pills, too many pills, and sleeping almost all the time."

"So she's been lethargic?"

"Or drugged," Ethan said.

The thought had crossed Ana's mind, but it was inconsistent with the fever as the cause of her unconsciousness. "Compile a meds list, would you?"

Ethan jotted down the names of the drugs and their dosages. "This bottle's almost empty. It looks like she's been through about twenty Vicodin since yesterday."

"Is there anything else your son might've told you, maybe how long she's had a fever?"

"Derrick didn't mention a fever"—Margaret gestured at the small garbage can—"but Emily threw up when he brought her home."

Ana called the hospital for orders.

"Who are you calling?" Margaret asked.

"The ER," Ana said, listening to the phone ring.

"County Memorial," Margaret said. "Emily absolutely has to go to County."

Ana knew Ethan's annoyed expression was because of Jared, though it was Wilson who answered.

"Wilson, it's Ana." She detailed Emily's symptoms and listened as Wilson returned conservative orders. "Regular saline and one gram Ofirmev for the fever," she said to Ethan.

The smell Ana had attributed to the congealed milk on the nightstand intensified when they transferred Emily from the bed to the gurney. Her nightgown stuck to her abdomen, held in place by a putrid, infected-looking discharge. Ana gently peeled the cotton away from Emily's skin, heat from the wound radiating through her gloves, and inspected the surgical site.

"The drain is clogged," she said. "We have to move her, *now*."

They hurried Emily out of the house, into the back of the ambulance, and headed for County with flashing lights and sirens blaring.

CHAPTER 51

This is not how I die.

Colby told herself this over and over, even after finding the pruners rusted shut. Her head ached, the pain spreading across her scalp and down her neck making it hard to concentrate. She closed her eyes, careful not to leave them closed for too long, and collected her scattered thoughts.

First thing she needed to do was stop the insulin.

Backtracking proved ten times harder than the initial trip, but she kept at it, making small gains until she resumed her starting position.

The IV site ached and had started to bleed. She considered ripping the line out with her teeth, but the sheath was too deeply embedded and secured with tape.

The only option was to chew through the tubing, if she could get to it.

She examined the setup. Two bags, one large and one small, hung from a rusted nail on the side of a wooden shelf. Gravity fed the line. A pile of refuse—red gasoline cans, trash bags, and boxes—blocked her from reaching it.

She scooted as close as she could to the clutter and pushed off her toes, thrusting herself forward. The cut where the glass from the broken light at home had embedded in her foot made her yell out in pain.

The chair toppled, landing her in an awkward half-kneeling position. A metal bur on the nozzle of an old gas can tore through her pants, and she screamed when it sliced through her skin. The cut burned, and the pins and needles sensation in her legs became much worse. She rested unevenly on the pile of trash and was too low under the line to reach it. She drew her knees toward her chest, moving like an inchworm toward higher ground. The sharp edge of the metal can bit into her shin, and she felt the warmth of too much blood pouring down her leg. She didn't need to see the cut to know it was deep. The next movement had the bur embedded.

"Please, oh please."

She put all of her remaining strength into a final maneuver, a push forward that had her inverted, like a hammock. She shimmied until she caught the line between her teeth and bit down hard, refusing to let go.

The skin in her arm lifted as the sheath fought against the tape. The near-blinding pain paled in comparison with the wound in her leg that she was certain needed stitching. She clenched her teeth so that the tubing was seated between her molars and sawed them back and forth. The cold temperature of the room made the plastic rigid, and she didn't feel like she was doing more than pinching the line. She repositioned the tube between her canines. A puncture would weaken the line and make it easier to bite into two. Her jaw ached, but she kept at it. A leak of fluid bathed her dry tongue, and she nearly cried out with joy. She spat, careful not to swallow the liquid rolling down her chin, and gnawed until the final thread broke. The tubing hung straight down, spilling the bag's contents onto the floor. The tension let off her arm and alleviated one of her many pains. A temporary wave of relief washed over her, the sense of accomplishment fortifying her will to fight. Severing the line was the first step, but if she was going to survive, it couldn't be the last.

CHAPTER 52

Sergeant Mike Richardson greeted Jared at the front door of the police station with a tense smile and an outstretched hand that seemed more a formality than a genuine greeting.

"Twice in one day, I've got to ask . . ."

Jared shrugged, unsure of what to say that would account for his reporting a homicide and a missing person less than twenty-four hours apart without implicating himself in either. "It's not my day, I guess."

Mike led him to his cluttered office down the hall, which smelled of cologne and room-temperature lunch meat. A thirteen-inch tube television sat on a shelf in the corner, and the weatherman on the screen delivered his lunchtime forecast. Part of a ham and cheese sandwich rested on a piece of white deli paper, and there was a faint mustard smear on Mike's chin.

"Can I get you something? Coffee? Soda? Sandwich?"

It had been hours since Jared's last meal, but the stress of the day had gotten to him. "No thanks. I'm not hungry."

"I imagine you're not." Mike wiped his face with a napkin, slipped on a pair of outdated eyeglasses, and looked over the paperwork that Jared was sure was his statement about Marco. "I suppose we ought to start at the beginning, Dr. Monroe." He pushed the rest of his lunch aside.

"Jared, please." Dr. Monroe, in Jared's mind, was his father.

"All right, Jared. When was the last time you saw or spoke with Colby?"

"Last night, around midnight." Mike started to jot down information, but Jared stopped him. "Wait, no. She didn't answer last night. I left her a message around midnight, saying I'd be coming to the house, but late. It's been since Monday, I think." Working long shifts tended to blur the days together.

"Coming to the house? What do you mean by that?"

Jared didn't realize the awkward phrasing until after he had said it. "I recently filed for divorce. I've been staying either at a hotel or in the hospital's on-call room. My lawyer sent a process server to the house with the papers yesterday."

"I see. What time was that?"

"Before noon, I think."

"And after that?"

"I finished my shift, met up with a friend, and the next morning went to see Marco."

"But you never saw or spoke with Colby?"

"No."

"Not even when you went home?"

Jared hadn't said he went home, but he knew it was implied. Ana had told Jared all about Mike, and as the questions hit closer to his night with her, he felt like he was being interrogated by her father. "I didn't end up going home."

"I see. Another night at the hotel?"

"Not exactly." Jared looked over Mike's shoulder at a breaking news report and a grainy rendering of his house on the television. Terri Tate stood on the edge of his front lawn, reporting the scene with a somber expression befitting grave news. "What's going on?"

Mike shook his head. "Word travels fast."

Jared strained to listen to the report, and Mike turned off the TV.

"Does your wife have any enemies, Dr. Monroe? Anyone who would want to hurt her?"

"Enemies? I don't know. I'd say after her stunt with Dorian Carmichael, *I* might be her biggest enemy."

The mention of Dorian's name piqued Mike's interest.

"Tell me about that."

Jared, confident that telling Mike about Colby's infidelity would stop the line of inquiry leading to Ana, rambled on about the night of the County Memorial event. "And that's why I filed for divorce."

"Do you have reason to believe that she's still seeing Dorian?"

Jared shrugged. "No reason not to."

"Any chance he'd hurt her?"

Jared was about to answer, when a ruckus erupted in the hall.

"Excuse me," Mike said. "What's going on?"

A midthirties officer with a thick, brown mustache and a name tag that read "Chipowski" stopped in his doorway. "You're going to want to see this."

"I'm in the middle of an interview, Chip."

"It can wait."

"It *can't* wait. I have a missing person to find."

"I know," Chip said, "and the woman who just staggered in said she knows something about it."

Jared craned his neck to see a pair of officers escort Noreen to the room across from them. She was filthy, her hair disheveled, and her right eye blackened. Her full bottom lip was split, and she was limping.

"Is that Noreen?" Jared said, barely able to believe it.

"You know her?" Mike said.

"I ought to. She's Dorian Carmichael's nurse."

CHAPTER 53

Emily opened her eyes and turned her head toward an unfamiliar, melodic female voice.

"Welcome back," the woman said. "I'm Dr. Cynthia Davis." Five foot six and dressed in a navy pencil skirt with a conservative but well-fitted striped top, she looked as much like an Ann Taylor model as she did a physician. Her sleek hair was tied neatly back, and a fringe of straight bangs emphasized her hazel eyes.

"Where am I?" Emily said.

Derrick leaned over the bedside railing, tears spilling from his swollen, green eyes. "You're at County Memorial," he said, and looked at Dr. Davis, who was noting Emily's vitals. "Is she all right?"

"Her temperature and heart rate are back to normal, and the antibiotics appear to be working. She's out of immediate danger, but there are no guarantees about the transplant. I'm sorry." Dr. Davis continued her examination. "Emily, an infection in your surgical wound has spread to your bloodstream. Can you tell me how you've been feeling since you were discharged?"

Emily looked at Derrick and then away. "Not great. Nausea, vomiting, redness around the incision, and my stomach hurt, but I thought it was the medication making me sick."

"Can you describe the pain for me?"

"It was a dull, kind of tugging pain."

"She didn't tell me any of this," Derrick said. "Emily, why didn't you say something?"

"I didn't want you to worry."

Derrick sighed. "I'd say that plan backfired."

Dr. Davis referred to the meds list Emily was brought in with. "You were taking all of your medications as prescribed?"

"Yes, she was," Derrick chimed in. "I gave them to her myself."

Emily shook her head. "I didn't take them all. I told you, a couple of them were making me sick, and I didn't want to throw up. We were supposed to be getting a nurse—"

Derrick cut her off. "I called a dozen times. No one called back, and no nurse ever showed up."

Dr. Davis lowered the bedside railing and folded back the sheet. "I'm going to take a look at your wound, Emily, if that's all right." Emily nodded, and Dr. Davis removed the dressing. "The drain was clogged, but we were able to get it working again." She pressed the upper-right quadrant of Emily's stomach, expressing a syrupy fluid from the drain. "I'm sorry. This might be a bit uncomfortable."

Emily looked away, unable to watch.

Derrick's cell phone rang, and he stepped away when Dr. Davis flashed him a look of warning.

Emily did her best to listen in.

"Yes, Dad. She's awake." Pause. "I don't know. I've left a dozen messages; he's not calling back." Pause. "Yes, Dad. I realize the kind of money you laid out." Pause. "Yes, Dr. Davis is taking care of her. I have to go, Dad. Love to Mom."

Emily could hear Bill, her father-in-law, speaking even as Derrick hung up the phone.

"I'm sorry about that."

"Everything okay?" Emily said.

Dr. Davis fixed Emily's gown and covered her with the blanket.

"Everything's fine, hon. You know how Dad can be."

She did, well enough to know that her health and wellness were more important now that the Warrens were invested in her surgery's outcome.

"Dr. Davis, not that I don't appreciate what you've done for us, but I wonder if you might explain why you're filling in for Dr. Carmichael, or if you're aware of his whereabouts. I've been unable to reach him since Emily's discharge, and I'm worried that he should be here, knowing her case as he does."

Emily knew it was his father talking.

"I assure you that I've been working in this research field for nearly ten years and that I am well qualified to handle Emily's case. I think you'll find me equally as skilled and cautious as my colleague. If you'd prefer to speak to the administration about replacing me on this case, it's your choice, but you'll be doing Emily a disservice. I understand your concern is for Emily's well-being, as is mine. With regard to Dr. Carmichael's whereabouts, I'm as much in the dark as you are."

CHAPTER 54

Mike stood across the interrogation room from Noreen and did his best not to intimidate her further. She avoided eye contact and chewed her fingernails between crying jags. Mike quietly instructed everyone, except for Coop, who had a way of putting people at ease, and Maria, the on-staff victim's advocate, to leave the room.

Noreen's hands shook, and when Mike pulled out the chair next to him for Coop to have a seat, she nearly jumped out of her skin. She kept her cheek turned, but Mike could see the bruises emerging from beneath her makeup. Her nails had been chewed back past the skin and the cuticle of her right thumb was bleeding.

"Are you sure you wouldn't prefer to go to the hospital?"

"No." Noreen shook her head. "I have to do this now, or I might never."

"Please, take your time."

Noreen lowered her head, and an expression of pained sadness washed over her face. Her shoulders rounded forward, and her tear-filled eyes glistened under the fluorescent light. "I was attacked last night, raped." The second word, she said more quietly.

"I had gone to talk to the doctor I work for about something we had done."

Mike, who knew from Jared that Noreen worked for Dorian Carmichael, tilted his head. "Something you had done?"

"Something Dorian made me do. He ordered all of the tests, and he did the surgeries. All I did was stay quiet about it."

"Who are we talking about?" Coop said, less versed in the case than Mike was.

"Dorian Carmichael."

Mike turned his attention back to Noreen. "What did you keep quiet about?"

"Four months ago, Dorian performed a uterine transplant on a patient named Stephanie Martin. I'm sure you've seen it on the news." Everyone in the room nodded. It had been a headline for weeks. "At the time, there was a shortage of donors, and Dorian came up with the idea that we could test some of our patients, under the guise of other illnesses, to find a match."

"Other illnesses?" Mike said. "As in, fake diagnoses?"

"There were so many people coming in for the surgery, Dorian said no one would catch on to the extra tests being ordered. I hoped we'd get a cadaver donor before any of this happened."

"But you didn't?"

"No. And the money Dorian was being offered to do the procedure was too much for him to refuse. He convinced a patient of his, Sydney Dowling, that she needed a hysterectomy for cancer because she was a match to Stephanie Martin."

Mike held up his hand for Coop, who was clearly beside himself, to be quiet. "But she didn't have cancer, did she?" He struggled to suppress his extreme emotions.

Noreen shook her head. "And then Stephanie Martin got sick. The transplant failed, and Dorian had to reverse the procedure. Marco figured out what Dorian had done, and he had proof."

"Marco Prusak, the pathologist at County Memorial?" Noreen nodded. All of the cases, except for Colby Monroe's disappearance, were starting to come together. "And Marco went to the hospital board?"

"No. He put a copy of the reports matching Sydney to Stephanie through the office mail slot. Dorian thought it was me. He came to my house, and he lost it. He was screaming and shaking. He said he was going to *take care of it.*" She paused for a minute, and Maria handed her a tissue. "Thank you." She was shaking again. "I didn't think he would kill him. I tried to get Dorian to turn himself in and"—she raised her hand to her blackened eye—"I could see how angry he was. I should've never let him in. I begged him to stop, but he was crazy." Fresh tears rolled down her cheeks.

"Don't blame yourself. This isn't your fault." Maria held her hand out, and Noreen took it. "The hospital will do a rape kit. They'll take photos and collect evidence. I hate to ask, but did he wear a condom?"

"It all happened so fast."

Mike had never been comfortable with sex crimes, and discussing the particulars made him less so. "Maria will go with you to the hospital and will stay there for as long as you need her to. As for Marco, you're implicating Dorian in a possible homicide. Do you have any proof that he was involved with the murder?"

Noreen wiped the tip of her thin nose with the tissue. "Isn't what I told you enough?"

Maria looked at Mike out of the corner of her eyes, her lips pursed, and her expression annoyed that he was further upsetting a victim.

"I'm afraid not, no."

"Then what if I told you I know something else."

Mike waited through a long pause before saying, "What else?"

"I saw a news report before coming here that said Colby Monroe was missing. Dorian *dated* Colby, until recently. I overheard them fighting over the phone, at the office, the night before last. He's obsessed with her, Sergeant Richardson, lovesick, and when he was on top of me, he called me 'Colby,' said he was going to 'miss me.' What do you think he meant by that?"

CHAPTER 55

Ana sat on the couch across from Jared, not even bothering to ask why he hadn't returned her phone calls, because she could see something was wrong.

"How did things go with Marco?"

Jared ran his hands down his stubbled face, the shadow of a dark beard coming in along his firm jawline.

"Marco's dead," he said matter-of-factly. "And you were right about Sydney and Stephanie Martin." He handed her two pieces of paper, lab reports confirming their suspicion. "Whoever killed Marco tossed his apartment, my guess, looking for those. There wasn't much more than information worth taking."

"Is that where you've been all this time? Did you call the police?"

Jared tucked a pillow under his arm, an easy normalcy replacing the awkward tension between them. "I'd have thought you would have heard by now."

"Heard what?"

"I've been with Mike all day."

"Mike who?"

"Mike Richardson."

Ana huffed out a breath, wondering why Mike hadn't called her. "Did you tell him about the reports, about Sydney?"

"No," Jared said, "but I don't think I have to. On top of everything else, Colby is missing. I went to the house to get some things, and she was gone."

"Maybe the divorce papers were enough to make her just leave? This is a good thing, right?"

"Wrong. There were signs of a struggle—blood and a vial of succinylcholine."

Ana pulled a face. "Succinylcholine? Who could get their hands on something like that?"

"Other than doctors, paramedics, and pretty much anyone who works at any hospital and has an access code, I don't know."

"You don't think someone killed Colby, do you?"

"After what happened to Marco, I don't know what to think. Noreen, Dorian's nurse, showed up at the police station, roughed up and crying. She looked like she'd been attacked, and whatever she said to the police was enough for them to finally let me go."

"Do you think she turned Dorian in?"

"I'd say so."

"Do you think he killed Marco and Sydney?"

Jared shook his head. "I don't know what to think, but why the hell would he hurt Colby? Something doesn't make sense, and Mike acts like he's onto me, as if I know something I'm not saying, or worse."

"He didn't really think *you* had something to do with all of this, did he?"

"Even I would think someone reporting a homicide and a disappearance in one day was suspicious."

"Are you worried about Colby?" Ana couldn't help feeling like the whole thing was some kind of setup. "I mean, what if she wants it to look like something happened that didn't? Maybe she and Dorian are planning to run off together or something."

"She's not like that, Ana, and after almost two decades of marriage, of course I'm worried. Mike said he had a lead, and that he'd call me as soon as he knew anything. I get the impression he doesn't like me much."

"He'd like you a lot less if he knew you were spending time with me. Still, I don't know why he didn't call me. He told me he'd be in touch as soon as there was a break in Sydney's case."

"It's not like you can call him. How would you say you got all of this information without mentioning me?"

It was a path she wasn't ready to go down. "I have no idea."

Ana's phone rang, and she held up a finger for him to be quiet before answering it.

"Hello?"

"May I speak with Anneliese Ashmore, please?"

"This is Ana." She didn't immediately recognize the heavily accented, male voice on the line.

"This is Gino from Matrazzo's Florist calling. You asked our delivery driver to look into an arrangement of roses delivered to Parker and Sons Funeral Home, no?"

"Yes."

"I'm sorry it took me so long to get back to you. I had to go back through quite a few credit card receipts."

"Were you able to figure out who sent them?"

"The flowers were ordered by a gentleman named Dorian Carmichael."

Ana's mouth fell open. "Did you say Dorian Carmichael?"

Jared stared at her with interest.

"Yes, miss. That's the name on the receipt. I hope that helps."

"Yes, thank you so much." Ana hung up the phone and blew out a breath. "I think I found a way to break the ice with Mike."

CHAPTER 56

Dorian lived in a modern colonial about a mile off Pine Grove Drive where the former woodlands had been developed into an affluent haven for the upper class.

Three squad cars rolled down the freshly plowed driveway.

Coop and Mike parked, blocking both sides of an end-loading, two-car garage. Ronald sealed off the driveway.

Coop, who was in the best physical condition and had three inches of height advantage over Dorian, was assigned the role of arresting officer, partly because of his stature, but also because Mike knew, given his relationship to Sydney, that he was too close for his motives to go unquestioned.

The three formed a triangle as they approached the front door, Mike and Ronald with their service pistols drawn.

Coop readied his handcuffs before knocking. "Police, open up."

"Can I help you?" Dorian cowered, his fearful expression having the questioning undertone of someone unsure of what came next.

Coop puffed out his chest. "Dorian Carmichael?"

"Yes."

"You're under arrest for the rape of Noreen Pafford. You have the right to remain silent. Anything you say can and will be used against you in a court of law." Coop stepped inside and grabbed Dorian's right wrist. He closed the metal cuffs down with a series of clicks and turned Dorian away from him, raising his hands high enough behind his back to be uncomfortable, before securing the left.

"Wait, what?" Dorian's eyes went wide. "There's been a mistake."

"You have the right to an attorney. If you cannot afford an attorney, one will be appointed to you free of charge . . ."

Mike presented the search warrant for Dorian's review. "Is there anything you want to tell me about what you did, or what I might find in your home? Are there any weapons in the house?"

"No, of course not."

Mike waved dismissively. "Take him to the car, Coop. Ron, start upstairs."

"Please, wait." Dorian pulled against the cuffs, and Coop tightened them another click. "I didn't do anything."

Coop pushed Dorian toward the sneakers at the door. "Slip them on, or you can walk to the car in your socks."

"Let me just talk to Noreen. We can call her. This is a misunderstanding. She'll tell you."

"Shoes," Coop insisted.

Dorian stepped into the untied sneakers, and Coop ushered him outside.

Mike pulled on a pair of gloves and booties, and did a sweep of the first floor, checking for medical equipment, needles and vials, anything to tie him to Marco or Sydney, as well as searching for clues as to Colby's whereabouts.

"Any luck?" Ronald leaned over the second-floor railing, his cheeks flush and his hairline glistening with sweat.

"No, nothing. If he has Colby, he's not holding her here. You?"

"Oh yeah. Come take a look at this."

Mike took the stairs two at a time and followed Ron to the office at the end of the hall. An L-shaped desk wrapped around the far wall. One of its drawers hung open.

Ron turned the label on a clear glass vial and showed it to Mike. "Succinylcholine"—he opened the drawer above it—"and insulin. Does this guy have an MO, or what?"

Mike sighed, frustrated that he couldn't skip trial and lock Dorian away for good for what he did to Sydney. It was his emotions talking and he couldn't afford to be emotional. "Leave everything exactly as you found it. Julian will document and collect the evidence as soon as he gets here."

Ronald snapped several photos of the open drawer, the click of the camera app making it hard for Mike to hear the noise in the background.

"*Shh.* Stop that a minute, would you?"

"What's the matter?"

"Do you hear that?" Mike took a few steps closer.

"Hear what?"

"Listen. It sounds like buzzing, or vibrating."

"Like a cell phone?"

"I don't think so." Mike followed the sound to the adjoining bathroom and turned his ear toward the cabinet under the sink. "It sounds like it's coming from in there." He opened the door and jumped back when a swarm of blue-and-green blowflies with orangish eyes flew out at him. "Jesus."

"What is that smell?" Ronald coughed and swatted the fly circling his head.

"You have your camera app up still?"

"Yeah."

"Give me your phone." Mike took a couple of shots of the shoe box, its lid askew, before knocking it the rest of the way off.

Inside, was a bundle of tissue paper coated in yellow larvae. Beneath it was a decomposing tongue.

CHAPTER 57

Colby shivered. Freezing, but dripping with sweat, she was lying facedown in a pile of refuse. The wound in her leg throbbed. The IV sheath, disconnected but still embedded in her arm, ached. Blood backed up the severed bit of line and dripped from the gnawed tubing. She felt weak; the effects of the insulin as it continued to metabolize were worsening even though she'd cut off the supply. Her only hope was an open soda can next to the remains of a long-forgotten lunch in the corner.

She considered that getting to the can could expend all of her energy only for it to be empty, but it didn't matter. She had to try.

With one arm facing up and the other down, there was little chance of the two cooperating. The chair was tipped completely forward, and her pant leg was snagged on the rusty metal can embedded in her skin. She was prone, almost kneeling, and needed to get onto her side if she was going to crawl. With the IV tubing disconnected, she had a bit more leeway. She planted her left foot firmly on the ground and pushed off the heap with her right hand, bracing for the fall. Her foot acted as a pivot point, and rather than tip on its side, the chair spun and Colby landed face-first on the concrete. It happened fast, she was unable to break her fall. Her forehead hit the cement floor. Fireflies sparked in her vision. The dull, insulin-induced headache magnified to an unbearable migraine. She let out a pained shriek and started to cry. The chair clung to her back, and her body sagged awkwardly beneath it. The rusty can let go of her leg, but when she fell, a new pain took hold. A meaty crunch, like ripping tendons in her ankle, accompanied her crash.

She lifted her head and looked through her tears at the can just inches away.

You can do this.

Moving with the chair fastened to her back proved harder than expected. She pressed her right palm to the floor and drew her knees to her chest, collapsing the chair around herself. Her face burned as she tilted her head, using her chin as an anchor point to drag herself along. Blood ran from her forehead and rolled down her eye as she inched toward the can, praying there was still something in it to drink.

Each movement brought new pain. Her knees and wrists stiffened from the cold and awkward positioning. She was spent, and her jaw had started an involuntary clenching motion she feared was an onset of mild seizures.

The next step was unconsciousness, followed by death.

She refused to let that happen.

Unwilling to risk food-borne illness, Colby nudged aside the remains of a moldy sandwich and went straight for the soda. There was no way to drink from her position, so she tipped the can on its side instead of placing her mouth over the opening. Dark slush filled a divot in the floor, and she slurped fast to get what she could before the concrete drank the liquid. There was less than a third of a can left, not as much sugar as she needed, and it had a smoky aftertaste that, only after she'd forced it down did she realize came from a cigarette butt, the filter of which emerged from the opening.

She spat a piece of soggy paper onto the floor and closed her eyes, disgusted with how low she'd sunk to survive. Her stomach growled, and her intestines locked in a vise grip, the radiating pressure of which forced her bladder to empty. The urine warmed her for a second before becoming cold and magnifying the already bone-deep chill. She shuddered, another seizure hitting, worse than the last. The metal chair frame clacked against the cement, and her body jerked violently until she was spent, too tired to fight. Her eyelids closed, and as hard as she tried to, she couldn't reopen them.

CHAPTER 58

Dorian paced the interrogation room, staring at the two-way mirror and wondering who was behind it. His mind raced with scenarios about how his consensual sex with Noreen had turned into rape. He worried that Noreen had somehow found out about his and Colby's trip to his cabin, and that the phony rape charge was some grand payback for her unrequited obsession. He was even more concerned that having had sex with her provided the proof.

Sergeant Mike Richardson opened the door and pulled out a chair. "Please, have a seat. Your attorney still hasn't arrived. Can I get you anything?"

Dorian shook his head. "No, thank you." He folded his slightly shaking hands on the metal table. "I don't need a lawyer, you know. I'm innocent."

"Sure looks like it, too, when the first words out of your mouth are, 'I want a lawyer.'"

"It was reflex. I didn't rape Noreen. I have no idea where this is all coming from. I panicked."

"Then you waive your right to counsel? Otherwise, we can sit here as long as it takes. I have time."

"I just want this over with."

"Is that a 'yes,' then? You're waiving counsel?"

"Yes, for now. I can stop and request my lawyer later, right?" Mike nodded. "Then let's talk."

Mike clicked his pen. "Where were you Monday?"

Dorian counted back three days and tried to remember his whereabouts. Monday was the day Kristin had given him the envelope. "When Monday?"

"Take me through the day."

"I made rounds early, around six, and went to the office to see an eight a.m. patient. Noreen didn't show up for work and hadn't called in. I asked Kristin, my receptionist, to try to get ahold of her, and when she had no luck, I got worried. I had Kristin cancel my day, and I went to Noreen's apartment."

"You knew where she lived."

"Of course. We've driven together to dinners, seminars, that sort of thing."

"What happened next?"

"I went inside and we talked."

"You mean, you argued. One of the workers who had been shoveling that day describes you as upset and panicked."

Dorian recalled the work crew. "I wasn't either of those things. I was concerned."

"As her boss."

Dorian sighed. "As more than her boss, maybe."

"Maybe?"

"Noreen has been coming on to me for years. Maybe I flirted, and maybe I liked the attention, but I wasn't the one initiating things. I turned her down every time, except for that day."

"Are you saying you slept with her?" Dorian nodded. "Why was that day different?"

No answer to that question was going to make Dorian look innocent, and he debated stopping. "I was being set up."

Mike narrowed his eyes. "For?"

"An envelope showed up at my office that morning." Dorian lowered his gaze. "Two pathology reports linked my first transplant patient to their donor, a donor I lied to in order to illegally procure a uterus."

"Sydney Dowling."

"Yes." Dorian felt sick admitting it. "The only person who knew was Noreen, and I had sex with her in the hopes that she'd be quiet about it."

"And when she refused?"

"She *didn't* refuse. We had sex, I fell asleep, and I woke up to her screaming at me. She found the reports in my coat pocket and was furious that I would think she was the one who left them at the office. She said she never saw them before, and she threw me out of her apartment."

"Then what?" Mike leaned back in his chair.

"I believed her. She was too angry for me not to. I figured the only other person who could have this kind of information was Marco Prusak. I went to his lab and ended up here, in a holding cell. I was here until bail was posted."

"And you hadn't talked to Marco before that? Hadn't gone to his apartment?"

"I don't even know where he lives. Ask him yourself."

"I'm guessing you haven't seen the news in the past couple of days."

Dorian shrugged. "No, why?"

"Because Marco Prusak was murdered."

"Murdered?" Dorian moved his sweat-slicked hands to his lap. "When? What happened?"

"Time of death puts his murder prior to your arrest, which, among other things, poses a different set of questions."

"What other things? What are you talking about?" Dorian panicked, feeling caught in something much worse than the damning
rape charge.

"I'm not inclined to divulge specifics. Let's talk for a minute
about bail. I checked your file. Tell me about the woman who
posted it." Mike's tone was alarmingly similar to the one he used
to tell him Marco was dead. "Tell me about your relationship with
Colby Monroe."

A pit of fear worked at Dorian's insides. "Is Colby all right?
Where is she? Is she hurt?"

"I was hoping you could tell me."

Dorian's suspicions about Noreen, and what she was capable
of, escalated to another level, and he prayed that wherever Colby
was, she was all right. A tear rolled down his cheek and he said,
"I'll take that lawyer now."

CHAPTER 59

Jared's slow breath was warm on the back of Ana's neck, and his fingers were intertwined with hers. A flurry of knocks came at her door, and when they didn't wake him, she tried to slip away before the next round.

"Where are you going?" Jared lifted his head off the pillow and smoothed his dark hair.

"Someone's at the door," she whispered, pulling the blanket up over his shoulder. "I'll get rid of them."

"Are you sure?"

"Positive." Ana moved the sidelight curtain and gasped.

Mike's bloodshot eyes held a familiar sadness, and he looked like he hadn't yet slept that night. She opened the door, and he walked right past her.

"We need to talk," he said.

Jared sat up and pushed the blanket to the end of the couch, his sleepy eyes a dead giveaway that he'd been there all night. "I'd better go."

Ana scrunched her face in preparation for the inevitable verbal lashing she knew Mike would wait until Jared left to give her.

Jared collected his things, put on his jacket, and grabbed his keys off the coffee table. "I'll call you later." He exited through the door to the garage where Ana had insisted he park, given the likelihood of unwanted attention. The garage door went up, and he backed out.

He was thankful Mike had parked on the street, since it helped avoid the awkwardness of asking him to move his truck.

"I can explain."

"He's a married man, Ana. What are you thinking? Do you know what people say about women who do these kinds of things?" She did know because she'd said such things about Misty. "Answer me. What is this, some kind of *fling*? I know you've been through a lot lately, but you can't just throw yourself at anyone willing to give you attention, especially when they're married."

"It's not like that, Mike. For one, he filed for divorce. And two, nothing happened."

Mike scoffed. "It looked like nothing happened."

Ana planted her hands firmly on her hips. "I know you didn't come here just to disapprove of my choice in men. I said nothing happened, and it didn't. End of story. What do we need to talk about?"

"We have a suspect in custody. After his nurse turned him in, Dorian Carmichael confessed to performing unnecessary surgery on Sydney."

"Did he also confess to murder?"

"No, but we're holding him on other charges until we can collect evidence that ties him to Sydney's case."

"I want to talk to him. If he was willing to admit what he did to Sydney, whether it was because his nurse called him out on it first or not, maybe I can get him to tell us everything. I need to know *why* he killed her."

"Ana, that's not a good idea. Besides, it's impossible."

"You're the sergeant. Make it possible." She drew a deep breath. "There's something I never told you, Mike."

"*What* didn't you tell me?"

"That day you told me not to go to Sydney's, when forensics was there searching the house, I had already been there."

"And you didn't think I needed to know that?"

"I found a card in her desk drawer for a doctor she hadn't ever mentioned going to, a Dr. Alan Sanders. He told me Sydney most likely didn't have cancer. Jared helped me figure out what Dorian did."

"*You're* the secret he was protecting," Mike said.

"What do you mean?"

"It seemed more than coincidental that Jared ended up giving not one, but *two* statements, if the cases weren't related. County Memorial staff said Jared and Marco weren't what anyone would consider friends, at least not close enough that he'd check on him. It wasn't coincidence at all that he went to his apartment. He went there for you."

"I wanted to have proof of what Dorian did before telling you. Jared went to Marco to get it."

"And did he get it?"

Ana handed the reports to Mike. "Since Dorian confessed, I don't see why these matter, but here's the proof that Stephanie Martin's uterus came from Sydney." Mike looked over the papers. "And there's something else. Remember the roses without a card at Sydney's wake?"

"Yeah."

"I had the florist look into who sent them."

"And?"

"It was Dorian Carmichael."

CHAPTER 60

Julian turned down Oakland Street and glanced at Elsa, sitting in the passenger seat.

Her deadpan stare had him worried.

"Are you sure you want to do this?" Before Sydney's murder, Elsa hadn't seen anything worse than a traffic accident. Julian, a decade older and with a new daughter of his own, had become instinctively overprotective.

"There's no guaranteeing she's even there," Elsa said, talking about Colby Monroe.

Julian nodded, but after hearing the grim details of what had happened to Marco Prusak, he expected the worst. "And if she is?"

Elsa shrugged. "I can handle it."

Julian parked in front of Dorian Carmichael's office and surveyed the surrounding houses. The two on either side were for sale and unoccupied, making the probability of witnesses slim. He exited his patrol car, produced the warrant, and climbed the porch steps.

A single set of tire tracks, belonging to a hideous, yellow 1970 AMC Gremlin, was the only sign of anyone having gone in or out, and it blocked the narrow drive that led around back. A sign on the door marked the office as "Closed," though when Julian turned the knob, it was open.

An unattractive young woman wearing a turtleneck, an oversized sweater, and a floor-length skirt worked an industrial-sized shredder.

Julian had no doubt the Gremlin was hers.

"Can I help you?" she asked, feeding a large stack through the machine.

Julian produced the warrant. "We're here to search the premises. Is anyone else here?"

The girl shook her head. "Just me."

"And your name is?" Elsa pulled out a pen and paper.

"Kristin Newman."

Julian surveyed the cluttered reception desk, littered with empty manila folders, and the overfull bags of ribbon-thin paper. "May I ask what you're doing there?"

Law stipulated that medical records less than eight years old couldn't be destroyed; longer, if they belonged to children. The year stickers on the folders' tabs said these were current.

Kristin chewed the inside of her cheek. "I'm purging deceased patients' records to clear out file space."

"Did Dr. Carmichael tell you to do that?"

"No," she said. "Noreen did, when she called in this morning."

Julian and Elsa exchanged confused glances.

Elsa moved in for a closer look at what was being destroyed. "Are you familiar with a woman named Colby Monroe?"

"The nurse at County?"

"Former nurse, but yes. Have you ever met her?" Julian pushed open the door of an empty unisex bathroom.

"Not that I remember, but she used to call a lot."

"Has she called lately?"

"Not in months," Kristin said.

Julian did a sweep of the first-floor exam rooms and, finding nothing, waved for Elsa to join him.

"I'm sorry," Kristin said, "but what are you looking for?"

"Could you please show us to Dr. Carmichael's office?" Elsa said, ignoring the question.

Kristin let the conversation drop. "Follow me." She lifted the hem of her skirt and led Julian and Elsa to the largest of several offices on the second floor.

Julian thanked and dismissed her, waiting for her footfalls to disappear before saying anything else.

The office was neat; the spines of the charts on Dorian's desk were flush with one another.

"Look at this." Elsa held up a schedule from days earlier and read a handwritten note aloud. *"Meeting with Mitchell."*

"County's CEO is named Mitchell Altman," Julian said, opening the two closet doors on the far end of the room. There were banker's boxes and reams of reports printed on continuous-feed paper, but nothing recent. "Add him to the list of people to talk to."

Elsa went through the files and found an old message tucked between the pages of a medical journal. "There's a message here from Sydney dated a week before her murder."

Julian took it from her. It was marked *urgent*, but it said little else. "Anything from Colby?"

"Nothing. I don't think she's here," Elsa said.

Julian paced the length of the room, wondering what he was missing. The blinds covering the window, which overlooked the abandoned garage, were half-lifted. "Elsa, look." He pulled them up the rest of the way.

A shovel sat propped against the side of the building, and the windows had been papered over. Snow-filled depressions surrounded the garage, but the Gremlin was parked at least twenty-five feet away, and there were no visible prints leading to the car.

Someone other than Kristin had been in there recently.

"Come on, she has to be down there." Julian hurried down the stairs and slapped his palm against Kristin's desk. "Are there keys to the garage?"

Kristin was on the phone, rescheduling an appointment. "I'm sorry. Can you please hold? Thank you." Kristin held the handset away from her ear. "Keys to what?"

"The garage out back."

"Not that I know of. No one uses it. It's supposed to come down in the spring."

Elsa pulled her Beretta from its holster.

Julian had already drawn his.

"Stay behind me," Julian said, his adrenaline rushing as he hurried down the snowy driveway and tried to lift the wooden roll-up door. His arm jerked under the resistance of the locked handle. "Dammit. Locked." He holstered his gun, squatted, and tried to force the door up. It gave slightly, then crashed back down. "There's got to be a way in here." He peered through the narrow gap around the edge of the paper, but was unable to see anything through the filthy window.

Elsa ran around the side and turned the side-entrance door-knob. "Julian, over here. There's a bunch of garbage blocking the door, but it's unlocked."

Julian plowed into the door with his shoulder, moving the clutter with the harsh sound of metal on concrete. To the left of the door, two IV bags, one of saline and one of insulin, hung from a nail in the shelf; on the floor was a woman's lifeless body. "Call for backup," he shouted, "and get an ambulance here, *now*."

CHAPTER 61

Julian forced his weight into the door and cleared a path just large enough for Elsa to squeeze through. Even at a hundred and ten pounds, she had to take off her belt to fit.

She took careful steps, each meeting with the collapsing of something else as she scaled the pile.

"Is she breathing?" Julian said.

"I don't know." Panic crept into Elsa's voice.

"Open the other door. Hurry."

"It's stuck." Elsa fidgeted with the lock and pounded the door with her fist.

"Hit it with something. It's probably jammed."

Elsa picked up a rusty pair of pruning shears and beat the knob of the lock until it gave. She lifted the door, and Julian rushed in.

Colby Monroe lay on the floor next to a brown stain that appeared to have come from a tipped soda can.

Julian pulled on a pair of latex gloves and pressed two fingers to the side of Colby's neck, feeling for a pulse. "She's alive. Elsa, grab the blanket in the trunk." He snapped several quick pictures to preserve the scene.

Colby was soaked through with sweat, her shirt clinging to her like a second skin. A faintly sweet urine smell emanated from her, and there was a rip in her jeans where blood seeped from a nasty wound that certainly needed stitching. Her left sleeve had been rolled up, and the remains of an IV line, clogged with blood, jutted from the crease of her elbow. The edge of the tubing was frayed, no, *chewed*, through, and her pale skin had a dusky hue that mimicked the concrete.

She wasn't dead, but she was close.

Julian tried to rouse her, but she wouldn't be wakened. She didn't make a single sound, no matter what he did. He patted her hand, her face, and lifted her eyelids, all the while calling her name.

The sirens grew louder as the ambulance drew near, and Elsa had barely come back with the blanket when Jim and Ethan arrived.

Jim emerged from the driver's seat. His sandy blond hair stuck out around the edges of his knit cap, and he pulled it down over his ears as he called out his orders.

Ethan wheeled the gurney behind him.

"What do we have?" Jim asked Julian.

"Colby Monroe, missing more than twenty-four hours, abducted from her home, and this." Julian held out the empty bags of saline and insulin.

There was a spark of recognition in both medics when Julian said her name.

"She's Jared Monroe's wife," Ethan said to Jim. "Hand me the glucose meter." He placed the meter to her finger and drew a single drop of blood. "She's hypoglycemic. We need to get her sugar up."

"Colby, can you hear me?" Jim shone a penlight at her eyes.

Ethan noted her elevated heart rate. "And tachycardic."

Julian called in to the station to let Mike know that they'd found her.

Jim pushed the blanket aside and lifted Colby's left sleeve. He examined the line taped in place and sighed. "Someone knew what they were doing. We have to start a new IV in the other arm. Let's get her inside and warm her up."

"I want to go with her," Elsa said. "She shouldn't be alone."

"She isn't alone." Julian gestured at Jim and Ethan.

Elsa had a big heart, and Julian knew it would eventually burn her out.

"What if something happens, and there's only a small window to take her statement? Someone should be there to find out what happened."

Though the excuse served Elsa's intentions, it made sense.

Jim and Ethan had Colby in the back of the ambulance by the time Julian and Elsa reached their agreement.

Ethan had called in for orders and was prepping a new IV and a bag of glucose as instructed. Colby remained unresponsive as he rolled up her right sleeve and expertly started the new line.

"We have to go," Jim said.

Elsa climbed up and sat on the bench seat, out of Ethan's way. "Julian, I'll meet you at County."

Jim slammed the back doors, climbed into the driver's seat, and resumed the lights and sirens.

Julian watched the ambulance speed off toward County only four blocks away.

CHAPTER 62

Wilson leaned against the counter, snacking on a bag of popcorn, and looked down at Jared, who was sitting in a chair behind the desk. "Let me get this straight. You spent *two* nights with her and nothing happened? Man, you're out of practice."

"It's not like that with Ana. It's different."

Neither mentioned a word about Colby in an attempt at leaving morality off the table.

"So, what's next?" Wilson wiped his mouth on his lab coat sleeve, which sat an inch above his wrist.

"I guess we wait and see."

The overhead page announced an urgent call en route.

Jared grabbed his stethoscope off the desk and buttoned his lab coat on the way to the sliding glass doors.

Cecelia waddled after him, holding her swollen belly with both hands and shouting. "Dr. Monroe, please wait."

"Not now, Cecelia. We have an emergency."

"But—"

"Whatever it is, it's going to have to wait."

She moved faster than a nine months pregnant woman, no matter how practiced, had a right to.

"Dr. Monroe, I need to speak with you. It's urgent."

"You definitely shouldn't be running in your condition," Wilson said.

Cecelia, out of breath, paused and leaned with one hand against the wall for support. The shouting had drawn the attention of everyone in the department, including the patients. "Dr. Monroe, this is Dr. Walker's call. Let him handle this one."

Just the mention of Simon Walker's name had Jared's hackles up. "He's chief of medicine, not an ER physician, Cecelia."

"But I triaged him this call. He already knows the case."

The ambulance backed in.

Jim hurried to open the doors, and Jared saw Colby inside.

Jared ran toward her, pounding his hands against the glass when the automatic doors didn't open fast enough.

A young, redheaded police woman jumped out of the back of the ambulance, her forehead beaded with sweat.

"Jim, what's going on?" Jared said. "Why didn't anyone call me?"

"Insulin-induced hypoglycemia. She's unresponsive, tachycardic, and hypothermic. We have her on a glucose drip, but she hasn't come to."

"Colby, can you hear me?" Jared shook her hand. "Colby, it's Jared. Wake up."

A green wool blanket covered her up to her chin, and only her right arm stuck out of it. Jared placed her hand on her chest, grabbed the side rail, and wheeled her fast enough through the ER that Jim had to jog to keep up. "Put her in room one. Wilson, get me a warming blanket."

"Doc, you should let me take this." Wilson certainly had the skill set, but Jared refused to give up the lead role.

Simon Walker came rushing down the hall, the white tails of his open lab coat flapping behind him. "Jared, you are off this case."

"I don't have time for this, Simon."

"Jared, I mean it. Get away from her."

Jared narrowed his eyes. "Why, because she's my wife? I can't objectively take care of family? You slept with her, too." He kept a determined pace, working to unfasten the buckles on the gurney.

Wilson exchanged an electric heating blanket for the wool one.

Jared's first thought was that the zippered, men's sweatshirt Colby was wearing didn't belong to him. His second was that, at that moment, it didn't matter. "Increase the drip on that IV. I need a glucose reading, now."

"I'll have you suspended for this." Simon kept at Jared, and Wilson stepped between them, running interference.

"Honestly, Simon, I don't care if you have me *fired*." Jared pulled the privacy curtain and continued his assessment.

Colby's left sleeve was caught on a chewed IV line that hinted at a fight for her life.

She'd always been strong.

Wilson attached the EKG leads and vitals monitor, and went to work on the tape. "We've got to get this line out to clot the bleeding."

"I need a picture, please," Elsa said. "It's evidence."

Jared held up Colby's arm, and Elsa snapped several shots.

"My name's Elsa," she said.

"Jared Monroe." The introductions were brief and hurried.

Wilson hit "Print" on the EKG machine, handed Jared the tracing, and repeated the blood-glucose testing. "Glucose level is up, but she's still low. Heart rate is stabilizing. Temperature is normal."

Jared noted blood on Colby's jeans. "Get me a surgical tray and a suture kit." He pushed the blanket off her leg and cut away her jeans. The cut was deep and embedded with rust. "Grab me a tetanus shot, too."

Wilson set a cleaning basin and suturing supplies on a cart and pushed it next to Jared.

Jared pulled up a stool at the bedside and lowered the railing. He flushed the blood and debris from the wound with an irrigation syringe of sterile water and scrubbed at the edges. The cut was jagged, hard to align. Blood, water, and dirt soaked the disposable pad under Colby's leg in a tie-dye pattern.

Elsa shivered and went pale.

"Are you all right?" Jared asked.

"I'm fine," Elsa said.

Wilson opened a folding chair and pressed down on Elsa's shoulders for her to sit. "Just in case."

Jared anesthetized the wound despite Colby's unconsciousness and hooked the suturing needle carefully through her skin. If she were awake, she'd insist on a plastic surgeon's skill to minimize the scar. Jared, knowing how vain she was, did the next best job. No matter what had happened between them, he was determined to pull her through. The cut took six stitches, and when he was finished, he snipped the line and peeled off his bloody gloves, wondering how, exactly, all of this had happened. He turned to face Elsa and asked the question he almost didn't want the answer to.

"Where did you find her?"

"In the garage behind Dorian Carmichael's office."

CHAPTER 63

Mike led Ana into an empty lobby where a uniformed officer stood silently by the metal detector. Benches lined the perimeter of the otherwise bare-bones room, the only decorations being signs relating to dress code and conduct. It was outside of visiting hours, but Mike had arranged for Ana to have a private chat with Dorian.

Standing there, waiting to be let in, she felt like she was going to be sick.

"Are you sure you want to do this?" Mike said.

Ana nodded. "Have you told Dorian that Colby's been found yet?" Jared had filled in the gaps of what little Mike had told her, Colby's condition raising more questions than answers.

"No," Mike said, "and I prefer you didn't, either. His lawyer will let him in on the news soon enough. I don't want to give him time to make up another explanation."

"Empty your pockets, please." The officer, a thirty-something-year-old man with a brush cut and piercing green eyes, held out an empty plastic basket.

Ana turned in her keys and wallet, having brought only what she needed.

"Feet apart, arms out at your sides, please." The man swept her, twice, with the metal-detection wand, sent her wallet through the X-ray machine, and handed her back her things. "You're all set." He pushed open the door to the visitation room.

Ana took a seat on a hard plastic chair along a C-shaped, metal counter where more than a dozen chairs on either side of her spoke of group inmate visits. A lump formed in her throat as she pulled the chair forward and leaned into the cold counter with her elbows. The echo of metal on tile gave her chills.

The door connecting the visitation room to a large holding cell opened, and the officer led Dorian in.

"Fifteen minutes," he said.

Dorian sat in the seat across from her.

Ana had met Dorian only once, on the day of Sydney's surgery, when he came out to the waiting room to tell her and Mike that Sydney had made it through. She had thanked him, a gesture that now angered her, and she had thought him both charming and handsome.

This defeated man, sitting head down, in handcuffs and shackles, was neither of those things.

A long silence passed between them before Ana, in an acknowledgment of their limited time, spoke. "What am I supposed to say, here?" She didn't know where to start.

"You're the one who asked to see me." Dorian looked up from his clasped hands, his expression emotionless and hard, despite the faint shiner beneath his eye that said he'd been beaten.

"You're the one who agreed to meet." Ana mustered the strength needed to be direct. "Why did you lie to my sister?"

Dorian didn't bother playing stupid. "Greed, narcissism . . ." He unlaced his fingers and held his palms face up. "Desperation? I don't know anymore. Would it help if I said I would take it all back?"

"Sydney lost everything—her husband and her chance at having a family—all for you to, what, give it to somebody else for money?"

Dorian shrugged. "It wasn't all about money. She was a donor match, and my program needed to move forward. I didn't think things through. I didn't see the harm I was doing until it was too late. I thought she'd accept the diagnosis I gave her and move on."

"And when she figured out you lied to her, you killed her for it."

"No, I didn't," he said, his stern tone full of conviction. "I admitted lying to her. Why would I kill her, and then tell the truth?"

It was the question she'd come to get the answer to.

"Then why did you send flowers to the funeral home?"

"What flowers? What funeral home? I don't know what you're talking about."

"Matrazzo's has your credit card on file. You sent three dozen roses to Sydney's wake. The florist said it was absolutely you who ordered them."

"Or someone with access to my credit card."

"Are you saying someone *else* ordered the flowers to make it look like it was you?"

"I've had some time to think in here, Ana, between beatings. What I did was unconscionable. I deserve to lose my medical license, but someone is setting me up for much worse. I'm not a rapist, a murderer, or a kidnapper, though someone's trying damned hard to make it look like I am. Someone"—he lowered his gaze—"is hurting people I love."

"People, or just Colby Monroe?"

Dorian's demeanor changed altogether. "What do you know about Colby? They won't tell me anything. Is she all right?"

Ana, desperate for leads in Sydney's case, exploited Dorian's obviously genuine concern. "I'll tell you what I know if you'll tell me who you think is setting you up, and why."

Dorian gnawed his bottom lip, as if contemplating an answer.

"What could be worse than what you've already admitted to?"

"It's not that, but my lawyer would have my head."

Ana pushed back her chair and stood. "Then I guess we're done here."

"Wait. Just wait a minute, please."

Ana sat down.

"All right. Okay." A long pause followed. "I slept with Noreen. I didn't rape her. She's been, I don't know, *obsessed* with the idea of us as a couple. I shouldn't have done it, I know that, but I thought she was blackmailing me. She was the only person who knew the truth about what happened with Sydney, or, at least, I thought she was. Marco Prusak knew, too, though I still don't know how or why he was so intent on ruining me."

"So, you're saying Noreen is framing you for murder, rape, and kidnapping out of what, disappointment? That's some ego you have."

"Not disappointment. Jealousy. Nothing else makes sense. I didn't kill anyone, and yet everyone who knew about the transplant is dead. I didn't rape Noreen, and I admitted to having sex with her. DNA will prove that I was careless, nothing more. I don't know how she got the bruises, but she's the only person with motive. Maybe she did it to cover her own ass. Maybe she figured she was covering mine. And Colby, why would I hurt her? What makes sense about that? But it makes sense that Noreen would hurt her, especially after making me say I didn't love Colby. I do love her, and Noreen could see it. That hurt look on her face, I can't get it out of my head."

"And you thought having sex with her would fix this?"

"Two minutes," the guard called through the door.

"I was stupid, I admit it. I've made a lot of bad decisions and there's a lot to set right, but I don't belong in here. Please, tell me what's happened to Colby. Is she okay? She can tell you that I had nothing to do with her kidnapping. They haven't charged me with it, but it's obvious they intend to. Did they find her?"

"Yes, they found her, at *your* office, but she can't tell anyone anything, not in her condition. She's in a hypoglycemic coma. Someone hooked her up to an insulin drip and left her for dead."

Dorian covered his mouth with his hand, and Ana couldn't help staring at the cuffs. "Is she going to be all right?"

"I don't know. She's in the County ICU."

The jingling of keys announced the guard coming through the door. "Time's up."

Tears spilled from Dorian's eyes as the guard tugged him out of the chair.

"Wait a minute," Ana said. "One more question." The guard waited for her to finish. "Do you think Noreen's behind Sydney's murder?"

Dorian sniffled. "I'd bet my life on it."

CHAPTER 64

Kim hunched over a microscope, reexamining a specimen she'd looked at a half-dozen times. A clear plastic container, the size of a 35 mm film case, held a dozen or so yellow larvae. A silver tray displayed Marco Prusak's tongue.

"You know, you haven't been in my lab this much in years. You keep it up and I'm going to think you have other reasons for coming here." Kim winked at Mike over her shoulder.

"I'll try not to make it a habit." Mike worked at a smile. "Any usable evidence?"

"Based on the blowfly larvae, time of death is confirmed as seventy-two hours ago. The DNA and wound patterns are a match. This is Marco Prusak's tongue." Kim discarded her gloves and rinsed her hands at the sink. "Come on. Let's get a coffee."

The break room clock read 11:00 p.m., but it felt much later. Halfway into a double shift, Mike felt strained, as if he were running out of time.

Dorian Carmichael's attorney had already met with the judge and district attorney. Given his admission of having had consensual sex with Noreen, and the lack of physical evidence, including that his prints were nowhere to be found, not even on the items taken from his house, there was a remote possibility of his being released on bail. Rumor had it that Dorian was calling the whole thing a setup.

Mike needed something tying him directly to either Sydney's or Marco's murders, or to Colby's abduction if he was going to thwart Dorian's release.

Kim hung her lab coat on a hook behind the break room door and tugged at the hem of her emerald-green sweater, which hugged her athletic figure and brought out the green in her hazel eyes.

In all the years Mike had known her, he'd seen her in jeans only a handful of times. A pity, really.

"Casual Friday?"

Kim shot him a playful but annoyed look and brewed a fresh pot of coffee. "Day off."

He didn't realize that she'd come in just for him. "Kim, I'm sorry."

"Don't be. We'll just say you owe me one. Can we be candid here?" Mike nodded. "You look like hell."

"It's nothing a shave won't fix." Mike ran his hand over the former scruff on his chin that had, without his really noticing, grown into a full beard.

"I don't just mean the facial hair. This case is tearing you apart, Mike. I know the connection to Sydney, and I know you well enough to know you're not going to stop until you make this case, but you have to be objective. When's the last time you slept? I mean, *really* slept, not just an hour here or there."

Mike couldn't remember a time since Sydney's death. "It's been a while, I guess."

"Then you know I'm right. You need fresh eyes, and I don't mean just mine. Everyone who tells you something you don't want to hear gets replaced by someone else. You've got me sorting through evidence, for Pete's sake. I'm an ME, Mike, not a CSI."

"It fits, Kim. It all fits." The lack of conviction in Mike's tone had even him doubting himself.

"It fits *too well*." Kim poured two cups of coffee. "I've been over the file a dozen times, and there's nothing that says the evidence you found at his house wasn't planted. Not a single print, Mike. Not Dorian's or anyone else's on those medical supplies. Your suspect is a well-educated man, levelheaded by all accounts, and he admitted to wrongdoing. He also vehemently denies everything else. There are a dozen accounts in the interview files from other staff at County Memorial who said that Dorian and Colby Monroe were secretly some kind of item. Why would he hurt her? What is her role in any of this?" Mike had been so busy persecuting Dorian that he hadn't really thought about that.

Kim pursed her full lips and blew across her coffee before taking a sip. "You asked me if there was any new evidence, but I'd say it's the opposite. The tongue doesn't look like any trophy I've ever seen, and I've been on enough serial homicides to spot a souvenir when I see one. That isn't what this is. The crude cutting doesn't fit. Dorian Carmichael is a surgeon, with microvascular training, correct?" Mike nodded. "Do you honestly think that someone with his skill set would be able to throw out all of his training to hack out a tongue with a kitchen knife?" She shook her head. "My gut tells me something isn't right. Someone wants you to find all of this evidence. Get some rest, Mike, put everything you *want* to add up out of your mind, and look at what's missing."

Mike finished his coffee in silence. He needed the knife, or the pad that matched the paper used for Sydney's suicide note, and he needed Dorian's prints on one of them. "You're right." He sighed.

Kim set her hand on his. "You're one of the best detectives I've ever known. You'll figure this out. You just have to look at the bigger picture."

Mike let her hand linger a moment longer, and gently pulled away. "Thanks for coming in tonight, and for the coffee. You're a lifesaver, Kim." He just wasn't sure whose.

CHAPTER 65

Ana scuffed her boots on the coarse mat inside the County Memorial ER, hoping she had made the right decision in going there. Hours of tossing in bed, of thinking about what Dorian had said, and of finding nothing useful on Noreen, had made Jared her last hope.

She approached the young, bottle blonde sitting at Cecelia's desk and wondered if Cecelia had finally gone into labor. The girl's tanned skin had an unnatural orange hue, in-line with her fake fingernails and lashes.

Ana had never seen her before and assumed she was another in a long line of temps that County hired because they were too cheap to have extra regular staff.

"May I help you?" the girl asked.

"I'm looking for Dr. Monroe, please."

Jared peeked out from behind a privacy curtain in triage. "Ana?"

"Hey." She waved her hand and grimaced.

"What are you doing here?" Jared looked in both directions down the empty hall and excused himself from his patient.

"I'm sorry," she whispered. "I've been trying to call."

Jared took his phone out of his lab coat pocket. "*Ugh*. The battery's dead. Come here." He led her into a small copy room and closed the door behind them. "Is everything okay? What's wrong?"

His nervous behavior had her feeling like a dirty secret.

"What do you know about Noreen Pafford?"

"Dorian's nurse, Noreen?" Jared reached for her hand, but she pulled away.

"She's unlisted, and I need to know where she lives."

"I'm not sure." Jared drew his eyebrows together and moved to touch her.

Again, she avoided him. "You're not sure, or you don't know?"

"She mentioned something at a Christmas party a year or so back about moving into Pemberton Trace, but I have no idea which unit, or if she did actually move there. What's wrong?"

"With?" Ana noted her own icy tone. Too many unreturned phone calls, being shoved in a private room, and Colby's resurfacing had her conflicted.

"With you? With *us*?"

"There's no *us*, Jared. You're married."

"Divorcing, Ana. What did I do wrong?"

Mike's words rang in her head: *home wrecker*.

"You didn't do anything wrong. It's been a rough day. Mike's on my case, and I went to see Dorian."

"You *saw* him?" Jared's expression went from wounded to angry. "And he what, blamed everything on Noreen? Is that why you're looking for her? What did he say?"

"Nothing. It doesn't matter. I have to go." Ana opened the door, nearly tripping over Wilson Quinn as she stumbled out into the hall.

"Ana, what did he say?"

"Jared, we have to talk." Flecks of what looked like potato chips speckled Wilson's beard.

"Not now." Jared waved him off. "Ana, wait. Please."

Ana kept walking.

The young blonde watched their escalating conversations with interest.

Wilson persisted. "Doc, it's important."

"*This* is important." Jared caught up to Ana and took her hands in his, a public display that caught her off guard. "I need to know what's wrong."

"People are watching." Ana squirmed, and when she tried to pull away, again, Jared held her firm.

"Let them. Please, talk to me."

"Jared, I mean it." Wilson set a hand on Jared's shoulder. "Colby's coming to."

Ana leered and pulled her hands away. "Don't worry about me, *really*. Go take care of your wife."

CHAPTER 66

"Noreen, it's Brandon. I have some bad news."

Noreen sighed. With her lawyer, it was always bad news. "What is it?"

"I got a call from Kelly McTiernan, Dorian's attorney. She says the judge is considering letting him out on bail. Apparently, there's nothing but circumstantial evidence."

"Circumstantial! Are you kidding me? After what they found at his house?"

"Crime lab says his fingerprints aren't on any of it."

"And that's enough? He's a rapist, Brandon. What am I supposed to do here?" Her mind worked out the possibilities even as she said it.

"I'll keep in touch. If he contacts you, call the police. It might be a good time to get away for a couple of days."

Get away.

"That's a great idea."

She hung up the phone and turned on the morning news. Terri Tate, who had inadvertently been one of her prime sources for information, appeared on the screen in front of a house she would've recognized anywhere as the one next to Dorian's office. Noreen turned up the volume, expecting to hear that the police had found Colby Monroe, dead.

"Breaking news in the case that has police baffled: Colby Monroe, who had recently been abducted from her Marion home, has been found, in an abandoned garage at the office of Dr. Dorian Carmichael, County Memorial's fallen star who is behind bars this morning on unrelated charges. County Memorial's CEO, Mitchell Altman, continues to be unavailable for interview. The hospital's Public Relations department claims 'no comment.' The victim is reported as being in critical condition. No other information is available."

Noreen let out a frustrated growl and threw the hairbrush in her hand across the living room.

"Shit!"

An untraceable burner cell sat in a box on the counter; it was something she bought for "just in case." She cut the box open with a sharp kitchen knife and followed the activation instructions. She jotted down the number and texted it to Brandon. The last thing she needed was someone tracking her position.

She fired up the laptop in the corner of the living room, searched for a high-end car rental place, and dialed the phone number.

"Good morning, Go Rentals. This is Chuck. How can I help you?"

"Good morning, Chuck. I'm looking to rent an SUV for a few days, something that will stand up to all this snow."

"I'm sure we can help you. I have several vehicles in mind—"

"I want a Land Rover LR2. Baltic Blue, please."

The man didn't immediately respond. "Let me take a look at our inventory. I'm not sure we have one of those in stock." Noreen listened as he pecked away at the keyboard. "Nope, I'm sorry. I have a 2014 Acura MDX, or a Lexus RX 350."

"Neither of those will work. May I speak with your manager, please?"

"Just a minute."

"This is Marcy. May I help you?"

"Marcy, I was just speaking with Chuck, and I have a request he doesn't seem to be able to help with. I guess I should've told him the whole story, but I'm hoping you can help me. See, my truck was in a terrible accident, probably totaled, and not my fault, but I'm going up to Bristol Mountain for the weekend, and I really don't want to explain what happened to my parents. They're meeting me up there and they're elderly, the concerned type, you understand? I don't want them worried. They wouldn't necessarily notice a different license plate, but they'd notice a different car. I need a Baltic Blue Land Rover LR2."

"I understand completely. My mom's the same way. You'd think they'd stop worrying by now." She let out a soft laugh. "Let me see what we have coming back in. Can you hold on a minute?"

"Absolutely. Thank you." Noreen listened as Marcy searched for an exact match to Dorian's SUV.

"You're in luck."

"Really?" Noreen almost couldn't believe it.

"Yep. Looks like we have a Baltic Blue LR2 scheduled to be returned later this morning. It'll need to be checked in and detailed, but we can have it to you by tomorrow."

"How about tonight and I'll vacuum it myself?"

"I'll do what I can to rush it. Will you be picking up the vehicle, or would you like it delivered?"

"Delivered, please, to unit thirteen, Pemberton Trace."

"Absolutely, we have a lot of clients there. We know right where that is. Is there anything else I can do for you this morning?"

"That will be it, thank you."

"I'll just need a good phone number to reach you at."

Noreen gave Marcy her home phone number, unwilling to risk anything tying her to the burner cell.

"We'll call you as soon as the car is in. Thank you for renting with Go Rentals."

Noreen hung up the phone and searched her key ring for the spare key to Dorian's cabin.

CHAPTER 67

"Colby, can you hear me?"

Colby's eyes opened, and she rolled her head to the side. "Jared?"

"Yeah, it's me. Wilson, hit that light, would you?"

Colby reached out until her IV line pulled, Jared doing nothing to close the distance between them. "Where am I?" She squinted at the brightness.

"You're at County, in the ICU," Jared said.

Wilson checked her vitals and did a repeat finger stick. "Glucose is back to normal. Vitals are good. Heart rate is stable."

"How long have I been here?" she said.

"About a day. What do you remember about what happened?"

Colby stared out the windows, struggling to piece together a series of disconnected events. "Not much."

"Maybe this will jog your memory." Jared held up the sweatshirt he assumed belonged to Dorian. "Where were you two nights ago?"

Wilson hung a fresh bag of saline and kept his eyes averted. It wasn't like him to be so quiet. Jared could tell he was uncomfortable. After what he witnessed with Ana, Jared couldn't blame him.

"Why don't you let me finish this?" Jared said. "One of us should get back to the ER."

Wilson looked more than a little relieved. "I'll meet you down there."

Jared lifted the blanket covering Colby's leg and peeled back the dressing. "So, two nights ago?" He had to get the conversation back on track. "What do you remember?" He could tell from the long pause and Colby's concentrating expression that she was filtering what she told him.

"You had left a message, and I came home late."

"Late from where?" Colby didn't immediately answer. "You were with Dorian, weren't you?"

Colby nodded.

"Can I ask you something?" As angry as he should have been, he didn't want another argument. He wanted closure.

"Shoot." She reached for the cup on the tray next to her bed.

Jared filled it with water, added a straw, and handed it to her. "Do you love him?"

Colby drew her lips into a thin line. "I think so, yes."

Jared sensed the answer before she said it. "Even after all of this?" Rather than acknowledge the instinctual hurt, he kept the conversation going.

"All of what?"

"This, Colby, all of what happened to you. He nearly killed you, and for what?"

"Jared, are you nuts? Dorian didn't have anything to do with this. I have no idea who it was, or why, but I know for a fact it was a woman."

"What?"

"I didn't get a look at her or anything, but her voice was definitely female."

Jared pressed the call button for a nurse to take over with Colby and searched his pockets for his car keys. "I have to go."

"Go where?" she asked.

He didn't know how to tell her, but it was Noreen who attacked her, and he'd sent Ana right to her.

CHAPTER 68

Noreen stood in the doorway of her spacious condo, wearing an oversized cardigan and a pair of skinny jeans. She was gym-fit, and attractive underneath the cuts, scrapes, and bruises. Her full lips spread into a wide grin and she said, "Ana, I've been expecting you."

"Really?" Ana said. "And why's that?"

"Because my lawyer called me and said you'd met with Dorian, who, from the sounds of things, is looking to make the case that I framed him." Noreen shook her head. "Would you like to come in?"

Instinct warned Ana to run, but she hadn't come this far to leave.

"Yes, thank you."

Noreen's expertly decorated and expensively furnished place hinted at nothing out of the ordinary, not that Ana expected displayed murder trophies or anything, but she anticipated that there would be something different about the home of a woman she assumed was a sociopath.

Noreen poured herself a cup of coffee and held up the carafe. "Can I offer you a cup?"

"Sure, thank you." Ana scanned for anything to support Dorian's claims.

"I can tell you're nervous," Noreen said. "I don't blame you, but you have to understand that Dorian would do anything, *say* anything, to get out of the spot he's in. That doesn't necessarily make it true."

"Doesn't exactly make it false, either."

Ana stood at the kitchen counter rather than taking a seat. No matter how even-keeled and casual their discussion, Ana intended to keep a straight shot between her and the front door.

Noreen stirred a packet of artificial sweetener into her coffee and took a sip. "Do you think the police would've arrested Dorian without evidence? That they would have held him this long without proof of what he did to me?" Her eyes glossed over with tears. "Do you know how hard it is to get a night's sleep after you've been raped?"

Ana felt like a jerk. "I'm sorry, I . . ."

"Excuse me a minute, please." Noreen set her mug on the counter and closed herself in a room down the hall that Ana assumed was the bathroom.

The sobbing echoed in the otherwise silent first floor, punctuated by Noreen blowing her nose.

Ana hadn't meant to upset her, but the time alone was fortuitous.

Papers covered the computer desk in the far corner of the living room that faced out the picture window. Ana waited for Noreen to come back, listening to the sounds of drawers opening and closing.

"Are you all right?"

"I'll be out in a minute."

A minute turned to two, and then five.

Ana decided to take a closer look. Old bills, receipts, and copies of recent OR and office schedules were tucked beneath the foot

of a closed laptop. Two manila folders of personal financial statements sat to the right of a small desk lamp, and when Ana moved
them, she gasped. Underneath was a purple notepad with a water-
mark image of flowers in the background.

It was the *exact* paper Sydney's supposed suicide note had
been written on.

Ana had been so engrossed that she hadn't heard Noreen come
back. She felt a sharp pinch in her biceps and let out a yell, instinctively grabbing her arm. A disorienting feeling took hold, and the
sensation of losing control hit her so fast, she couldn't fight back,
or run. She pressed her palms to the desktop and struggled to draw
a breath. Her legs buckled, and she collapsed, paralyzed on the
floor at Noreen's feet.

"On second thought," Noreen said, "maybe you were right to
insult me."

CHAPTER 69

A transporter, a young girl wearing maroon scrubs and white sneakers, pushed a wheelchair past Derrick and Dr. Davis, halting their heated conversation.

"What do you intend to tell her?" Dr. Davis's stare was hard to read.

"I don't intend to tell her *anything*, unless I absolutely have to." Derrick could see that wasn't the right answer.

"You can't keep sitting on her like this. Emily's going to see the news sooner or later."

"And by the time she does, hopefully the Dorian Carmichael story will have fizzled itself out."

"I spoke with Mitchell Altman this morning, and we both agree it's best if we can get Emily home as soon as possible."

"The *CEO* agrees? Based on what, his vast medical experience? No. All due respect, Dr. Davis, but sending Emily home too soon was the catalyst for this whole series of events, and from what I hear, might've been for Stephanie Martin as well."

Dr. Davis bristled at the mention. "This wasn't my mess, Derrick. I'm cleaning it up the best I can, but you have to work with me. Terri Tate has been relentlessly trying to identify Dorian's second patient, *Emily*. The longer you let her remain here, the more likely it is that someone will talk, that you will lose the benefit of privacy. The care Emily's getting here, she can get at home."

"Then you try to sell her on that, see how she reacts." Derrick worked to smooth the anger from his face and pushed the door to Emily's room open. "After you."

Dr. Davis mustered a smile and walked into the room with an act of confident cheer. "Good morning, Emily. How are you doing today?"

Emily's color had returned, and she'd even managed to dampen and comb her hair, the curls much less unruly than they had been.

"I'm feeling better, thank you. Is everything all right?"

"Fine, why wouldn't it be?" said Dr. Davis.

"You and Derrick were out in the hall awhile. I was worried."

"No reason to worry. I was just giving Derrick the good news."

"Good news?"

"The new drug regimen is working better than expected," Dr. Davis said. "Mind if I have a look?" She gestured at Emily's abdomen, and Emily moved her hands aside.

Derrick stood by her bedside, trying not to give anything away with his expression. He'd never been good at hiding his emotions, especially with Emily.

"The redness is gone, and the discharge has stopped. Looks good. Looks real good."

"Good enough that she can go home?" Derrick played along, expecting Emily to shoot the whole thing down.

"Home?" Emily asked, as if it were the last thought on her mind.

Dr. Davis smiled. "I don't want to get your hopes up, but yes, I expect that you'll be able to go home tomorrow and that, as long as you take all of your medication as prescribed, you're on the road to a full recovery. I need you to promise me something, though, okay?"

Emily nodded, not putting up half the argument Derrick expected. "Sure, what is it?"

"The minute you feel anything out of the ordinary, you tell someone."

"You don't have to worry about that," Emily said. "I've learned my lesson."

CHAPTER 70

Jared pulled into Pemberton Trace at sixty miles per hour, tires sliding on a faint coating of fresh powder, in complete shock that he hadn't drawn police attention.

He almost wished he had.

Ana's snow-covered Jetta was parked in a visitor's spot outside one of the buildings. Even though he expected it to be there, seeing it was a shock.

He pulled in next to it and slammed his car into park. His hands shook as he pulled the keys from the ignition, rushing out of his car so fast that he left the wipers in the "on" position.

"Hello." He knocked on the first door he came to, praying that someone would answer. "Hello, please, open up." He knocked faster and louder. Still, no answer. He went to the next door and pounded on it until his fists hurt. "Hello?"

A middle-aged man in an expensive, pin-striped business suit answered the door. He was halfway through tying a Full Windsor, his red tie draped over his left hand. "Can I help you?"

"I'm looking for Noreen Pafford." The man seemed to be trying to place the name. "Short hair, about this tall? Blond highlights? She's a nurse."

"Oh yeah. I know who you're talking about. She lives in unit thirteen, around back." The man smoothed his tie flat. "Is everything all right?"

Jared ran off without answering.

"Noreen, open up." He knocked progressively harder. The man had followed him. "Noreen, hello? Open up." He jiggled the door handle and found it locked.

"Hey, guy, you're making me nervous."

The last thing Jared needed was a confrontation, but he'd deal with one if he had to. He kept knocking, determined to get in.

"Guy, seriously." The man produced a cell phone from the holster on his belt. "Do I need to call the police?"

"Yes," Jared said. "And ask for Mike Richardson. Tell him Ana's in trouble." He ran around to the front window, trudging through a foot of packed snow, and squinted to see through the mostly drawn curtains. Cold seeped through his pant legs, and his socks soaked through as the snow melted. Peering into the lifeless space, it was obvious the house was empty.

Jared rushed past the dumbstruck neighbor, who held his phone out to the side.

"What are you waiting for? Get going on that call. Mike. Richardson."

Jared raced back to his car. Heat poured out of the vents full-blast, and he shoved his feet under the dash, straining to pull out his wallet and Wendell Cobb's business card.

He plugged his cell phone into the charger and dialed. The call, placed to Wendell's private number, was immediately answered.

"Wendell, it's Jared Monroe."

"Jared, I'm glad to hear from you. I was beginning to worry."

"Listen, I need a favor."

"If it's about Colby, I haven't heard anything back from her lawyer and—"

"It's about Dorian Carmichael."

There was an immediate, dramatic silence. Wendell cleared his throat and let out a deep breath. "Jared, what are you up to?"

"I don't have time to explain. Dorian's in lockup, and if there's anything you can do to get him out, I'll post bail."

"As your lawyer, I seriously advise against that."

"And as your client, I'll take that under advisement. I need him out, now."

"I—"

"Dammit, Wendell, I know you can pull strings. I need him out of there. Do it and call me back."

A brief pause followed. "I'm not sure I can."

"Make it happen. The sooner, the better." Jared spun out of the parking lot, headed for the county jail.

CHAPTER 71

The precinct hummed with activity, the background noise making it hard for Mike to hear what Coop was saying.

"She's what?" Mike shouted into the receiver.

"Stephanie Martin is dead. I found out when I went to County to question her."

"What about Colby Monroe?"

"She's been taken to Radiology for testing, but she's awake. I gave the charge nurse my card, and she says she'll call as soon as Colby is back in her room, but it'll be a while. I'm on my way back to the office. I'll see you in ten."

"See you then."

There was no guaranteeing Stephanie knew anything about her organ donor, or the lengths Dorian had gone to, but she was, up until recently, the only living lead to Sydney.

Mike checked his cell for a return message from Ana, who hadn't been answering his calls all morning.

He stared at the picture of her and Sydney on the corner of his desk. The photo had been taken almost a decade earlier, and the two couldn't have looked happier, or more like their mother. The chestnut hair with a hint of red in the sunlight and the slight tilt to the corners of their smiles were mirror images of hers, but their serious eyes were their father's.

Ana's father had pulled Mike's ass out of the fire more times than he cared to count, and he loved Sydney and Ana more than anything in the world. Losing a friend who had put his life on the line in exchange for Mike's was the closest Mike could imagine to losing family, until now. Mike was almost glad his former partner wasn't here to see this.

"Mike, you have a call on line two." The voice of Dorothy, the switchboard operator, boomed through the speakerphone.

Mike wiped the tears from his eyes and pushed the button.

"Sergeant Mike Richardson speaking."

He was answered by a moment of silence and the unsure voice of a man who eventually identified himself as Peter Ross.

"I'm not sure exactly what to say here. I was told to call you."

"Told by whom?" said Mike.

"I don't know his name."

Mike was starting to get annoyed. "You were told to call me by someone you don't know, and you're not sure why. I'm sorry, but if you have nothing to tell me, I have to go."

"The man drove a silver BMW, and he was at Pemberton Trace apartments. He came to my door asking for Noreen Pafford, my neighbor, and he seemed agitated. He kept knocking on her door and looking in her window. I told him I was going to call the police, and he told me to ask for you, specifically."

Shit, Jared Monroe.

Mike had watched him leave after the second round of questioning, and he remembered his car.

"Did he say anything else?"

"He did. Someone was in trouble. I can't remember the name he said. I barely remembered yours. It was a girl's name. Something with an 'A,' maybe."

"Ana?" Mike's heart hammered in his chest.

"Ana, yes. That's it. I wasn't even going to call, but—"

Mike hung up the phone and dialed Dorothy's extension.

"What's up, Mike?"

"Radio out, find out who is closest to Pemberton Trace, and get them over there, immediately."

"Is everything all right?"

"Dorothy, just do it," he shouted, and snatched his keys off his desk. His thoughts turned to Dorian in county lockup, his theory changing from murder to conspiracy.

Noreen and Dorian were in this together.

He dialed the warden on his way out the door.

CHAPTER 72

Ana woke to the sound of a slamming door and the smells of leather and pine. She was bound to a wooden kitchen chair, her ankles taped to the legs, and her wrists together behind her.

"Where am I?"

Noreen didn't immediately answer.

"You know, I've been hearing some interesting stories about you. Here I felt a little guilty about kidnapping the grieving sister, the do-gooder medic with the tragic past." She filled a cup of water at the sink and pressed it to Ana's lips. "Drink." Ana drained the entire thing in three gulps. "Rumor mill at County says you're quite the little home wrecker." Ana didn't bother to argue. "I have friends there, too. It's how I first knew about Dorian and Colby Monroe, not that they weren't obvious. I mean, she had guilt written all over her. Funny, isn't it? You and I, and this whole six degrees of separation thing? He's with Colby, you're with Jared, and now you're at Dorian's cabin. Someone has to make him understand that he can't just have every woman he wants. When this is all over, he'll be locked away for good."

Any doubt that Dorian was onto something had disappeared with the needle stick.

"Are you going to kill me, too?"

"Too?" Noreen smirked. "Are you calling me a murderer?"

"Is there another way to say it? I can see your issue with Colby, but what did Marco or Sydney do to you?"

Noreen sat in the chair across from her. "To me? It was more about what they did to Dorian, at first, not that I wasn't implicated." She looked at her watch. "Now it's about what's right. My lawyer called, you know. A courtesy to let me know my 'attacker'"— she used air quotes—"is about to be out, roaming the streets. Apparently another *friend* of his, Jared Monroe, knew someone who could pull a few strings. You wouldn't know anything about that, would you?" Ana didn't, but she refused to answer on principle. "Doesn't matter. If Dorian puts two and two together, he'll find us, and nothing will happen to you until he does."

"So you *are* setting him up?"

"I was trying to help him." Noreen slammed her palms on the table. "You think he was the least bit thankful? No. He accused me of blackmailing him, had sex with me to keep me quiet, and then ran off with Colby. I mean, who the hell does that?"

"You *framed* him for rape."

"And murder." Noreen regained her calm. "This all started with your sister. Yes, we lied to her, but if she had let it go, she'd still be alive. She was relentless. Second opinions, constantly calling the office, looking for reports that didn't exist—I should've just manufactured a report that said she had cancer and the whole thing would've dropped there, but she just kept coming."

"Sydney was like that."

"You're telling me."

"But you didn't have to kill her."

"Didn't I?" Noreen shrugged. "I don't see that I had a choice."

"How did you convince her to meet you at a place like the Aquarian?"

"Same way I got you to knock on my door. Leave a trail of bread crumbs. Works every time. I gave Sydney just enough information to implicate Dorian, and offered to help her make him pay for what he'd done. Isn't it funny how if there are a male and female suspect, the finger always points to the man? All I had to do was tell Sydney that I was sorry, set up a meeting at the Aquarian, a place layered in enough prints to keep the police busy for a decade, and play the 'girl code.' Sister solidarity and all that shit. A couple of drinks, a long chat, and some zopiclone in the bottle—she didn't see it coming. The thing about medicine, Ana, and I'm sure you can appreciate this, is that we know everything about our patients. Dorian had written that prescription for Sydney's insomnia, but she refused to take it. I had it filled in her name. I knew her pharmacy, her date of birth, and it's not like they asked for ID or anything. It should've been painless. She should've gone to sleep, permanently. That crackhead motel manager would've found her and the note."

"You spelled my name wrong," Ana said.

"Did I?"

"You used two 'n's.'"

"Doesn't matter. I suspected the medical examiner would figure out what happened and rule it a homicide. There was still no reason to implicate me. Anyway, the zopiclone made Sydney sick. She kept saying she had to throw up. She shoved her finger so far down her throat, I thought she'd gouge out her windpipe. I tried stopping her, but she wouldn't listen. I shoved more pills down her throat when she went unconscious, but she came to and made herself sick again. She wouldn't stop asking for you. She begged me to call you, kept begging me, until I hit her with the succinylcholine."

"Same drug you used on me."

Noreen nodded. "Only, her I let die."

"Why are you telling me this?"

Noreen shrugged. "Because, really, the big picture is kind of impressive. Because you asked me if I was going to kill you, too, and the answer is yes. Not because I have anything against you, but because it's the only ending that fits. You've led everyone in Dorian's direction, and what makes more sense than for him to silence you? I'm walking away from this, Ana, and Dorian's taking the fall."

"You *hope*."

"I'm a woman, Ana, and we're cast as victims, not villains. I don't need hope. The ball's already in motion."

"And if you're wrong?"

"We're *never* wrong." Noreen smiled and took a bottle of red wine from a rack on the counter. She rummaged through a drawer, found a corkscrew, and used it. She whiffed the bottle's opening and seeming pleased, poured herself a glass. "To Sydney." She raised it in toast.

"And Marco?"

"I told Dorian to find an outside lab to run the tests. I *warned* him that running the donor tests through County was too risky, but he wouldn't listen, and you know what got him pinched? A grudge. Do you believe that? Took the better part of two hours of torture to get *that* out of Marco. He was determined not to talk." Noreen swallowed the rest of the wine and poured herself another glass. "Dorian was a resident on a transplant team, years ago, when Marco's daughter, Jasmine, was born with biliary atresia. She was put on the transplant list by a month old, but Jehovah's Witnesses don't believe in transplants, at least not unless they can be done without blood transfer. There wasn't a facility within five hundred miles willing to help with that. Every surgeon told Marco and his wife, Faith, that their daughter wouldn't survive without a transplant, everyone except for Dorian. He gave Faith false hope that the transplant was unnecessary, and their daughter died because of him. I guess we know how Marco felt about that. Everything he'd done over the past decade was to bring Dorian down. It only took me a few months."

CHAPTER 73

Warden Joe Jenkins couldn't have sounded more apologetic.

Mike was crushed by the news.

Ana was in trouble, and Dorian Carmichael, potentially a coconspirator with Noreen Pafford, was about to be released on bail.

Mike wondered why Noreen had him locked up in the first place.

As an alibi, for when Ana went missing.

"Shit. How did this happen?" Mike sped down Main Street in his patrol car. He came to a congested intersection and flipped on his lights. "Come on, move it."

A short siren blast cleared the way.

"I don't exactly know. The attorneys have been working on it all morning. Apparently Dorian Carmichael's attorney convinced Judge Coleman that Dorian was being set up. The only thing I know is that they said there weren't prints tying him to any of the evidence, not even on what was found at his house, and, Mike . . . your name came up."

Shit.

"I knew that was going to happen sooner or later."

"We've known each other a long time, and I don't believe for a second you didn't cover your bases, but maybe this case is too close to home for you to be working on."

"Joe, don't even start. It was Ronald Graham who found the evidence, and both he and Coop were with me the whole time. Ron was the first upstairs, end of story."

"I believe you, Mike, but it's not me you have to convince."

"Is it too late to change Coleman's mind?"

"Orders are already written up, and bail is on its way. Carmichael should be out within the hour."

"Who's posting bail?"

"Jared Monroe."

CHAPTER 74

The county correctional facility was a concrete fortress surrounded by high fences and razor wire and was secured by dozens of armed guards. The flat face of the building loomed several stories over a weathered parking lot.

Jared pulled into a front-row parking spot and waited.

It took less than a half hour for Wendell to call back with details of Dorian's release and another forty minutes to finalize Jared's posting bail.

Jared watched the minutes tick by and waited for word from Ana that never came.

Anger, jealousy, and embarrassment, all emotions Jared wasn't used to, bubbled to the surface as he recalled Colby's response when he asked her if she loved Dorian. Colby had been through a lot, and even though Jared was falling for Ana, hearing her admit that she was in love with Dorian had stung.

The front door opened, and a guard escorted Dorian out. He looked like hell and walked with his head down and shoulders rounded.

Jared left the driver's side door open and walked toward him with a balled-up fist that connected with the shiner just under his left eye as soon as he was within arm's reach.

Dorian's head whipped to the side. He staggered and nearly fell.

"Hey." The guard who had been watching from the doorway rushed toward them.

Dorian held up his hand. "No problem here. I deserved that."

"That's for sleeping with my wife." Jared cracked his knuckles to release the tension in his joints.

Dorian scooped up a ball of snow and held it to his face. "I know you didn't bail me out just to take a swing at me. What are you doing here?"

"Get in the car and we'll talk."

Dorian got in and put on his seat belt without saying a word.

"Tell me where to find Noreen."

Dorian turned on the heat and warmed his wet hand in front of the vent. "How the hell should I know? In case you didn't hear, she's the one who had me locked up. We haven't exactly been in touch."

"Dorian, I don't have time for this. Your pathological need to screw everything that walks has Ana in trouble. You want out from under this nightmare, you tell me where Noreen would go if she wasn't done ruining you."

"Ana told you, didn't she?"

"Told me what?"

"That Noreen was setting me up."

"No, she didn't. Colby told me it was a woman who attacked her."

"She's all right?"

Jared could see his relief. "Yes, she'll be fine. Now where would Noreen go if she was, in fact, framing you?"

Jared pressed his hand to the back of Dorian's seat and looked over his shoulder, speeding backward out of the parking spot. His tires squealed as he exited the slow-opening gate and floored it.

"Give me your phone."

"What?"

"Give me your phone. My battery is dead." Dorian's hands were shaking.

Jared unplugged his phone from the charger and handed it to him. "Who are you calling?"

"Counselor Kelly McTiernan, please. This is an emergency. Where's the 'Speakerphone' button on this thing?"

"Hold that button on the side."

A woman's voice came over the line. "This is Kelly."

"Kelly, it's Dorian Carmichael. Who knew I was getting out on bail?"

"What?"

"Who, other than you, knew I was getting out?"

"Wendell Cobb, the judge, and opposing counsel. Why?"

Dorian hung up the phone without answering her. "I know where Noreen is. Get on 490 East."

Jared merged onto the highway doing a solid eighty-five miles per hour. "Where are we going?" he asked.

"Noreen's lawyer knew I was getting out on bail, and I'm sure he told her as a precaution, right? You say she has Ana, who, besides being your apparent *girlfriend*"—Jared scowled at Dorian's tone—"is sister of the woman whose murder I'm being framed for. Noreen alleged rape to get me behind bars, but she's been setting me up for worse. She can't stand the fact that I'm in love with . . ." Jared didn't need him to finish his sentence to know it was Colby, and, at the moment, he didn't even care. "If she has Ana, she's planning on finishing what she started, and putting a smoking gun in my hand."

"You've got a real way with women, Dorian. Anyone ever tell you that?"

"They didn't have to. Head toward Bristol Mountain," he said. "Noreen's at my goddamned cabin."

CHAPTER 75

The Merlot made Noreen light-headed, and after only two glasses, she couldn't tell whether she was warm from the fireplaces, or the alcohol.

"You think I'm crazy, don't you?"

"Depends." Ana shrugged.

"On?"

"On whether or not you *want* to kill me, or you feel like you have no choice."

Noreen smirked, her buzz making her a little more truthful than normal. "What if it's both?"

"Then yes, I'd say you've gone crazy."

In lucid moments, Noreen had come to the same conclusion, though she wasn't sure how or when it happened. She didn't start out enjoying any of it, but power was its own drug.

"You know, Dorian told me he loved me."

"And you believed him?"

"Yeah, I guess I did." After all the years she had spent earning his affection, changing everything about herself, and making herself into someone like the women he flaunted, she needed to. A tear rolled down her cheek before she could stop it.

"You all right?"

"Never better." Noreen tore off a length of tape, the adhesive of which kept sticking to her gloves, and covered Ana's mouth with it. Ana was an unavoidable, eventual casualty—a loose end—and Noreen refused to let her manipulate her into feeling bad about that. She shook off the sadness and forced a laugh. "You're good. You almost had me." She lifted the green glass bottle to the firelight. Half a bottle of wine and she was sniveling. She set the bottle on the counter and opened the dishwasher, more out of habit than anything else, to put her glass inside. Two wineglasses sat side by side in the top rack, one of them rimmed with lipstick.

Noreen threw her own glass as hard as she could against the wall, shattering it into hundreds of pieces.

"Do you know how hard I tried to get Dorian to bring me here with him for a weekend?" Noreen said, even though Ana couldn't answer her. "I begged, Ana, and I'm not the begging type. Just once I wanted what all of these other women get. Do you know what I got instead?" Ana shook her head. "A spare key and, 'Have a nice time. Place is yours whenever you want it.'" Her gloved hands shook as she bent down and collected the largest of the glass pieces. "Bastard." A jagged shard broke through the glove and embedded itself in her left hand. She let out a pained cry, pulling the glass from the cut, and peeled off the glove, which was quickly filling with blood. "Shit."

She wrapped a kitchen towel around her hand and made a fist to keep the pressure on it, searching for anything she could use to slow down the bleeding. The cut was deep, too deep, and needed stitches, something that would have to wait. She opened the cabinet under the sink and reached behind the dishwasher soap for the first aid kit.

Despite being right-handed, she found that something as simple as opening a gauze pad seemed a monumental task. The wrappers were the pull-apart type and required a dexterity she couldn't manage with only one good hand.

She could feel Ana's stare at her back.

Ana was a paramedic, and her only option.

Noreen set the kit on the table in front of her.

Blood soaked through the dish towel, enough for it to drip.

"I need your help." Noreen peeled the tape from Ana's mouth, the irony of the situation not entirely lost on her.

"Why would I help you?"

"Because it's what you do. You help people, and you hope I'll let you go."

"Will you? Let me go?"

"No, but I'll be merciful." Noreen reached into a cardboard box of medical supplies and pulled out a syringe and a vial of succinylcholine. "Sydney went quickly, once I injected her, Ana. She was gone in a couple of minutes. I can make this easy, or hard." Her hand throbbed, the pressure of the too-tight towel turning her fingertips cold and dusky. "Your choice."

"Fine, but not for that reason."

Noreen didn't care why; that Ana was willing to help was all that mattered. She took a chef's knife from the holder on the counter and cut the duct tape holding Ana's hands. She replaced the knife and put the whole set in the living room, out of reach.

Ana stretched her arms and shoulders. "How bad is it?"

Noreen held her hand over the sink and slowly unwrapped the towel around it. The cotton fibers stuck to the edge of the cut, which bled faster when she pulled it. "Not terrible, but it could take a couple of stitches." The gash was short, but deep. She rinsed her hand under a stream of cool water and tried not to pass out. "What do we have in there?"

Ana sifted through the medical kit. "Nothing to stitch with. The best I can do is Steri-strips and a bandage."

"Is there antibiotic ointment?" Noreen patted her hand dry and turned to find Ana holding a pocketknife.

She knew she should've checked her.

CHAPTER 76

Mike's Dodge hummed down I-490, the tires eating up the snow-dusted highway at almost ninety miles per hour as the vehicle struggled to keep up with Jared's BMW. Tourist traffic congested the roadway as they drew near to the Bristol Mountain Ski Resort and Jared veered effortlessly through it. Mike jerked the steering wheel hard to the left, and the truck pitched, threatening to roll. He'd kept several car lengths between him and Jared to avoid being recognized, but he was beginning to lose him.

"Come on, come on." Mike pressed down on the accelerator and switched lanes.

Jared crossed over two, gaining three car lengths between them.

Thick traffic gathered near the exit where a construction zone funneled the steady stream of cars down to a single lane less than one mile ahead.

Mike gripped the steering and aimed for the front of the pack.

Jared veered out into the shoulder, and his tires spun. The car fishtailed sideways.

Traction and four-wheel drive had Mike gaining on him, but he couldn't catch up. He pulled into the right lane, and a horn sounded, long and loud. He'd cut off a Camry he hadn't even seen. The close call had his heart hammering in his chest.

Cars alternated turns, merging as the left two lanes formed a single-file line.

Jared sped around them.

Mike could only watch him fade off into the distance with no idea where he was headed. He picked up his cell and dialed Coop, hoping he'd been able to make sense of what was happening.

"This is Coop."

"Coop, it's Mike. Any luck?" He had been calling Ana for hours with no answer.

"Nothing. I can't get a trace on her cell."

"So her phone's off?"

"Off and the battery's out of it, most likely. Otherwise, I'd still get a trace. Where are you?"

"Eastbound on 490, about ten minutes out from the Bristol Ski Resort. I lost sight of the doctors in a construction zone and have no idea where they're headed. Any ideas?"

"Not yet, but Julian called. They found a print."

"Where?"

"On the bottle of succinylcholine found at the Monroe house. You're never going to believe who it belongs to."

"I can't believe a lot of things lately," Mike said. "Who?"

"Noreen Pafford."

"You're kidding me." Noreen had sat in front of him, answering his questions with the fluid ease of truth and the trademark signs of a victim. If the whole thing had been an act, it was well researched and well rehearsed. He rolled down his window, waving his arms and shouting that he needed to get through due to an emergency, but few people yielded to his frantic display.

Traffic went from a crawl to a standstill, and Mike recounted
every painful detail of Sydney's homicide investigation. He repro-
cessed the crime scene, wondering what, if anything, they had
missed. The autopsy had been inconclusive in that it didn't point
to a particular agent, though the succinylcholine found at the
Monroes' house posed a likely possibility. Dorian had been forthcoming about his lying to Sydney about having cancer, and his
medical license had been fast-tracked for revocation. He had also
admitted to consensual sex with Noreen. Mike's well-honed gut
didn't peg Dorian as a rapist, or a murderer, and despite the damning evidence, there wasn't a single fingerprint tying him to any of
it. The only print belonged to Noreen, a suspect he had immediately discounted because she was a victim, and if he was being
honest, because she was female. He thought back to the day after
Sydney's murder, when he returned to the Aquarian to get the surveillance tapes from Samuel and was called over by the least help-
ful eyewitness he'd ever interviewed. She had given him one solid
piece of information: the person leaving room 11 was a woman.
Tunnel vision had him thinking only of Misty. He couldn't believe
he hadn't thought of Noreen as a suspect sooner.

CHAPTER 77

Emily tuned the television to the news channel, and Derrick snatched the remote from her hand.

"What are you doing?" she said.

Derrick changed the channel to a game show and feigned momentary interest. "We've had enough bad news for one week."

A commotion had started in the hallway, one that normally Derrick would've complained about at length, but now avoided like the plague. He had been keeping her isolated, away from the news and local TV, and she knew there had to be a reason.

"What's going on with you, lately? First our doctor disappears, and then you quarantine me. I know you well enough to know when something's up."

Derrick ran his hands through his hair and paced, alternating his gaze from the wall clock to the door. He smoothed the front of his pleated khakis and blew out a long breath.

"Hello, are you going to answer me?"

Dr. Davis ducked into the room, closing the door quickly behind her. Her once-comforting smile fell flat, and she flashed an unmistakably concerned look at Derrick. "It's time."

Derrick took the small overnight bag from behind the lounge chair and started packing.

"Time for what?" Emily asked nervously. "What's going on?"

Dr. Davis bagged Emily's toiletries and handed them to Derrick. "Everything's going to be fine," she said. "Don't worry." She stepped on the floor pedal to lower the bed and put down the railing. "I'm going to have you swing your legs slowly around to me, and we're going to get you dressed in some more comfortable clothes."

Emily clutched her blanket to her chest, tugging against Dr. Davis, who was trying to pull it down. "*What's* going to be fine? Derrick, why are you packing?" She looked right into Dr. Davis's eyes. "You told me I had to stay for at least another couple of days." It wasn't that she wasn't happy to be dressed and elated to be going home, if that was what was happening; it was the hurried way in which it was happening that had her worried about a repeat of the last time she was discharged.

"Plans changed, hon." Derrick handed Dr. Davis a pair of loose-fitting pants and coaxed the blanket from Emily's hands.

She grabbed his wrist and pulled him close. "Why did they change?"

Derrick lowered his eyes. "Because the press knows that you're the second transplant patient."

Emily's spirits sank. Hers was a time-bomb kind of secret. Being the mayor's daughter-in-law meant there was no expectation of privacy, even in a matter as personal as this one. She planned to come out with her story after a successful pregnancy, but it seemed that now she had no choice.

A middle-aged, blond nurse with a name tag that read "Trish" hurried through the door with a wheelchair, shouting for Security to help her.

The burly guard, late-twenties, dark skin, and with biceps as big around as Emily's thighs, forced the crowd back.

Dr. Davis helped Derrick ease Emily up. "What's going on out there?"

"Mitchell is trying to clear the news crew out, but they're not moving." The nurse parked the chair next to the bed and put on the brakes.

Emily flashed Derrick an angry look. "Is that why you've been keeping me away from the news?"

"No, not at all," he said, but she could see he was lying. He untied the strings on the back of her hospital gown, and a chill crept up her spine. She shivered, and he quickly pulled the fleece over her head. "Is there another way out of here?"

Dr. Davis slid Emily's feet, one at a time, into her pant legs and shook her head. "Out of the hospital, yes. Out of this wing, no."

Emily slid slowly forward. Derrick and Trish stood on either side of her to catch her weight.

"Ready?" Dr. Davis said.

Emily nodded and stood.

Derrick, careful not to lift her arms, accepted most of her weight. A jolt of sharp pain radiated through her incision, and she froze in place until it subsided.

Dr. Davis pulled Emily's pants up to just below her wound dressing and folded over the top so that the waistband rested low on her hips. She pulled the wheelchair forward, and Derrick helped Emily into it.

The transfer had taken everything Emily had. "I'm not sure I can do this."

Derrick handed Emily's bag to Trish. "I don't think you have a choice. If we don't get you out of here, they'll never leave."

Dr. Davis made sure that Emily's feet were settled on the footrests and held her hand on the doorknob. "There's a nurse—her name is Jane Allen—already on her way to your home."

Emily had heard before that a private nurse was coming, but it was nice to have a name this time. She turned to Derrick. "Is this why you have been avoiding watching the news?"

He nodded, but Emily could see from his expression that it wasn't the whole truth.

"Ready?" Dr. Davis said.

Derrick disengaged the brakes. "Ready."

"I guess." Emily, knowing she had no choice in the matter, buried her face in her steepled fingers and pressed her elbows into the armrests. She held a shallow breath as Dr. Davis opened the door.

The security guard cleared the way ahead of them.

Camera flashes went off in her periphery.

Terri Tate stooped down to her level, shoving the microphone in her face. "Emily, how did you feel when you heard your surgeon was stealing organs for transplant? As a recipient, are you worried where yours might have come from?"

Emily kept her lips pressed together to keep her mouth from falling open. Compared to the most terrible reasons for which she had thought Derrick was keeping her away from the news, this was worse.

The security guard stepped between her and Terri Tate and wedged some space. "Back off," he said in a deep voice.

Terri was not easily deterred. She moved around him and kept going. "Are you concerned about the first transplant patient having died from complications?"

Emily, determined not to let the ambitious reporter get the best of her, kept her head down.

Derrick shouted over the dull roar that neither he nor Emily had any comment.

"What about the fact that Dr. Dorian Carmichael has been arrested for rape and is a possible suspect in a recent string of murders? Are you concerned for your safety?"

At this, Emily couldn't help looking up. Flashes went off in rapid-fire sequence, some so close, the light made white spots in her vision. She glanced over her shoulder at Derrick, who couldn't make eye contact.

"That's enough." The guard all but shoved the cameraman and Terri Tate aside. He pressed the elevator call button, and when the door opened, kept anyone else from entering.

The chair's wheels thudded on the metal threshold, jolting Emily and causing a radiating pain in her stomach that made her whimper.

"Are you all right?" Derrick steered her into the back corner.

"No," Emily said through clenched teeth. "I don't think I am."

CHAPTER 78

The wine had given Ana the advantage.

"Don't move," she said, thankful for the pocketknife she'd taken from her glove compartment.

Noreen held the towel to her injured hand, her eyes shifting to the ringing burner cell on the table. "I need to answer that. It's my lawyer."

"You need to sit the hell down." Ana slid the knife through the tape holding her ankles. "Sit." She stood, and her knees nearly buckled from the tingling numbness of returning blood flow. "I mean it, Noreen. I've had enough."

Noreen took a few steps toward the chair Ana pulled out for her. "All right. All right. I'm sitting."

Ana kept the knife pointed at her, but couldn't stop her hands from shaking.

The phone rang again.

"He's not going to stop calling. I need to answer that."

Ana, needing to keep her occupied, reluctantly agreed. "Make it quick, and not a word about this, you understand me?"

Noreen nodded and flipped the phone open. "Brandon, hello?" *Silence.* "How long ago?" *Silence.* Ana fastened the end of the roll of duct tape to the table and cut several long strips. "Okay, thank you for calling." She hung up. "Dorian's out of jail, and my guess is he's on his way."

"Hands behind your back." Ana cleared her throat to steady her wavering voice.

"You're not cut out for this," Noreen said, doing as Ana instructed.

"I'll take that as a compliment." Ana reached for a strip of tape, and Noreen delivered a sharp kick to her right knee, catching her off guard. The knife skidded across the table and crashed to the floor.

Ana stumbled and fell.

"You should." Noreen gained a quick advantage, grabbing Ana by her hair.

Ana scrambled to her knees and crawled for the knife.

Blood dripped from Noreen's hand as she tried to wrestle Ana to her back.

Ana chalked the lack of pain response to the alcohol, which had Noreen's equilibrium off. Though strong, she moved with the back-and-forth motion of someone just off a ship.

Ana threw her elbow back as hard as she could, jabbing Noreen in the ribs. Noreen lost her hold, and Ana gained ground, the knife only inches away.

"Get off me," she shouted, and stretched her arm to the end of her reach.

"Not a chance." Noreen landed a solid, disorienting punch to the back of Ana's head.

Ana saw stars, her vision momentary white lights in a fog. She blinked hard and fast, praying for the sensation to pass. A second blow knocked her flat, this one so crushing, Noreen screamed, too.

Ana's head pounded, her neck stiff and her thoughts scattered, as though she were on the brink of unconsciousness.

One minute, Noreen's weight was on top of her, and the next, she was gone.

Even in the twilight of her injury, Ana realized the danger.

Noreen had the syringe of succinylcholine before Ana could recover.

"Stick with being the good girl," Noreen said, injecting the full dose into her. "You don't have the killer instinct." She shook the blood from her injured hand and stood over Ana, rolling her onto her back and leaving her to gasp, like a fish out of water.

The relaxant dissolved the tension from Ana's stiff muscles, and she melted into the cool floor, aware that her time was short. She closed her eyes, unable to draw even a single puff of breath. She could've easily suffocated to death, but when Noreen fitted her with the CPAP breathing mask, she knew that wasn't the plan.

CHAPTER 79

Jared turned off NY-64, onto the yet-unpaved Lakeside Lodges Road. The wind and snow had picked up substantially, and his tires, packed with fresh powder, skidded on the gravel.

"How much farther?"

Dorian held the armrest with a white-knuckled grip and pressed his lips tightly together as if he might throw up. "A mile, maybe less."

There were no indications of life, only half-finished construction and lot markers with "For Sale" signs.

Jared kept his eyes on the road, which didn't even register on the GPS. "What are the chances of a plow coming through any time soon?"

At the current rate of snowfall, even if they could get to Ana, there was no guaranteeing they'd get her back out.

"Slim to none. It's a private road, and the builder's not keen on paying out of pocket to keep it clear."

Jared's blood pressure went up a few points. "Said builder realizes this is a ski destination, yes?"

Dorian grumbled. "Most of us have trucks, and it isn't a problem."

The narrow road straightened through a clearing, and Jared picked up speed across the straightaway.

"You might want to slow down there, friend."

"I got it, don't worry." The wind had cleared some of the snow, and his tires finally had some grab.

"Jared, I'm serious. Slow down."

Jared sped up his wipers. This close to Ana, he only wanted to go faster. "Will you just let me drive?"

"Jared, watch out!" Dorian pushed his feet firmly into the floor mat and nearly slapped Jared in the face as he reached out to grab the back of the driver's seat with his left hand.

Jared slammed on the brakes, which was exactly the wrong thing to do given the circumstances. The BMW spun three hundred sixty degrees. His biceps ached from fighting the skid.

"Steer into it," Dorian shouted, and tried to grab the wheel.

"Get off me." Jared threw his elbow and hit Dorian in the ribs.

"Steer into the skid and get off the brakes. Hit the gas."

Dorian's counterintuitive advice came too late. The car went into the ditch, rear end first, whipping both of them back, hard, in their seats.

Jared clamped his hand on the back of his neck, the stiffness automatic and headache-inducing. "You all right?" He stretched gently to either side, wondering if he hadn't just sustained a mild concussion.

"I think so." Dorian unlocked his knees, pulled his feet back, and unclenched his hands from the seat back. "You?"

"I'll be fine." Jared tried to open his door, but snow held it closed.

Dorian unfastened his seat belt and pulled the passenger door handle. The door opened, and the wind flooded the seat with fresh snow that melted on impact. He turned his face away from the icy cold and pulled it shut. "You think you can get the car out of here?"

"Not without calling a wrecker, but if it gets dragged out, it's probably drivable."

"We're too close for both of us to sit here and wait this out. Call, wait for help, and I'll run ahead. We're going to need a way out of here."

His plan made sense.

Dorian's safety wasn't Jared's first or even second concern, but he wasn't dressed for the cold, and if something happened to him, he wouldn't make it to Ana. Jared checked the fuel gauge, and finding the gas tank more than half-full, figured the car's heat would suffice. He unfastened his seat belt and unzipped his coat.

"Here, take this." The bulky winter coat was almost impossible to get out of, and he had to push the driver's seat back to clear the sleeves. Every bit of what Jared had done for Dorian directly linked to Ana. He reached under the passenger seat for the emergency roadside kit he'd never taken more than a Band-Aid out of and quickly found two flares. "Light these when you get out there."

Dorian put the coat on and lifted the hood. "This Ana girl means a lot to you, doesn't she?"

Jared nodded. "More than you know."

CHAPTER 80

The traffic broke, and it would have been smooth sailing if Mike had any sense of which direction he was headed. He pulled off the highway, his truck barely fitting in the half-cleared shoulder, and answered his phone.

"Mike, it's Coop."

"Any news?"

"Elsa went by Noreen's place with Julian, and they found Ana's car in the parking lot, under enough snow to say it's been there a couple of hours, at least."

"What about Noreen?"

"No answer. Her place is abandoned."

"Put out a BOLO. Get her information from the DMV."

"It won't help."

"What do you mean 'it won't help'?"

"She's not driving her car. You know we wouldn't go this far outside of the lines without the proper authorization for anyone other than Ana, but Elsa and Graham knocked on doors. One of Noreen's neighbors said she's driving a rental, a dark blue SUV. She said she didn't know car makes or models. I did some digging, and it turns out Noreen rented a dark blue Land Rover LR2 from a place called Go Rentals that specializes in high-end vehicles, and, Mike, it's worse than that. The car's identical to Dorian Carmichael's."

"Shit." Mike slammed his palms into the steering wheel hard enough that a jarring pain radiated into his aging shoulder, one that had been dislocated and shot in his first year on the force.

"Dorian didn't rape her, did he?" Coop asked.

"My gut tells me no. Any luck tracing Ana's cell?"

"None, but . . ." A voice in the background interrupted, and Mike strained to listen. "Where? Okay. Off 490?"

"Coop, what's going on?"

"Are you sure?"

"Sure of what?" Mike shouted.

"Dorian Carmichael owns a place on the other side of the Bristol Mountain Ski Resort, off 490. LoJack on the rental puts Noreen there. I'm sending backup."

"How do I get there?"

"Mike, you're off duty. Wait this one out."

"Coop, I'm not going to ask again. How do I get there?"

"Hang on." The sound of clicking keyboard keys filled the silence as Coop searched for directions. "Take 490 to NY-64, head toward Bristol. There's a private access road, Lakeside Lodges Road it's called, but I doubt it'll show up on your GPS. Dorian's place is the last on the right."

Mike turned on his directional and sped out into traffic with barely a glance over his shoulder. He slammed his foot on the gas and weaved between cars, which were now fewer and farther between.

A long silence followed as he considered his next move.

"Mike, you still there?"

"Yeah, I'm here, Coop. Listen, I need everything you can dig up on Noreen. Find out whatever you can and get back to me."

"I'll do what I can, but my guess is you'll see her first."

CHAPTER 81

The basement was cold and damp, the only light coming from a single bulb suspended from the ceiling. Pain shot up Ana's ankles as if she'd been hobbled, the result of having been dragged down the stairs. The blunt-force injury made her wonder if she managed to escape, could she run or even walk.

It didn't matter.

She wasn't getting out of this.

The continuous positive airway pressure machine was the only thing keeping air in her lungs, and she lay helpless with each artificial breath.

Noreen looked a mess. Her wispy bangs clung to the droplets of sweat covering her forehead, and her once-styled hair stood on end in a way that made her look deranged. *Appropriate, considering.* Even injured, she'd managed to tape Ana securely to a lounge chair and start an IV line, the insulin dripping at an almost imperceptible rate.

She intended for Ana's death to be slow and agonizing.

Noreen checked her watch and wrapped another layer of medical tape around the blood-soaked compression bandage on her hand.

"It didn't have to be like this."

It didn't, but she wasn't going to just roll over and die.

"You could have helped me. I would've given you the succinylcholine, and this would have all been over quickly."

Already the panic was setting in, even as the injection wore off.

Ana's chest expanded, and she drew her first partial breath, independent of the machine.

Noreen put a stethoscope in her ears and listened to Ana's lungs before taking off the CPAP mask.

The cool burst of air on Ana's sweaty skin made her shiver. She gasped, a full, unaided breath rushing into her lungs.

Noreen listened again. "What did you really think was going to happen?" She hung the stethoscope around her neck. "Did you think you were going to kill me, or just hurt me enough to get away? I know you, Ana. I've known girls like you. You want me to answer for what I did, but I'm too smart for that. I have a plan. You aren't walking out of here. And for what it's worth, neither am I." She covered her hand with her sleeve and unscrewed the lightbulb, leaving Ana in complete darkness.

CHAPTER 82

The speedometer registered a steady eighty miles per hour as Mike closed in on the Bristol Mountain Ski Resort. He let his foot off the accelerator and took a hard right onto NY-64, steering a bit with the unavoidable skid.

Traffic picked up as he closed in on the mountain, the die-hard skiers and snowboarders with gear strapped to their roofs, driving undeterred. A Subaru Outback cut in front of him and proceeded to do thirty-five as the driver searched for the parking lot entrance. Mike honked and waved his hand for the middle-aged female driver to get out of his way. She flipped him off, but pulled over, allowing him to regain speed.

Heavy snowflakes fell on his windshield, and the wipers turned them into a packed dam. He cranked up the defroster, heat making the problem worse.

Ice coated the end of the driver's side wiper and prevented the rubber from making contact with the glass. Mike rolled down the driver's side window and reached for the blade on the upswing. The seat belt held him in place, and he had to loosen it to be able to reach. He leaned forward, the heavy snow pelting the side of his face, and caught the edge of the blade. He pulled it back and let it go with a slap against the glass, breaking off a small chunk that barely increased visibility. A second hard thump cleared the rest, but Mike nearly missed his turn. He fought the instinct to slam on the brakes as he jerked the wheel to the right and sped through the desolate construction zone. The truck tires spun, then gained traction. Mike squinted to see what looked like fresh tire tracks in the nearly deserted road. The red casing of an extinguished flare stuck out from a mound by the ditch.

"Shit."

A silver BMW had careened off the road and was back-end first in the ditch. A trail of footprints led away from the car, the headlights of which were half-shrouded by a cloud of exhaust. Mike didn't want to stop, but when the passenger's side door opened and Jared Monroe stumbled out of the car, he had no choice.

Snow covered Jared's dark hair and settled on his eyelashes. His feet sank through the snow, halfway up to his knees, and he waved his arms for Mike to stop. He wasn't even wearing a coat.

"What the hell are you doing? Are you crazy coming out here?" Mike shouted through the open window and turned up the heat. The fan drowned out Jared's answer. "What? I can't hear you."

Jared held up a finger, turned off the car, and pocketed the keys. He pulled himself up the embankment, holding on to a long sapling branch, and staggered onto the road, shivering. "I need a lift."

Mike reached across the passenger seat and pulled the door handle. "Get in."

A clear thread dripped from his nose and he sniffled, holding his bright red hands in front of the vents.

"How much farther?" Mike asked, not bothering with small talk.

"Less than a quarter mile, last house on the right. Dorian should already be there."

CHAPTER 83

Dorian couldn't believe how far Noreen had gone.

A Baltic Blue Land Rover, exactly like his, sat parked in the cabin's driveway.

He thumbed the lever of the front door handle, and stumbled inside. Extreme heat hit him head-on, the contrast in temperature breaking him out in a sweat.

"Noreen?"

A half-empty bottle of wine sat on the counter next to a stack of sterile gauze wrappers, a bottle of peroxide, and a lightbulb.

"Noreen, are you here?"

The silence gripped Dorian's body like a vise.

"Come on, Noreen, this isn't funny."

He walked through the great room, looking around and behind things in case she was hiding.

"Noreen, answer me."

The sound of tossed sheets catching a breeze echoed in the loft.

Dorian stood at the base of the stairs, contemplating arming himself. The sound came again, and with each heavy step on the hardwood he regretted his decision not to.

He reached the loft bedroom, and the scene sucked the breath out of him.

Noreen rolled onto her side, her head propped up on her hand and her elbow sinking into the mattress. She was naked, except for Colby's shirt, which he'd torn the buttons off in a lustful fury. "Took you long enough," she said, a smile spreading across her face.

"Where's Ana?"

"I have no idea what you're talking about." Noreen, a white gauze bandage taped to her palm, patted the bed for him to come join her.

"That's bullshit, Noreen. What are you doing here?"

"You told me to help myself to the place whenever I wanted, remember?"

He reached for his phone, and her demeanor did a pendulum shift.

"Don't you dare!" She produced a syringe from behind her and removed the cap with her teeth. "Sit." He hesitated. "I'm not going to say it again." She pushed herself up and tucked her legs underneath her. Her half-exposed breasts heaved with each heavy breath.

Dorian took a careful step toward the bed and sat on the end, as far away from her as he could get. "What do you want?"

"That's the million-dollar question, isn't it?" Noreen lowered the needle, keeping her thumb on the plunger. "You know, I heard you made bail. I thought you might be headed to the hospital, but Colby can't exactly talk to you from a coma, can she?" Dorian didn't bother telling her that Colby had come to. "You told me you loved me, Dorian. You made love to me, remember? After you'd been in jail, the first time? I never told you that Mitchell called me, did I? He wanted to know what you were looking for, ransacking Prusak's office, but I covered for you. I always cover for you. I went to post your bail, but you were gone. You didn't even have to call me, and I was right there, in time to see you leave with *her*. Where did you say you were that night? At the office, finishing charts, burning the midnight oil and all that?" She tugged on the shirt. "Nice job on the buttons."

Dorian's nostrils flared as he sucked in a deep breath. "I'd say we're more than even. I lied to you about where I was, and you lied about me raping you."

"But did I? I mean, there's DNA, and there's that thing with Marco, and the evidence at your house. All of what's happened makes you look, frankly, guilty. I did what I did to Sydney to keep you, to keep *us*, from being exposed. Marco should've minded his own business. Ana, too, for that matter. Everyone could've just gotten past this, and you could've loved me."

Dorian curled his upper lip. "Love you? You make me sick."

"Make sure you tell that to your attorney." Noreen emptied the syringe into her thigh, her body went limp, and she stopped breathing.

CHAPTER 84

The room temperature solution felt like ice water running through Ana's veins, adding to the already bone-deep chill of the dark basement.

"Help!" Her voice was dry and gravelly.

"Ana, where are you?"

It was Jared.

"Jared, help."

"Ana, where are you?"

Mike was with him.

"Mike, I'm downstairs."

The switch clicked on and off, a thin sliver of light bathing the wooden stairs in a white glow.

Mike ran into the darkness and collapsed at her side. "Are you all right?"

Jared fumbled with his phone, and the bright white flashlight pierced the darkness.

Ana squinted, having been in the dark so long that her eyes couldn't immediately adjust.

Mike pulled at the tape holding the IV sheath in place.

Jared turned off the drip, checked the IV bag labels, and all but knocked Mike out of the way.

"Here, hold this." He handed the cell phone to Mike. "I need both hands."

Mike kept the light trained on the IV site.

"How long have you been hooked up?" Jared said.

"Minutes, not longer."

"Ten? Thirty? How many?" Jared brushed Ana's hair back from her face, and even in the dim lighting, she could see his concern.

"Somewhere in between." Ana leaned her head back against the chair and sighed. She felt terrible, but things could've been so much worse. "How did you know where to find me?"

"Noreen isn't as smart as she thinks she is." Jared pulled the sheath from her hand, holding pressure on the site until it stopped bleeding.

Ana closed her fingers around his. "Thank you," she whispered, and turned to Mike. "I'm sorry I didn't tell you. I wasn't sure—"

"I'll be mad at you later. Right now, I'm glad you're alive." He welled up with tears. "What can I do to help?"

"I need something to cut this with." Jared pulled at the layers of duct tape.

Mike handed Jared his pocketknife. "Here."

Jared cut the tape and eased Ana forward. "Can you walk?"

A surge of pins and needles came and went as blood pumped through her extremities. "I think so." She tried to stand up, and her light-headedness turned to vertigo. The room spun and her knees buckled.

Mike reached out to keep her from falling, but Jared beat him to it. He cradled her in his arms like a child and lifted her.

Ana wrapped her arms around his neck and nestled against him. He smelled of cologne and car exhaust, and felt like safety.

"She needs sugar—juice, candy, something," he said to Mike.

"I'll see what I can find in the kitchen."

CHAPTER 85

Dorian held Noreen under her armpits and dragged her off the bed. The give of the mattress made it nearly impossible to do CPR. Her heels hit the floor with a thud, and her shirt, Colby's shirt, fell open. A bright red dot from the friction of Dorian's hands against her ivory skin filled the space between her breasts. Dorian's shoulders, arms, and hands ached from nonstop compressions.

"I'm not going to let you die," he said, unable to reconcile his feelings for her. Weeks ago, he'd have considered her a confidante, a friend, and a necessity. She had been part of his daily life for years, helped build his practice, and it seemed impossible she'd have ever set him up. Guilt surfaced, the feeling that all of the flirting and false hope had been too much for her, and that she was more fragile than he had considered. None of that mattered now. He needed her to live in order to get out from under the disaster she'd made for him, and for her to pay for what she'd done.

He pinched her nose, delivered two more breaths, and shouted, again, for help.

"Jared, *dammit*, will you answer me? Help!"

He'd heard him arrive with someone else, but he had no idea who.

Sergeant Mike Richardson, not at all the person he'd expected, appeared at the top of the stairs.

His breath caught at the realization he was about to be arrested, again. He interlaced his fingers and thrust the heel of his hands into Noreen's chest. Her legs fell open, exposing her completely.

Mike kept an indirect gaze, his head turned from the blatant, if not vulgar, nudity. He pulled a pair of handcuffs from his back pocket.

"It's not what it looks like," Dorian said. "She shot herself up with something and stopped breathing."

"Succinylcholine," Mike said.

The symptoms fit.

Dorian pinched Noreen's nose and covered her mouth with his own. He delivered two breaths, and her chest rose with each inhalation. "Where's Jared? I need his help."

"He's downstairs, with Ana. Noreen had her tied up in the basement."

"Is she all right?" Dorian asked between shallow breaths.

"Jared says she's going to be fine."

Dorian looked at the alarm clock on the nightstand next to the unmade bed and calculated the elapsed time. He'd been at CPR for more than five minutes. He'd heard of those who had performed CPR for hours until help arrived, and had been successful. He didn't know how they managed.

He gave Noreen two more breaths, and she gasped.

Finally.

"Jesus. Thank God." Dorian sat back on his heels.

Noreen stared at the ceiling for a moment, languid and seemingly confused. The wail of police sirens filled the room.

Noreen, as if she knew they were coming for her, rolled her eyes toward Dorian.

In them, he saw nothing but hate.

CHAPTER 86

Ana sipped a glass of orange juice that did nothing to soothe her nausea. She was tired from the insulin, but thankful to be alive, to be with Jared, and to see justice being served.

The front door opened, and several uniformed officers filed in. The swirling squad car lights reflected off the snow, the walls, and the windows.

Mike read Noreen her rights and a list of charges ranging from kidnapping to murder. She stared blankly ahead, almost catatonically, dressed in a pair of ill-fitting sweats that Mike told Dorian he took from the bedroom dresser.

Dorian couldn't have looked more relieved that he wasn't the one in handcuffs.

Noreen's gait had a psychiatric-ward shuffle to it as Mike handed her over to Coop for transport.

"Are you sure you're okay?" Mike set his hand on Ana's shoulder.

"I'll be fine."

Jared held her shaking hand; an act that Ana could see from Mike's steely stare upset him.

Ana pleaded silently for him not to react.

Mike must've understood the look in her eyes, or he'd have never backed off.

"Dorian, I'm going to need to take your statement regarding what, exactly, I walked in on."

"Whatever you need." Dorian stared out the living room window, watching Noreen go. The swirling lights appeared, and then disappeared, shaking him from his trancelike state. He took a second orange juice carton from the refrigerator and set it in front of Ana. "You need to keep drinking."

"No more juice." The acid from the last one left a sour taste and a burn in her stomach. She held up her hand and he pushed it closer.

"Drink."

"Ana, please," Jared said.

"No. More. Juice. I'll throw up."

The crime-scene unit's arrival interrupted their debate.

"Sergeant Richardson." Ronald Graham nodded in greeting.

"Ana, are you all right?" Elsa rushed into the kitchen, and Mike steered her away.

"She's fine," he said. "Did you call EMS?"

"They're on their way."

Ron opened his kit on the kitchen table.

Mike handed him the lightbulb from the kitchen counter. "Start in the basement. That's where she was holding Ana. You'll need this."

"Are you sure you're all right?" Elsa asked Ana from across the room.

"I'm positive." Ana, who had never been one for being the center of attention, stood to prove her point. A haze settled over her vision, and she was unsteady on her feet.

Jared tried to have her sit back down, but she refused.

"I need to move," she said. Her stiff knees ached, but she took a few steps, holding on to the counter. She looked out the window at the fresh snow covering the newly arrived cruisers, and filling the tracks of those that came before them.

Some things covered up more easily than others.

Her wounds weren't so effortlessly erased.

The familiar blue-and-white ambulance barreling down the driveway struck her with dread.

"I don't *need* an ambulance."

Jared tucked her hair behind her ear and smiled. "Well, you can't ride with me. My car's in the ditch."

Ethan rushed through the door in an obvious state of panic. "Where's Ana? Is she all right?" His eyes settled on Jared's hand on Ana's shoulder. "Oh thank God." He dropped the strap of the medic bag off his shoulder and hurried her toward the sofa.

Jared immediately bristled.

"Ethan, you don't have to do this. I'm fine, really," Ana said, sitting down.

Ethan dropped to his knees and grabbed Ana's wrist to take her pulse. "What happened?"

"Insulin. Noreen put me on an insulin drip."

"I need a glucose meter," Jared said.

"All due respect, Doc, you're not my contact on this one. Back off."

Ana reached down, unzipped the familiar bag, and searched for the meter.

Ethan gently nudged her away. "You're the patient, remember?" He set the test strip and punctured her finger. "Ninety-seven, almost normal."

"Test it again," Jared said.

"No, *don't* test it again," Ana said. "Can you give us a minute?"

Jared reluctantly agreed.

"What's going on here?" Ethan asked.

The question wasn't health related; it was personal.

"Honestly? I don't know." Jared's doting behavior, the openness with which he attended her, and his obvious feelings for her, had them in new territory. "I never meant to hurt you. You're important to me, Ethan. You're my—"

"Friend." He spat the bitter word. "I know."

"Is she good to go?" Mike asked impatiently. "I want to make sure she gets a good once-over."

Ethan nodded and packed up his bag.

"I don't want to go to the hospital." Ana picked at the adhesive on her clothes and skin, and Mike stopped her.

"If you're medically cleared, I'll take you home after we're done collecting the evidence we need." He patted Ethan on the back. "Load her up."

Ethan held out his hand and Ana took it, grateful for the olive-branch gesture. "I assume you want to walk?"

She smirked. "Unless you want to carry me."

"I'll ride along," Jared said.

"No, you won't. Chain of custody. I'm going with her. You're the one who put the car in the ditch?" Mike asked Jared. Jared nodded, and Mike tossed Dorian his keys. "Then *you're* driving. You two came out here together, you can go back together, and you can both give me your statements when you return my truck."

CHAPTER 87

With Ana safe, the tension between Jared and Dorian returned with a vengeance.

Jared took his coat off the hook by the door, leaving Dorian to freeze.

Dorian followed him out into the cold and unlocked the truck. "Do you see a snow brush anywhere in there?"

Jared rummaged behind the seat and handed one over without saying a word. He considered briefly helping Dorian clear the snow and decided to wait in the passenger seat instead. The truck bore the ghost of heat, enough that Jared couldn't yet see his breath.

He watched Dorian scrape at the ice dam under the wipers and tried not to fixate on the image of the shirt one of the investigators had come downstairs with.

Anger was a reaction Jared wasn't sure he should have anymore.

Dorian climbed in the driver's side, started the truck, and turned the defrosters on high.

Jared fumbled with the buttons on the radio, finding the presets tuned to country music, talk radio, and easy listening, which he settled on for lack of anything better.

"Thanks for the help." Dorian warmed his hands in front of the heater vent and adjusted the mirrors.

"That was Colby's shirt the cop brought downstairs." Jared looked straight ahead, into the vanishing tree line, as he asserted his observation.

Dorian looked over his shoulder, neither confirming nor denying the fact, and backed down the driveway with the truck in four-wheel drive.

A quarter mile down the road, the BMW was still in the ditch, buried under a heap of fresh snow with no sign of help coming.

"Good thing we didn't wait for a wrecker."

Jared wasn't amused. "You really don't have anything to say? Colby was there, wasn't she?"

Dorian pressed both hands into the steering wheel, stretching his shoulders and back. "Yes, she was."

A door had opened between them, one Jared was reluctant to walk through. "How long?"

"A few hours?" Dorian seemed confused by the question.

"How long have the two of you been sleeping together?"

"A year or so, not counting the few times she broke it off."

Jared thought about the times Colby had tried to reconcile their marriage and wondered if her trying to fix things was out of guilt. "She told me she loves you." The words almost wouldn't come out.

"And where does that leave us?"

Jared wasn't sure which "us" Dorian was referring to. "You and me? Nowhere, at best. You and *her*? That's up to you two. Either way, I'm done."

"You were leaving, anyway." Dorian glanced over. "You served her with divorce papers. Did that have anything to do with Ana?"

"Coincidental timing. Don't put me on your level, Dorian. *I* didn't sleep with her."

Dorian chuckled. "But you wanted to. That's the difference between you and me, Jared. I go after what I want. Life's too short. I don't know what happened with you and Colby, other than she says you stopped paying her attention. At this point it doesn't even matter. She's in the hospital, alone, probably scared, and she's been through hell. She cheated death, Jared, and I'm betting, knowing her, it's changed her perspective. This thing with Noreen . . ."

"Totally your fault, by the way."

Dorian waved his hand. "I'm not taking credit for Noreen's lack of mental well-being. There was no way I could've seen any of what happened coming, but I am sorry for any part I might have played in it. Whatever misguided motivations I had for the surgeries, the God complex is gone. I'm an unlicensed, unemployable, center-of-the-media-circus freak show, and you know what? All I can think about is Colby, lying in that bed, wondering if anyone cares if she lives or dies. *I* care. Yes, there's some baggage between her and me after this, but we have another chance, all of us. I saw the way you looked at Ana, Jared. And I've seen you with Colby. Night and day, my friend."

"You're really giving me relationship advice right now?"

Dorian shrugged. "Someone has to. What point does it serve holding on to someone you don't love anymore?"

"I do love Colby, and I'm sure, on some level, she loves me. We're just not *in* love."

"The difference between being happy and settling."

Jared didn't want to admit it, but Dorian was right. After all Colby had been through, she needed someone to care for her in a way that he couldn't bring himself to. The lies had to stop somewhere.

His relationship with Ana couldn't move forward until they did.

CHAPTER 88

The ambulance backed up to County Memorial's emergency room entrance, and Ana, feeling more or less her old self again, banged on the door to be let out.

"Give me a minute, would you? You are the worst patient ever." Ethan smiled, but Ana could tell he wasn't kidding.

Mike stepped down and held out his hand.

Ana took it, still a bit unsteady.

Ethan struggled to unfold a locked-up wheelchair parked in the ER's vestibule.

"Those things always stick," Ana said. "And no way am I being pushed around like an invalid."

Ethan let out a frustrated growl and chased after her. "Wait up, would you?"

Mike led Ana to the check-in desk. "I appreciate everything, Ethan. I have her from here."

Ethan started to argue, but Mike wouldn't have it. "She's fine. Go." His no-nonsense tone made the soft suggestion seem anything but optional.

Ana flashed Ethan a strained smile, listening to the building commotion behind the admission window. "I'll call you when I'm home."

A heavy-set woman wearing pink flowered scrubs with a stethoscope around her neck waved for Ana and Mike to come around back. "We have a room set up for you."

The woman handed Ana a gown for her to change into.

Julian, whom Mike had called en route, waited by the door.

Julian handed him a paper bag, which Mike promptly handed to Ana. "I'll take her statement when she's ready." He spoke as though Ana were invisible, an off-putting but sensible move, considering the circumstances.

Mike was too close to the case, and everyone knew it.

Julian was only observing protocol.

Ana pulled the curtain for privacy, changed into the gown, and bagged her clothes as evidence. She stumbled when she took off her socks and grabbed the railing to keep from falling.

"Are you all right in there?" Mike said.

A pain shot up Ana's big toe, the one she had caught on a bed wheel, and she took a deep breath before answering. "I'm fine. Stubbed my toe is all." She settled in on the bed and reached for a blanket. "You can come in."

Mike parted the privacy drape but stopped before walking through it.

A woman frantically shouted Jared's name.

Mike let the curtain fall shut. "You shouldn't have come here."

Jared's shoes appeared under the curtain next to Mike's.

Ana ran her fingers through her hair and licked her dry lips.

"Dr. Monroe, we've been trying to reach you," the woman said.

"Where's Ana?" Jared asked.

"This isn't the time or place, Jared. You shouldn't be here."

"Dr. Monroe, we've been calling you all day. It's your wife. She's asking for you."

Wife.

Even if Ana hadn't been eavesdropping, the three were close enough that she'd have heard their whole conversation.

"I am dealing with an emergency."

"Yeah, but—"

"I'll go to her room when I'm finished."

"But—"

"Go."

The woman walked away, and Jared spoke softly to Mike. "I know you think you're protecting Ana, but she doesn't need protecting from me. I want to be in there with her."

"With her? When everyone here knows you, and your *wife*? The last thing Ana needs is negative attention. It's not my place to comment on whatever you two started, but it's messy, and this isn't the place to straighten things out."

Ana sighed.

Mike was right.

Her heart broke at the idea of Jared at Colby's bedside, but it wasn't right to be jealous. She had no place in their lives, and Jared had no right dragging her into them. The line between friend and more had blurred. Their situation defied logic, and if she was being honest, she didn't see a way out of it.

The curtain opened, and Mike walked in, his expression disapproving. "I'm sorry," he said. "You deserve better."

The doctor arrived to examine her before she could argue.

CHAPTER 89

Three uniformed officers ate burgers and chicken wings at a corner table of the Barfly Tavern, a pitcher of soda between them. Mike nodded in their direction and headed for Anthony, who was sitting, head down, at the bar.

The day had taken too many turns to count, running into Anthony another in a long line of coincidences.

"Nestor, a Sam Adams, please, and one of whatever Anthony's drinking." Mike hung his jacket over the back of the bar-high chair next to Anthony's. He slipped the wallet from his back pocket and set it next to his keys, which Dorian had returned along with his truck. Mike had strong feelings about both him and Jared Monroe, but right now, he needed to forget both of them.

Nestor set a frosted mug of beer in front of Mike and turned to Anthony. "Another Jack and Coke?"

"Just a Coke this round, thanks." Anthony spun a worn band around his left ring finger.

"You okay?" Mike said.

Anthony kept his eyes on the television running behind the bar. "I was a shitty husband, Mike."

Mike, knowing it wasn't entirely true, shook his head. "Sydney wouldn't have agreed, not overall."

"I hope that's true. I heard what happened to Ana. Is she all right?"

"I just brought her home from the hospital. She's tired, but she's going to be fine. She wants some alone time. After all she's been through, I can't blame her."

"And you arrested another suspect?"

"Word travels fast." Mike, uncomfortable with discussing the case, nodded and changed the subject. "I don't mean to pry, but what's with the ring?"

Anthony stared at the worn platinum band, and his eyes filled with tears. "I missed her today, is all. I found this in a box while I was unpacking and"—he shrugged—"I don't know, I just wanted to wear it."

"Unpacking?"

"I got a place over by the firehouse, a three-bedroom brownstone with a lease-to-own option. Figured it's time, right?"

"Misty's probably got a nursery set up already, huh?" Mike hated the idea that Anthony's mistress was having his child, but he could see that Anthony needed support, not criticism.

"No. No nursery. No baby, either." He went back to spinning the ring, his eyes fixed in a ninety-mile stare across the bar. "The day Sydney died, Misty was spotting, remember me telling you?" Mike nodded. "Doctors didn't think much of it at the time, said the baby seemed healthy, but it was so early, you know? She miscarried a couple of days later. I tried thinking of a reason to stay, but I kept coming back to the trapped feeling that had me with her in the first place. If she hadn't gotten pregnant, I would've tried to work things out with Sydney. I mean, I *did* try, but it was too late. The brownstone came at the right time. It belongs to an aunt of one of the guys at the station. She got put in a nursing home a couple months back, so I was able to move right in."

Mike wasn't sure if he should be extending condolences or congratulations. "I'm sorry," he said, sympathy feeling more right.

"Thanks." Anthony shrugged. "I'm not sure if I am or not. Don't get me wrong. I'm sad about the baby, devastated, but Misty . . ." He drew a deep breath, then continued. "Things with her weren't like when I was married. Even the rough patches, those were the best days of my life. I wish I could've told Sydney that."

Regret was a burden Mike was too familiar with. Seeing Anthony's torture made him reflect on his own life, and on the emptiness of being alone to suit a job that was slowly destroying his faith in humanity. The time had come to fill it. "Excuse me a minute, would you?" He opened his cell phone and dialed Kim's number.

CHAPTER 90

Emily settled in on the couch, thankful to be home and that the crowd of reporters had been cleared from their front porch. Terri Tate was relentless, and it took three police officers and crowd control to finally put an end to the harassment.

Emily picked up the remote control off the end table and tuned in to the Channel 9 news. A still photo of County Memorial popped up in a window on the upper-right-hand corner of the screen, and a red-and-white banner announced "Breaking News." She turned up the volume and tucked the remote under her arm where Derrick would be less likely to grab it.

Terri Tate appeared on the screen, her expression artificially somber. A row of landscape lighting cast the hospital in beacons of white.

"This is Terri Tate coming to you live from County Memorial Hospital where CEO Mitchell Altman was arrested earlier today for his role in the scandal that has rocked this once top-seated medical facility. Sources close to the case allege that CEO Altman received over one hundred thousand dollars in exchange for his cooperation with Dr. Dorian Carmichael's organ-harvesting scam." A recording of an expensively suited bald man interrupted the broadcast. His hands were cuffed behind his back, and he kept his red face turned away from the cameras. A vein throbbed in his forehead. Another man, an on-staff lawyer according to the scrolling news bar on the bottom of the screen, attempted to cover the camera lens with his hand. The live report resumed. "In related news, Dorian Carmichael, a former person of interest in the murders of Dr. Marco Prusak and of his patient, Sydney Dowling, was released on bail and has since been exonerated of the most serious of charges. His medical license, however, has been revoked indefinitely pending an ongoing investigation. Noreen Pafford, Dr. Carmichael's nurse, was arrested earlier today and is being held without bail at the women's correctional facility. Details of the charges against her have not yet been made public. Speculation on the future of County Memorial's uterine transplant program heralds an uncertain future, though one family has come forward to express its sincerest hopes that the surviving patient, Emily Warren, meets with success." The feed cut to a prerecorded session between Terri and an older couple filmed earlier that day. "I'm here with Charles and Vivian Harmon, who recently lost their daughter, Janice, to a tragic car accident. I'm terribly sorry for your loss."

Vivian, a late-fifties, athletic type with an enviable build, wore a tailored navy blue suit and stood next to Charles, a slightly older man with thick, gray hair. "Thank you, Terri. It's been a difficult time for us."

"Vivian, you called our station earlier, when you saw footage of Emily Warren, Mayor Warren's daughter-in-law, being released home. You said you had a message for her."

"When Dr. Carmichael approached us about the possibility of donating Janice's uterus, we were reluctant. Janice was a practical woman—beautiful, smart, top of her law school class, and youngest to make partner at her firm—she believed that if she were ever in a position to help someone, she should do it. We were against organ donation of any kind. The thought of someone harvesting parts from your only child . . ." Vivian drew a breath and paused. "It's gruesome, and I couldn't help feeling that something was being taken away from her." Charles set his hand on Vivian's shoulder. "Janice was the greatest gift of my life. Her smile lit up a room, and I'm proud to call her my daughter. Family is the most important thing. That's my message to Emily. Janice was so focused on her career that she never married and never had children. I feel like part of Janice is alive somewhere, that part of her can still create life. There's a barrier around Emily, understandably so given the circumstances and all that's happened." She locked her aged, blue eyes with the camera as she delivered her personal message. "Emily, I've tried to reach you, and if you're watching, I want you to know that none of the ugliness of what's happened applies to you. I can imagine you're wondering, after what happened with the other patient, who your donor was. Charles and I don't want you to feel any doubt, or guilt. We wish you luck in creating your own family."

Emily wiped the tears from her eye as the prerecorded clip returned to a live feed.

Even Terri Tate looked touched. "A heart-wrenching message, for sure, and a hopeful one. Emily, we all wish you the very best. This is Terri Tate signing off from County Memorial Hospital. Thank you and good night."

"Can I change the channel now?" Derrick reached out for the remote. "I think that's the closest to good news we're going to get."

"The woman's mother is right. I would've felt guilty, wondering if somewhere another woman couldn't have children because of me. They didn't have to come forward."

Derrick leaned over and gave Emily a kiss. "They didn't have to, but I'm glad they did."

"Me, too," she said. "Me, too."

CHAPTER 91

Ana turned off the news and shook her hair loose from her ponytail. She finger-combed the tangled strands and tucked them behind her ears, debating, for a second, about calling Ethan. She told herself the nightmare was over, but her mind wouldn't let it be over.

She scrolled through her cell phone contacts and stopped at Ethan's number, deciding quickly that it was better to be alone for the right reasons than to call him in a moment of weakness. Her leaning on him was as unfair to him as Jared's giving her false hope had been to her. All of the visits, the nights spent on her couch, the comforting and listening, exactly what she needed when she needed it, had her believing in an impossible future.

Your wife's been asking for you.

The nurse's voice echoed in her head. She hadn't done anything wrong, but she felt like she owed Colby an apology. She reached to turn off the lamp, and the white beam of headlights panned across the living room. She looked out the front door at an unfamiliar white Tahoe parked in her driveway, the cargo area of which was piled so high with clutter that it blocked the light from the lamp-post on the other side of the yard.

Ana prepared to tell whoever it was that they had the wrong house.

The driver's door opened, but no dome light came on. A dark silhouette reached across the front seat, and when a car passed, its headlights illuminated his face.

Jared.

Ana rushed to open the door, not caring that she looked eager. The late hour said as much about why Jared was there as the bag slung over his shoulder.

"May I come in?" he asked.

"Of course, yes." She felt a little tongue tied.

"I'd have come earlier, but I had to pack." Jared made no assumptions. He didn't set his bag down, or get comfortable.

Ana locked the front door out of habit.

"Look, I'm sorry I didn't stay with you in the ER. I shouldn't have let Mike make me leave. I wanted to be there, but he—"

"Has a way of intimidating people."

Jared nodded. "He cares a lot, and he wants the best for you. I do, too. That's why I left Colby."

"Jared, she's sick." Ana couldn't believe she was defending her, but the woman had nearly died. "I don't want to be to blame . . ."

"You're not to blame for anything, and I didn't leave her alone. Dorian's with her."

"Oh?"

"That's why that nurse was looking for me. Colby wanted to be discharged, against medical advice. A lot has happened in the last few days, most of it terrible, and before all of it, Colby and I were trudging along, subsisting on broken vows and the fear of what came next. We couldn't even sleep in the same room, and I couldn't face her after what she did with Simon and Dorian. There were reasons, I'm sure, for her to blame me. I didn't pay her enough attention and I wasn't there enough, but we grew apart a long time ago. I knew, before I caught her with Simon, that she'd been cheating. I guess it's a mixed blessing, right?" Ana raised her eyebrow. "Her telling me she is in love with Dorian relieved me of any guilt I felt about being in love with you." Ana was speechless. "Ana, I love you. There's something about you that just gets me, and if you give me the chance, I'll prove to you that I can make you happy."

Ana kissed him to stop him from talking. She wrapped her arms around his neck and pulled him down to her. He gathered her up and smothered her in combustible kisses until they were both out of breath.

"I don't want to presume anything," he said, a peaceful, dazed look settling over him. "I'll start looking for an apartment first thing in the morning—"

"Yes," Ana said, already unzipping his coat and stealing another kiss. "You can stay, as long as you want to."

"You mean beyond tomorrow?"

"And even the next day."

When he set down his things, she knew he'd never leave.

EPILOGUE

The surgical team worked in unison, tending Emily who was consciously sedated and seemed only vaguely aware of her surroundings.

Derrick stood by her side, near the chest-high drape that separated her engorged stomach, painted Betadine orange, from her face, which held the listless expression of someone drugged and distant.

"Can I hold her hand?" Derrick asked.

The anesthesiologist, a middle-aged man whose hazel eyes were barely visible past the reflection in his glasses, nodded.

"Are we ready?" Dr. Davis, dressed in blue surgical scrubs, looked to him for confirmation.

"All set, Dr. Davis."

Sweat beaded on Derrick's brow as she pressed the tip of her scalpel into Emily's stomach. He turned his face toward Emily and locked her gaze. Her ivory skin looked pale against the surgical cap covering her hair. Dark circles, from long nights with no sleep, swallowed her tired eyes. The last month had been hard on her; the weight gain, the constant urinating, and the stress of prelabor contractions. One of the conditions of her pregnancy was that the baby be delivered by cesarean, the only safe way, considering the transplant.

Emily was reluctant to ever have surgery again, but as they counted down the days, excitement replaced both her and Derrick's fears.

This was their miracle.

"How are you doing?" Derrick whispered.

"Good," Emily slurred.

"You're going to feel a little bit of pressure." Dr. Davis widened the opening, reaching inside of Emily and manipulating the tiny infant until she could coax the baby into the bright light of the operating room.

Derrick squeezed Emily's hand, and she, as best she could, squeezed back.

"Is everything okay?" she asked.

"We're almost there," Dr. Davis said.

Derrick pressed his lips to Emily's hand. "You're doing great, honey."

Emily winced, and tears rolled down her cheeks.

A nurse rushed in from the corner with a receiving blanket draped over her hands. There was a sound of wet suction, and an infant's cry filled the room.

"It's a girl." Dr. Davis held out a pair of scissors for Derrick to cut the umbilical cord, but he shook his head.

"I can't," he said, crying with joy. His heart swelled with pride as he looked at the perfect, tiny being he and Emily had created. "It's a girl," he said to Emily. "She's beautiful." He smothered her with kisses, and she, in her dazed state, managed to kiss him back.

The nurse carried the baby to a station in the corner. She cleaned her up, weighed and swaddled her, and held her out to Derrick.

"Six pounds, three ounces."

Derrick, who had never handled a newborn, held his daughter tight to his chest, rocking her until she stopped crying. Her slate-blue eyes glistened from the ointment the nurse had put in them, and despite what the books he had read said about infants' eyesight, he could tell she was looking at him. He bent down for Emily to see her. "She looks like you," he said through tears.

"No," Emily said. "She looks like *you*."

Dr. Davis laughed. "And the arguing begins. Have you thought of a name?"

They'd tossed a hundred around during Emily's pregnancy and kept coming back to the donor, Janice Harmon, who had made the whole thing possible. Janice wasn't the best name for a baby, but they were determined to work it in.

"Sabrina," Derrick said. "Sabrina Janice Warren. You like that name?" he asked the baby.

Emily smiled. "Sabrina Janice Warren, *our daughter*. I like the sound of that."

AUTHOR'S NOTE

Succinylcholine is an injectable drug used as part of anesthesia and in emergency medicine to facilitate the passage of an endotracheal breathing tube. It paralyzes all of the muscles in the body, including the lungs. Succinylcholine acts within seconds, and its effects typically last less than ten minutes. Body enzymes break the drug down quickly, making it difficult for a crime lab to detect its presence postmortem. Tests for breakdown substances, known as "metabolites," do exist, but the testing is difficult and results are controversial. Succinylcholine has been considered by some to be a near-perfect murder weapon.

Insulin is used to control blood sugar levels in people whose bodies cannot naturally produce enough of the hormone. Too much insulin reduces the blood glucose (sugar) level to a point that the brain cannot function. Overdose of insulin leads to a condition called hypoglycemia, which can cause a person to lapse into a coma, or even die. There are numerous cases of insulin being used as a murder weapon. Unlike succinylcholine, insulin is slow-acting, and its effects can be easily detected and reversed.

Like succinylcholine, it metabolizes quickly, making it difficult, but not impossible, to prove that a victim has died from its effects.

Succinylcholine, and to a lesser degree, insulin (unless someone is diabetic), are difficult to obtain outside of the medical community. While both have been used in real-life murder cases, this is purely a work of fiction. Details of the crimes within, as well as locations, are hybrids between fact and fiction, altered to meet the demands of the story.

In other words, don't try this at home.

ABOUT THE AUTHOR

After the author's fifteen years of working in health care, Belinda Frisch's stories can't help being medicine influenced. A writer of dark tales in the horror, mystery, and thriller genres, Belinda tells the stories she'd like to read. Her fiction has appeared in *Shroud* magazine, Dabblestone Horror, and Tales of the Zombie War. She is the author of *Cure, Afterbirth, Fatal Reaction, Better Left Buried,* and *The Missing Year.* She resides in upstate New York with her husband and a small menagerie of beloved animals.

Visit her blog at: BelindaF.blogspot.com